FINDING *Jack*

Other Books by Melanie Jacobson

Perfect Set

Southern Charmed

Painting Kisses

Always Will

Twitterpated

Second Chances

Smart Move

Not My Type

The List

FINDING *Jack*

MELANIE JACOBSON

A note to my Facebook readers:

Thank you for taking this wild and often silly journey with me. It was so fun to write this for you each Friday. But...those were always rough draft posts. When I went in to revise, I realized that I understood Emily's character much better, and that meant making some changes that went a little deeper. You'll see some differences from the story you followed on Facebook, but I hope that in every case, it's a change for the better. Some will surprise you (Shaun had to become Sean because I have a real-life nemesis named Shaun. Story Shaun wasn't supposed to be a good guy, but it turns out…he is. So I couldn't do my nemesis Shaun the honor of keeping the spelling the same.) Some will delight you (you get more information about what Emily's apartment looks like, and it makes such perfect sense). And some will make you really happy (I gave you an epilogue. I do NOT do epilogues). Thanks for taking the journey with me. I hope you find Emily's story deeper, richer, and more interesting but just as funny.

Chapter 1

I stared down at the red stilettos. Granted, Nordstrom lights were extra flattering, but these pretty girls would look good under a half-dead parking garage bulb. I turned them from side to side, admiring them.

"Are they too much?" I asked my best friend Ranée.

She arched one of her perfect eyebrows at me. "Um, hi, we're here because you got a promotion?"

"I don't mean too much money. I mean...*too much.*" I made a point of examining my pedicure peeking through the peep-toe so I wouldn't see the eyeroll I knew was coming. It didn't matter. It dripped from her voice.

"If by 'too much,' you mean you're worried that Paul will think these are over the top, then yes. He will. But that doesn't make them 'too much.' Buy them. Buy them now. In fact, buy them in every color and wear them on every date with him."

"You're ridiculous," I said even as I debated whether I needed them in black.

"Then at least get them in black," she said.

It was fate, obviously. I waved the salesgirl over and told her I'd take them in black too, and she hurried to package them before I changed my mind.

Ranée hopped up from the try-on sofa. "I'm going to go see if I can find my brother a shirt for his birthday. Come find me in the men's department when you're done paying."

Five minutes later I found her riffling through lumberjack shirts. I wrinkled my nose. "Does your brother have to wear plaid flannel because he lives in Oregon?"

"It's not my favorite either, but this is about getting him something he wants. And he'll wear one of these."

"It just feels like such a cliché. Does he also have a bird tattoo and drive a Subaru?"

"No and yes, and stop being so judgey." She nodded at the picture on top of the clothes rack. "I think you'd do better with a guy like that anyway." It showed a guy tethered to the side of a rock face. He was wearing the same flannel shirt she'd just pulled from the rack.

"Definitely not. Rock-climbing man-bun guy? No. Flannel is strike one. Man-bun is strikes two and three."

"That's hair-ist."

"Hair-ist is not a thing."

"Yeah, it is. It's like elitist or racist. You're just biased against long hair."

"Only on dudes. And only because it's repulsive."

She picked up a different flannel. "Whatever. I'll get this one for my brother and then we can start Phase Two of the Emily Riker Rules the World celebration."

"Not the world. Just a—"

"Whole fleet of computer programmers!"

"Fleet," I said, testing the word. "I don't think a group of coders would be called a fleet."

"Then what? A herd?"

"No. They definitely don't travel in herds. They're more like...pods. Pods of coders."

"And you're the boss of your own pod."

"I'm queen of the pod people," I said, wrapping the arms of the flannel shirt around my neck to create a cape.

"Just put the red shoes on and you're Queen of Everything."

I slid my arm through hers and tugged her toward the register. "All I want to be queen of is the sofa. Hurry and pay."

An hour later we were at another register, this time debating our grocery store candy choices. I grabbed a king-sized Reese's four-pack. "Done! Pick and let's go. Tina Fey is waiting for us."

Ranée pushed a lock of blonde hair out of her eyes while she studied the display. "The beautiful thing about a *30 Rock* marathon is that it's there whenever we need it."

"Right, but the ice cream won't be, so hurry up before it melts."

Suddenly she snorted and reached for a paperback on the checkout rack. "Those shoes are wasted on Paul. They're going to make him nervous. You need this guy. He'd totally appreciate red stilettos."

I snatched the romance novel she was brandishing at me. It showed a long-haired man in a kilt who seemed to have lost all of his shirt buttons, but the woman in a flowy dress clasped to his chest didn't seem to mind. "Is this Fabio? Why are you obsessed with me suddenly dating Fabio?"

"Because Fabio can handle your shoe choices. Paul can't. And that's not Fabio. Fabio is blond."

"Why do you even know that?"

"Why do you even know who Fabio is?"

"I don't know. It's just one of those things that everyone knows. Like Kenny G. No one's ever heard his music but everyone has still heard of Kenny G."

She pointed to the ceiling. "Hear that music? That's probably Kenny G. Now you know. And I'm just saying, your soul wears stilettos and it needs more than a Paul. I bet Paul loves Kenny G."

"I don't know what is with you and long-haired flannel guys today but no. And right now, I don't even want to think about guys at all. I want ice cream, chips, and 30 Rock."

"Fine," she said, returning the book to its shelf. "But this is just proof that I know you better than you know yourself."

"Then you know how much I want to binge sugar and TV right now. Let's get out of here."

"All right," she said, but she ran her finger over the chisel-jawed face of the long-haired half-dressed Scottish hero. "But I'm right about this."

If only I would've remembered how far Ranée would go to make a point.

If. Flipping. Only.

Chapter 2

I was on mile three on the gym treadmill and chapter seven of a new Sarah Eden audiobook when my phone started blowing up. Instead of hearing the dulcet tones of Sir Toby, I got:

"But darling, you've never—"

Buzz

"in as long as I've"

Buzz

"how dare you"

Buzz Buzz Buzz

"cannot countenance such"

Buzz Buzz

I growled and snatched my iPhone from my armband and quieted Lord Toby to check the alerts. It had better be a forty-car pileup with every person I'd ever known involved if it was going to interrupt my audiobook and work out.

Oh, it was a wreck all right. Seven Facebook notifications and two more going off as I looked, all saying stuff like, "Hot, girl!" or "When did you and Paul break up?"

And then a text from Paul. `What's going on?`

I stopped the treadmill and hopped off so the impatient bro-dude waiting for a free one could have it while I investigated the situation. Two screen taps later and I was staring at a picture of me with a guy I'd never seen before in my life. A guy with his arm around me. It was posted under my name and "I" had apparently captioned it, "New beginnings."

Only I remembered that picture. It used to show me and my cousin in a selfie from his sister's wedding. His body had been photoshopped to look more athletic, and the face? This face was a seriously hot guy with high cheekbones, a mysterious half-smile, big dark eyes, and a slight five o'clock shadow. I would normally drink that in like a midwinter hot cocoa, but the whole effect was ruined by his fall of long brown hair.

Long hair.

I deleted the photo and stabbed Ranée's speed dial number.

"Hey, Em." Her voice was so innocent it was guilty.

"I already took it down but not before Paul texted me to ask me what was going on."

"Took what down?"

"Stop. You only sound guiltier. I know you hacked my Facebook."

"Hacking is a really strong word coming from someone who left her laptop open."

"In my bedroom!"

"The door was open."

"Just so we're clear, I'm going to kill you."

"No, you're not."

"Believe it. I have to go fix this." I hung up and posted a quick "Roommate hacked my Facebook" status before I logged out so she couldn't do it again. Then I sent Paul a quick text. "Sorry, Ranée thought she was being funny."

He sent back a question mark. I tried again. "Ranée was pranking me with that picture. I don't know who that guy is. Nothing to worry about."

His reply was slow in coming, not pinging me until I was back in my car. "I don't really get her."

Yeah, no kidding. I heard that from both of them about each other at least once a week.

It took me a half hour to get home through traffic. When I opened the door to our apartment, Ranée jumped off the couch and ran for her room, but she wasn't fast enough to keep me from getting my foot in her door.

"I left some Panda Express on the counter. We can talk after you eat." She said it through the crack.

"Open up. You're being ridiculous. Do you honestly think I'm going to hurt you?"

She flung the door wide. "Of course not, dummy. You'll just lecture me to death, but it'll be half as long if you do it on a full stomach." Then she pushed me hard enough to get my foot out of the door and shut it again.

I scowled at it. "Junk food is why I had to go to the gym tonight, and you're the reason I didn't work off last night's celebration. I lost my treadmill to Facebook drama."

"That was your choice," she called, unapologetic. "It's orange chicken. And fried rice."

I scowled for another second. But I really did love orange

chicken. So I went into the kitchen. Ranée gave me five minutes before she came out.

"Have the happy food endorphins reached your brain?"

I finished my bite. "I think I won't kill you."

"Come on, it was funny." She sat down on the other side of the table.

"Tell that to Paul."

"Ha. I could diagram a knock-knock joke for him and he still wouldn't get why it's funny."

"You just have very different senses of humor."

"No. I *have* a sense of humor. He doesn't. *That's* the difference."

Normally this would be where I rolled my eyes at her, but I didn't want to take them off my next piece of chicken. "You're way too hard on him."

"He didn't laugh once during our Marx Brothers marathon last week."

"He didn't?"

"No."

I hadn't noticed, but that was surprising. Everyone laughed during the Marx Brothers. "He's just not an old movie fan." I wasn't exactly sure if that was true. We didn't watch a lot of movies together. "But I don't want to talk about Paul anymore. I explained the picture and he's fine. But I'm really worried that you suddenly know how to do Photoshop. There's no way this ends well for me. Or anyone who knows you."

She waved away my concern. "Relax. I didn't do it. I know a guy."

I set my fork down to study her closely. "Ranée. People

who 'know guys' usually have mob connections or crack dealers."

"Shut up. Not like that. I mean one of my brother's friends is kind of internet famous for his Photoshopping skills. People send in Photoshop requests. Usually, he'll give you some hilarious version of what you ask for. Look." She tapped her phone a few times and pulled up Twitter then handed it to me.

The account belonged to someone calling himself @crankymtnman. She'd picked a tweet from someone who sent him a picture of a woman our age looking down with her hands over her mouth in happy surprise. The tweet read, "Hey, @crankymtnman, I told my mom my boyfriend of 2 weeks proposed to freak her out, but he didn't. Can you make it look like he did? Any man will do." His reply was a photoshopped picture of a Gringotts goblin down on one knee proposing while she looked delighted.

I handed it back to her. "That's pretty funny."

She nodded. "Sean really likes him. I've met him a couple of times. He's a funny guy. You should check out his feed some time. He nails it. If you're lucky, he'll actually do what you ask, but usually he messes with the people who request his skills."

"So Cranky Mountain Man decided to mess with you, huh?"

"No, his real name is Jack, and he did exactly what I asked him to."

"Photoshop me with some corny romance cover guy?"

"Corny or hot?"

"Hot until the fake hair makes him corny."

"Interesting," she murmured.

"Stop being mysterious. Why is that interesting?"

She tapped her phone again and turned it to show me a picture of Sean with the guy from the picture I'd deleted. "Because I asked him to Photoshop you with a long-haired hot dude to give you a vision of what was possible. That hot guy is Jack himself, and the hair is one hundred percent real. I've never seen him use himself in a photo hack before. I'll tell him you thought he was hot, but I think I'll skip the corny part."

And she was out of the chair and down the hall, thumbs flying, before I could even dive for her phone.

Chapter 3

I checked first thing in the morning to make sure Ranée hadn't gotten into my Facebook again. None of the notifications raised red flags. I looked at Ranée's page to make sure she wasn't up to any shenanigans there, and when that was all clear, I texted Paul.

`Are we still on for dinner tonight?`

He texted right back that he would pick me up at 7. He didn't play games where he waited a certain amount of time to call or return a message. It was one of the things I liked about him.

I half-wished I could reschedule our date for the next night. I always started Fridays with a tingle of anticipation for the weekend, but usually by quitting time I was dragging myself home and longing to be absorbed into the Clan of the Bedding to rule there as its queen. In pajamas. And thick socks.

But Paul wanted to take me out to celebrate my promotion too, and after Ranée's prank I owed him more than getting shuffled into a different calendar box so I could nap. Okay, fine. Not nap: so I could binge watch the new season of *The Crown*.

I couldn't blow off Paul for that, not when he was taking me out to Pacifica, the best seafood restaurant in the Bay Area. I didn't think I was a fancy food person until my mom and stepdad took me there for my graduation from Berkeley, and I discovered that I could love foods that sounded imaginary--like truffles and sablefish--as much as I loved Panda Express. I'm a complicated woman.

Work flew by, but I still came home as tired as expected, except Paul was due in an hour and I had no time to be tired. I splashed cold water on my face, posted a short status about going to Pacifica to celebrate with him, and went to get ready, pulling my new shoes out of their box. Time to let these girls out to play. I added a picture of them to my post. They deserved a little recognition. Heck, they deserved their own Instagram account.

He rang the buzzer of our apartment exactly at 7, and I was glad that Ranée was already out for the evening. His punctuality had gotten on her nerves ever since she'd come home one night to find him waiting on our doorstep, staring at his watch. Apparently, he'd gotten there five minutes earlier but was waiting for the exact minute he'd told me to expect him before he knocked. Ranée thought that was stupid, but then again, Ranée hadn't liked him from the start, so she used anything and everything he did as ammunition. That's when she started calling him Proper Paul like it was a bad thing. But that was another thing I liked about Paul. I was a project manager because I had exceptional organizational skills, but Paul was next level. It was nice not to have to worry about the details when he was around.

I opened the door and smiled at him. "Hey, you."

He stepped in and hugged me. He leaned down for a kiss, but I turned my head, and he dropped it on my cheek. "Don't want to smudge my lipstick. You can do that later." His easy affection was another one of the things I liked about him. It was also the biggest reason I could ignore Ranée's complaints that he was too uptight. He was so comfortable with open displays of affection—little touches, long hugs, kisses regardless of who was watching. Uptight men didn't do that. Uptight men—like my dad—were stingy with their hugs and affection.

"You ready for dinner? I checked the traffic and we need to get on the road if we want to make our reservation on time."

He lifted my coat from the hook by the door and held it for me. He didn't say anything about my dress, a sleek black number. But when I turned and tied my coat, his eyebrows rose as his glance fell to my red stilettos.

"Are those new?" he asked.

"Yeah. A little treat for getting the promotion. Do you like them?" The glint in his eye said that Ranée was wrong, and that Paul was very capable of appreciating these shoes, but then the glint disappeared as worry clouded over it.

"They're nice, but it's kind of a walk from the car to the restaurant. Are you going to be okay?"

So...maybe a small part of me wished that the glint would have stayed, and that he would have offered to...I don't know, carry me up to the restaurant door or something so long as I kept on the sexy red shoes. Not that I needed help walking in them. I was well-practiced in heels. But it was sweet in its own way for him to worry about my comfort.

"I'll be fine." I smiled and scooped up my purse and locked the door behind us.

On the drive over, we talked about work. He asked me about my new duties and caught me up on what was happening at his accounting firm. At the restaurant we ordered and went right back to shop talk, something that was easy to do with jobs as similar as ours.

The plates the waiter set in front of us looked delicious, but the excitement of the week had finally caught up with me, and I struggled to focus on the conversation until a series of electronic chirps broke through my end-of-the-week fog. Suddenly the flaky fish in my mouth tasted about as good as if I'd licked the tablecloth.

I gave my phone a quick glance. It was all Facebook alerts telling me someone had commented on a post Ranée tagged me in. I had a feeling I knew what was up, but I turned it to silent and tucked it back into my purse. I could deal with it—and Ranée—later, but then Paul's phone—which of course he'd remembered to set to silent—started up with a persistent series of buzzes as it vibrated.

Paul frowned. "Why's it going nuts? Something going on?"

"Let's just turn them off and enjoy dinner." Because now I knew for sure that Ranée had once again put her Jack friend up to no good.

Paul's forehead was already furrowed as he reached for his jacket pocket. "I'll just make sure that there's nothing wrong." He slid his finger across the screen and the furrows turned to gullies. He glanced from me to the phone and back again. Finally, he shook his head. "Why does this guy say he's here with you right now?"

He turned his screen to show me a picture of me wearing a sparkly silver dress, sitting at a table very similar to our linen and crystal covered one, except in the picture I was leaning against a man with a face that was getting way too familiar way too fast.

There was Jack again, his stupid hair up in a stupid man bun while the rest of him was all business casual, striped button down with a sleek watch on an arm resting comfortably around my shoulders.

I snatched up my phone and found the photo. *Emily Riker was with Jack Dobson at Pacifica.*

I untagged myself while I offered Paul a tight smile. "It's Ranée messing around again. I'll text her really fast."

He nodded like he wasn't concerned but his hands stayed curled around his fork and knife.

STOP WITH THE PHOTOSHOPS. I typed like I was doing a keyboarding speed test. **TAKE THE PIC DOWN**.

I shot Paul another apologetic smile. "Sorry, should be handled in a minute." He waved like it was no big deal but then his fingers curled right back around his knife.

But the alerts didn't stop. I rolled my eyes at Paul to show him how exasperated I was and turned it off. "That should solve it," I said. "Time to focus on relaxing."

"And celebrating," he added. "You're a project manager now. That's a big deal." He called over the waiter to bring two glasses of champagne.

We toasted my rise through middle management and had a comfortable evening talking work and life, topping it all off with rich chocolate cheesecake. But somehow neither the bubbles nor the dessert was able to scrub the bad taste of Ranée's newest prank from my mouth.

Chapter 4

"I'm really sorry," I said to Paul again at my front door. "Why don't you come in for a little while? We can watch some Fallon and shake off the weirdness."

"There's no weirdness," Paul said weirdly.

"Are you sure? You still seem pretty unhappy about all of this." Honestly, it was kind of getting on my nerves. I could understand being annoyed by the situation, but it made no sense to be annoyed with me. I'd obviously had nothing to do with it, and I'd clearly tried everything I could to fix it.

"I'm just tired," he said. "And yes, it does bug me that Ranée won't let this drop."

"But why?" The more I thought about it, the better I thought the question was. "Do you feel threatened by it? It's just a prank."

He sighed and ran his hand over his face. "You're right. But I'm worn out enough from work for it to irritate me more than it should, and that's as good a reason as any for me to head out. Sorry I'm being lame. I think I need a good night's sleep."

Fat chance. Paul was a chronic insomniac who rarely slept more than four hours a night, but I nodded. “I totally get it. I’ll call you tomorrow.”

He hugged me and pressed a short kiss against my lips, so short that I could tell how tired he really was. Paul usually left me with pretty great goodnight kisses. I’d told that to Ranée once in an effort to defend him, and she said it was probably because he’d done an intensive kissing technique analysis complete with diagrams.

Okay, that was almost believable. But I didn’t care because I was the beneficiary of either his analysis, his experience, or his natural talent. Or all three. Good kissing was good kissing.

I fell asleep before Ranée got home, and she was still asleep when I woke up, so I set to work trying to crack the prank mystery without her. It was still up on her Facebook wall with about fifty reactions and a string of questions. “Who is this?” “Cute couple!” “Did she break up with Paul?”

I contemplated dragging Ranée out of bed for answers, but there were friendlier rattlesnakes than a just-woken Ranée.

I examined the picture more closely. It was another Photoshop, but how’d this Jack guy do it? I didn’t own a silver dress like the one “I” was wearing in the picture.

I did a Google image search for the restaurant name and hit the jackpot deep on the tenth page. Or the “Jack”pot. I snorted at my own joke. He’d stuck our heads onto another couple who’d celebrated on a different night at Pacifica. There was the sparkly silver dress but on a brunette, and there was the button-down shirt on some other dude.

He was tagged in the picture too.

Wait.

I didn't even have to wait for Ranée to wake up to solve this. I clicked on his name to find the messaging link. Time to stop this idiocy.

EMILY: The photos are weird. Knock it off.

I got the "..." typing dots. Then they disappeared. Then they reappeared. It happened at least three more times. Finally, a message popped up.

JACK: Hi.
EMILY: Stop
JACK: Sure.
JACK: But
JACK: What are we talking about?
EMILY: The pictures on Ranée's FB.
JACK: Uh…brb.
JACK: Those were not me.
EMILY: That's not you in the picture?
JACK: No, that's me.
EMILY: Did you Photoshop that picture?
JACK: Yes.
EMILY: Then take it down.
JACK: I didn't post that. Isn't Ranée your roommate? Can't you take this up with her?

My fingers hesitated over the keyboard. It was a fair question. But Ranée had refused to delete it so far. And there was the whole issue of her being scary in the morning.

I dropped my hands to my lap. Now I felt kind of dumb for yelling at this guy for doing what Ranée had asked. I was about to close the laptop and wait for her to wake up so I could yell at her instead when another DM popped up.

JACK: Are they really freaking you out?
EMILY: Yes to the millionth power.
JACK: MILLIONTH? I could have understood to the thousandth power but the millionth is just hurtful.
EMILY: Funny…except not to my BOYFRIEND. Will you stop Photoshopping pics of us?
JACK: Sorry. Yes.
JACK: Wait, there's an US?

I should have left it there. I really should have. But for reasons I couldn't really explain, I did a fast and much sloppier photo edit on his mountain biking picture, cropping his head then pasting it onto the body of the first image I found under a search for "bodybuilders." Now his bike-helmeted head was on top of a big old muscle guy in a tiny speedo. Then I pressed send.

EMILY: No more doing Photoshops for Ranée. You're enabling her, and she needs NO encouragement. Stop supplying her or I'll start putting up this kind of garbage all over the place.
JACK: Uh…that wouldn't bother me. But I get why you're bothered. Can we start over?
EMILY: ???

The longest chain of "..." in the history of modern communication disappeared and reappeared. At last a message popped up.

> JACK: Hi. I'm Jack. Sometimes it's short for Jacka...never mind. I kind of know your friend Ranée. Every now and then I take a joke too far. I think I recently did that to a girl named...you. So could we start over if I swear not to do any more favors for Ranée?

Was he serious? He wanted to be friends? I could understand that he'd only been doing Ranée's bidding, but he'd caused some friction between me and Paul, and I was still irritated about having to smooth it over.

> EMILY: That's a nice offer, but no thanks. I just can't deal with your man bun.

That should shut him down permanently. I closed the chat window and wandered into the kitchen for a bagel. When I finished eating it, I discovered I hadn't shut down Jack at all. Another message was waiting for me.

> JACK: I was going to let this go and stay out of your hair, but then you had to go and make a crack about mine. This man bun is my crowning girly. I thought you were a better woman than that.

I couldn't let it go. Only an incredibly evolved human could have left such a perfect typo alone.

I was not evolved.

EMILY: Your crowning *girly*? I mean…you said it.

JACK: I MEANT GLORY. MY CROWNING GLORY.

EMILY: Your subconscious knows the truth even if you don't. Not that there's anything wrong with that. You do you.

I waited for another smart remark, but not even the dots appeared, and I realized I'd spent a full two minutes waiting for them. Which was stupid. The whole point of sending a message at all had been to get him to stop paying attention to me, so mission accomplished.

I shut my laptop and took it to my room, then changed into my workout clothes for my kickboxing class. Or as Ranée called it, my "kickdancing" class. I had just scooped up my keys when my phone chimed with a DM alert. I didn't like the little lurch my stomach gave because my brain told it that it might be Jack.

"Shut up, both of you," I told them. And then just to break a ridiculous habit before it started, I swept my phone into my gym bag without even checking it.

Which would have been a totally boss move if I hadn't checked it the second my kickdancing—BOXING—class finished. And there it was, a message notification from Jack.

Well. I wasn't going to read it. Who cared? It wasn't a big deal. I was in a relationship with a good guy, and I wasn't the kind of girl who was going to get distracted by the next hot guy that came along.

Not that Jack was hot. Because man bun. Maybe if it weren't for that he'd be the kind of guy I'd notice. But that was a moot point.

I drove home and threw myself on the sofa, trying to figure out what I wanted to do to relax. Normally simply walking through the door would do the trick. Ranée and I had met when she worked in marketing at my software firm. We'd clicked right away, and even though she'd taken a job with another company shortly after, we'd decided to share an apartment. Our personalities complemented each other, but so did our tastes. My preference for minimalist lines married with her love of bright pops of color produced an upbeat mid-century design scheme inside our cozy apartment.

I'd found the perfect charcoal gray vintage sofa and she'd livened it up with lime green throw pillows. It was like this throughout our living room and the dining nook/kitchen. The perfect symmetry of my furniture lines and the cheerful splashes of her color always calmed me when I got home, no matter what kind of day I'd had. But right now, I still felt buzzy with unspent emotional energy.

Maybe mindless celebrity stalking would do the trick? I curled up with a *People* magazine.

"Where have you been?" Ranée asked, padding out to the living room in bare feet. She had toilet paper shoved between each of her toes. They sported a shiny new shade of purple.

I sat straight up again. "Take that picture off your Facebook."

"Why? It's funny."

"It's not even kind of funny. I've already smoothed things over with Paul." Probably. I texted him on the way to the gym to see about grabbing a movie later, but he said he was snowed with work. It had happened before, so it could be true. It was true. Probably? "But I yelled at Jack, and now I'm going to yell at you."

"You yelled at Jack? Poor Jack. That's not nice."

"Neither is putting him up to stuff like this! Take it down, Ranée."

"Fine." She hobbled over to a kitchen chair, plopped down, and pulled her phone from her pocket to delete the picture. "There. Done."

"Good. Now promise not to do it again."

She gave me a "no deal" grimace.

I turned my back on her and settled onto the couch with *People*.

"What are you reading?"

I didn't answer.

"Emily?"

I ignored her.

"You're giving me the silent treatment?"

I licked my finger and made an elaborate point of turning the page.

"Very mature, Em."

I'd learned through three years of experience that it was the only thing that would work. I turned another page.

"Ugh, all right. I won't post any more Fabio Photoshops."

"Aw, thanks, Ranée. How nice of you. You couldn't if you wanted to. Jack won't do any more of them." I settled down to enjoy the magazine for real.

"I thought my magazines were too lowbrow for you."

"They are. Unless they have Chris Evans on the front. Which this one does. Now shut up so I can concentrate on finding out what he's looking for in a woman."

"Why would you need Captain America when you've got Paul? He's Captain All-American." She grabbed her water bottle for a swig and set it down abruptly. "Wait. I just realized that Captain America is the most boring superhero. Of course he's your favorite."

"Uh, no, Superman is the most boring superhero."

"Oh yeah. That's right." She took another swallow. "You know which superhero you really need in your life?"

I could already sense where this was going. "Don't say it."

"Thor."

"Because big pecs and long hair. Got it."

"Tell me he's not hot."

"Oh, totally. You know, *after* he got the haircut in the last Thor movie."

She opened her mouth like she wanted to argue the point then shrugged and settled into the easy chair and drew her knees up to her chin so she could peer down at her toenails. "Will Paul let you have purple toenails?"

"Paul doesn't *let* me do anything. Can you lay off him?"

She shrugged then drummed her fingers on the table for a minute. I refused to let her know it was bugging me. Suddenly the drumming stopped. "What do you mean Jack won't do any more Photoshops? How do you know?"

"He said he wouldn't."

She hopped up and hobbled over to plunk down on the

other side of the sofa. I moved my feet so she wouldn't sit on them. "You talked to him?"

"I sent him an IM. He was really nice about it."

"If he said he wouldn't make any more then why did I get the silent treatment anyway?"

"I wanted to make you say it."

"You're the worst." She pulled the magazine down so it lay in my lap. "Pay attention to me. Let's talk about Jack. Did he say anything else?"

"I don't know."

"That's the kind of thing you know or don't know."

I tugged at the magazine but she wouldn't let it go. "He sent me another IM."

"What did it say?"

I jerked the magazine back and leafed through it. "I don't know. I haven't read it."

"Why not?"

"Because I don't care?" I wish I hadn't ended that as a question. I hadn't meant to.

She rested her chin on her knees and studied me as closely as she had her toenail polish. I didn't like it so much. The staring. Her toes were cute. "Interesting," she murmured. "Maybe not checking his message is making it more important than it actually is. It's like...like Harry Potter! When he's not supposed to look in that whatchamacallit mirror, but the harder he fights it the more he wants to."

"The Mirror of Erised, and that's not exactly how it went."

"Nerd."

"You know that's not an insult, right?"

"You know you're just being a coward by not looking at his message, right?"

I threw up my hands. "I will do anything to shut you up right now." I climbed off the sofa and grabbed my gym bag, digging through it until I found my phone. With my best you-are-so-ridiculous side eye at Ranée, I opened the message.

And gasped.

Chapter 5

The message was from Jack, all right. It was another picture, but he'd Photoshopped himself again, this time astride a gray dappled unicorn on a beach, his long hair streaming in the breeze, the sky behind him filled with kites. He was wearing linen pants and no shirt, and he had a fake barbed wire tattoo around his bicep. But the best part was the crown of flowers he wore. He'd captioned it, "I AM MANLY, NOT GIRLY."

I laughed. And kept laughing.

"Let me see." Ranée snatched the phone from my hand. "Oh, now this is some of his best work yet. Can you really say no to that?" She handed my phone back. "I mean, compared to—"

I could tell by the look in her eye that it was going to be some kind of anti-Paul remark, so I held up my hand. "Enough. I can't even tell you how old that's getting."

She shrugged. "Thank goodness Paul won't see those DMs."

"Why are you saying it like that?"

"Like what?"

"Like I'm hiding something."

She tsked. "Ah, baby girl. I didn't say anything like that. That must be your guilty conscience talking. And if you feel guilty it must be because there's a little spark there that Paul wouldn't like."

"You're ridiculous. I don't feel guilty even a tiny bit. Jack and I were forced into this conversation because you put us both in an awkward position."

"So, you're done talking to him?"

I set the phone on the coffee table and picked up the magazine again. "I think so. I don't want to give him the wrong idea."

I expected an argument so when she stayed quiet, I glanced up from an article debating who wore a yellow latex dress better. Since the answer was neither, I gave Ranée my full attention again. She opened and closed her mouth twice without saying anything. "What? Spit it out."

"It's just...I don't think Jack usually bothers staying in touch with someone after he does a Photoshop request. I mean, if you look at his Instagram, he doesn't really interact beyond posting the pictures even though his followers are constantly trying to get his attention on there and Twitter."

"So?"

"So you obviously have his attention."

"I don't want it."

"But why not? He's hot, and Sean vouches for him."

"Because I have a boyfriend!"

She held up her hands in surrender. "Okay, okay. I'm just saying, he's provoked more emotion from you in a single day than Paul has the whole time you've dated him."

"That's a point for Paul."

"Fine," she said, flouncing toward her bedroom. "I won't try to save you from a boring relationship anymore...today."

I stuck my tongue out at her, but as soon as she closed her door, I opened Jack's message again.

EMILY: Fine. Not girly. You're practically an Old Spice commercial. You should be so proud.

I couldn't really explain why I'd responded. It made much more sense to let the conversation die like I'd told Ranée I would. Maybe it just seemed like a shame to let all the effort that he put into the Photoshop masterpiece go to waste.

But I definitely didn't want him to think I wanted to keep the conversation going just because, so I sent a quick follow up message.

EMILY: Also, does acknowledging your non-girliness guarantee me that I'm not going to get tagged in any more posts?

JACK: No. Just telling me that you didn't like it was enough to do the trick. Again, sorry.

I mean...it was a pretty decent thing to say, especially since it hadn't even been his idea. My fingers almost tapped out another reply, but I caught myself. I set it down instead and went back to celebrity gossip.

But my phone buzzed again, and I snatched it up.

JACK: Also, girl isn't an insult, and I wasn't offended when you said that. Girls are cool. I just want you to know that I know that.
EMILY: Appreciate your wokeness, but if we're going to be truly politically correct, I don't think we say "girls." I think we're supposed to say "women."
JACK: Point taken, but I actually meant girls. As in small humans. Which sounds weird. Some of the toughest, coolest people I know are girls.

I believed him. It surprised me, but I did. So I said so.

EMILY: I get it. My nieces are tiny and fierce and amazing. Anyway, we're good. Best wishes, etc.

At least now the conversation had closure, no weird, half-finished thoughts on either side.

And now that the situation was settled, I sent Paul a text letting him know that the Photoshopping would stop. His reply was terse. "Good."

I couldn't explain why that bothered me, but it did. I mean, I'd be annoyed if some woman started Photoshopping him and tagging him on social media. Probably. Maybe? I might just think it was funny. But I could definitely understand why it had bugged him. But saying "Good," like I was a child who had obeyed, or his secretary at work who'd done as ordered...

I'd been on the verge of suggesting a do over and going somewhere nice to eat, my treat, but now I didn't want to. I didn't have anything to make up for. Instead, I downloaded a fantasy novel my mom had been raving about and curled up with it in my room.

When Paul texted in the late afternoon to see if I wanted to go to dinner, I took a raincheck and then claimed the TV remote when Ranée left for the night. When she came home close to midnight, I was polishing off some mint chip ice cream and finishing up the last season of "Jane the Virgin."

"Big night?" She pushed my feet off the sofa and settled in the other corner.

I waved my ice cream spoon at her and puffed my cheeks out. "The biggest, hashtag no regrets. Did you do anything fun?"

"Sushi and an escape room with some of the girls in accounting. Hey, I was wondering..."

Her tone was far too casual to fool me. "Yeah?"

"Was there more to your DMs with Jack than I saw today?"

"Huh? No." And even though I hadn't said or done anything wrong, and even though I had nothing to hide, a pang of guilt darted through my chest for a blessedly short second. "Why do you ask?"

"I just got the most interesting phone call. You sure you didn't say anything that could be...misconstrued?"

Wait a minute.

Had I?

"I feel like you're getting at something, but I don't know what," I said. I couldn't think of anything I'd hidden about my DMs with Jack because there wasn't anything to hide.

"Sean called me. He wanted to know if I was in the mood

for a road trip up to see him. And maybe bringing my roommate along too."

I dropped the spoon. "Are you suggesting that your brother wants you to come up to see him, but this is a trick to get me up to Jack's neck of the woods?"

"You have no idea how literal that is." It was a grumble. Ranée didn't much care for the woods. Her idea of a good time outdoors involved a beach and frou-frou drinks. "But yes, I think that's what Sean was getting at. He wasn't exactly subtle."

"That is so weird and over the line. No, I would not like to go see some random dude from the internet. I wouldn't like to do that AT ALL."

She sighed. "I want to convince you that you should live a little, but yeah, in this case it's over the line. I was mainly worried that I'd missed out on some juicy DM that would inspire such love in Jack's heart."

"No. Ugh, this is no bueno. He seemed like a totally normal guy. I mean besides the thing where he was willing to go along with your idiotic scheme in the first place." I climbed off the couch and tossed my empty ice cream carton in the trash. "It's definitely time for me to go to bed. My day has officially reached it's crazy quotient."

Ranée's answer was a yawn, and I wandered off to my room, happy to read myself to sleep and quit worrying about Jack.

When a call from Paul woke me up the next morning, it was a reminder that there were still sane men with healthy boundaries in the world, and one of them was mine. "Hey," I said, blinking the sleep out of my eyes.

"Sleeping Beauty, huh? You're missing a beautiful day."

"Yeah? Good weather?"

"Not a wisp of fog anywhere. Let me take you out to breakfast."

I struggled to sit up. I had a far too co-dependent relationship with my comforter. I realized I had no desire to leave it and snuggled down further instead. We needed more time together, my bed and I. "I have a better idea. Why don't you come by after I'm more awake, and I'll make you breakfast?"

A DM chirp sounded in my ear. I stifled a sigh when I realized who it probably was. Great.

"Cooking for me, huh? Sounds great. When should I come over?"

I sniffed my shirt. No stink. That meant I didn't need to shower, and I could make an omelet in 15 minutes flat, so I did some genius-level computations and figured out how much more quality time I could give myself and the comforter. "An hour?"

"See you then."

Yessssss. Forty more minutes in bed, five to change and brush my hair, and then fifteen to cook. I wiggled down and pulled the covers up to my chin. This was happiness. People talked about trying to bottle it like it was a scent or a potion. Nope, it was just a down comforter. Come to think of it, I could stay in bed for fifty-five minutes if Paul and I just cooked together. That was a fun couple thing to do.

I closed my eyes. Bliss.

Until my DM alert pinged again. I snatched up my phone to tap out an annoyed, "Go away," but Jack's first message caught me by surprise. All it said was, "SORRY SORRY SORRY." Then he'd followed up with an explanation.

JACK: My idiot friend Sean just told me that he tried to talk Ranée into coming up here and bringing you with her. I had nothing to do with that. This time I'm staying out of your inbox for real. Just didn't want you to be stressed for no reason. Sorry again.

Relief washed over me.

EMILY: Thank goodness. Have to admit, I thought for a second there that everything had escalated quickly. Like maybe have-SWAT-on-speed-dial kind of quickly.
JACK: I know. Seriously. That was all him. I won't bother you again.

I realized that the relief I felt wasn't about him leaving me alone. It was…I wasn't sure I could explain it. It was more like I'd left our exchange yesterday feeling like he was a good guy, and it was nice to know it was true.

I spent another half hour bonding with my blankets and then finally climbed out of bed to brush my teeth, wrangle a ponytail, and put on some hummingbird leggings and a thin, comfy sweater. I was in the middle of pulling all the ingredients out when Paul rang the doorbell, an hour to the minute after we'd hung up.

"Hi," he said, stepping inside and dropping a kiss on my cheek. I smiled. Looked like he was back to feeling like himself.

"I'm glad you're here."

"Oh, hey, did I not give you enough time to get ready? I'm

sorry. You didn't have to rush for me."

"No, I just thought it would be fun to do this together. Come on into the kitchen."

Confusion wrinkled the corners of his eyes. "What are you—oh. No, I meant...never mind."

But he'd flicked a glance at my outfit. I quirked an eyebrow at him. "Something wrong with my clothes?"

His cheeks flushed slightly. "No, not at all. Forget it. I was obviously being an idiot."

A cough sounded in the hallway. OF COURSE Ranée had been there to overhear that whole exchange. Of course she had.

I refused to look at Ranée, knowing her face would be lit up with glee over Paul declaring himself an idiot. Instead I grabbed his wrist and pulled him into the kitchen. "You chop onions, I'll make a green salsa."

Ranée wandered into the living room and settled on the sofa where she'd have a clear view of what we were doing. "Can I get one?"

I waved her off with a spatula. Nope. She didn't want an omelet. She wanted fodder to use against Paul. I mentally willed him not to give her any ammunition. My ESP must have worked because he kept his conversation to the crazy hours he was keeping at work and questions about the food prep. She finally grew bored and disappeared into her room again.

Paul glanced over as I chopped some cilantro. "I don't like cilantro, remember?"

Of course I remembered. We'd had an entire conversation when we'd first started dating about how he thought it tasted like dish soap and how I thought he was crazy. "I know that, Paul." I couldn't keep the irritation out of my voice.

His eyebrows shot up. "Sorry. You seem, um, irritable today."

"Only when you show up to my house and start nitpicking me when I'm trying to do something nice for you."

"Whoa, I'm not nitpicking you."

"You implied my clothes were slobby, and you're micromanaging what I'm putting on your omelet."

He went back to slicing the mushrooms I'd switched him to. "Sorry," he said after he had one portioned into perfectly sized pieces. "I can see why I was coming off like that. I didn't mean to sound critical."

I shrugged. "It's fine."

He winced. "If there's anything I learned about women from my mom, it's that 'fine' never means fine."

"I mean it." I didn't mean it. But I didn't feel like getting into it. I just wanted to get the omelets in the skillet. "Why don't you sit, and I'll get these cooked."

He almost looked as if he would argue, but smart man that he was, he closed his mouth again and busied himself with setting the table while I poured the eggs into the skillet. I used the few minutes it took for the omelets to set to let go of the temper that had been rising since he walked in.

They cooked up perfectly, and I slid his onto his plate with a smile and took a seat across from him.

He dug right in, making appreciative noises as he ate, then he smiled back, a touch of hesitation in the curve of his lips. "It's really good."

"Thanks." My mom had taught me to make them when I

was twelve. I couldn't cook a lot of things, but omelets I could do.

"No, seriously, I don't think I've ever had a better omelet. Like this is French chef good."

"All right, that's enough. You're already forgiven. You don't have to go that far."

A look I couldn't quite read crossed his face, and it surprised me. We'd been dating five months. I thought I knew all his expressions except maybe extreme pain.

"Emily..." He set his fork down. "I meant it, it's an excellent omelet. But I get why it sounded forced. Do you feel like we've been off-kilter for a while?"

This was another thing I liked about him. He wasn't afraid to face things head on. It was all part of his extreme efficiency. He'd rather solve something than wait for it to solve itself, and it was something I needed to be better about. I could do it at work, but when it came to relationships I tended to wait for problems to magically go away by ignoring them.

"Off-kilter." I tried the phrase out to see if it was the right one to describe the way things had been lately. "Yeah, that's a good way to put it."

"I know I'm working a ton right now, and it makes it hard to give everything in my life the attention it deserves. I worked up a spreadsheet to help me strike a better work-life balance."

In the distance, approximately the distance of Ranée's room at the end of the hall, I thought I heard a snort when Paul said "spreadsheet," but he didn't seem to notice as he went on. "I've realized in some ways it's easier for me to carve out longer blocks of time less frequently than it is to try to string together shorter blocks of time more often. Interesting, huh?"

"Um..." I realized I was failing to see his point. "That's...wow."

"I'm not communicating clearly. Hang on." He pulled out his iPhone, tapped a few things, and handed it to me. It was a chart with color-coded blocks labeled with things like "work" or "gym" or "Emily." I showed up in one large pink block on the Saturday column.

"I don't really want to be pink." It was a joking complaint so I could buy time to process the weird, gut-level reaction that was happening. It wasn't warm fuzzies or happy tingles. More like...indigestion. Except my omelet was too good for it to be indigestion. This was not annoyance. Or uneasiness. But it was definitely somewhere between the two.

"The color is beside the point." His tone was a tad impatient, which happened sometimes when he wanted to talk shop and I wanted to goof off. But my goofing off was good for him, which he recognized when he pulled his head out of his...spreadsheets.

He took the phone back. "What color do you want to be?"

"Azure, and make it honey-scented."

He blinked at me.

I sighed and took the phone from his hands, turning it face down on the table. "I don't want to be a checklist item. I don't want to be something you fit in around everything else."

"But that's the whole point. I'm happy doing anything with you, but I want us to be able to spend real time together, not the time we can grab at the end of the day or in between other things." His blue eyes shone with sincerity, and I grinned and leaned forward to steal a quick kiss.

"All right. I understand what you're saying. This weirdness between us has got to go. What is it even about? I want to be done with it."

He reached over to play with my hair, one of my favorite of his habits. "I'm not sure. I think it's because we were both getting so busy at work and then all of a sudden you're showing up in pictures with another guy. I felt...threatened."

I pulled away. "That had nothing to do with me, and I'm not going to apologize for it again."

"I know," he said. "I'm sorry, that came out wrong. I'll rephrase. I got insecure, but I think it's because I've felt disconnected from you. So I have an idea. Let's go to Napa next weekend and reset. I'll work like a maniac to clear all my work so I can leave it behind, and we'll forget the rest of the world for a while."

Napa was a magic word right on par with bibbity-bobbity-boo. But this time, it didn't cast a spell over me.

And that...that was a problem. A big one.

"Paul," I said, gently pulling his hand away from my hair so the section he'd been winding slipped through his fingers. "A trip to Napa sounds so good, but work is crazy for me right now too. It isn't a good time for me to leave for a whole weekend. Even if I could make the time—which I can't—I don't think my mind would be on Napa. Or you."

His face fell, and he rearranged it to hide his disappointment, but the visible effort made me smile. "Stop. You look like I just told you that you can never have a puppy."

"I feel about that disappointed," he said, sighing.

"Don't. It's helping me see your point about trying to carve out big chunks of time instead of lots of little ones. Don't worry about it." I slid my hand around his neck, tickling the hair perfectly trimmed along his nape. He loved when I did that, and it won a reluctant smile from him. "We'll be fine. I just have to find the groove with this promotion, and we'll be back to usual."

A tiny shadow flitted through his eyes, but finally his smile widened. "Fine. A long weekend is out of the plan, but can you give me Saturday?"

I was going to protest, but he swept in for a kiss and stole the words. I gave up with a laugh. "Yes, I can give you Saturday."

"Thanks for the sacrifice." He smiled, but I could sense ragged edges that he wasn't quite letting me see.

"Stop," I said, softening the order with another kiss. "It's not a sacrifice. I want to spend next Saturday with you. No subtext."

"I'm going to make it so worth it." He was already on his phone, probably pulling up a spreadsheet to plan it.

I laughed again and took his phone from his hand and set it on the table. "Be present. I'm here right now, you're here right now, so what should we do?"

I didn't expect him to say, "Window shop," but that's what he did.

"Window shop?" I repeated like it was a German word I was learning to pronounce.

"Yeah. Let's run over to that new pedestrian market and see what they have. I've been looking for interesting pieces to put in my office to give it a cooler vibe."

Well. It wasn't as fun as any of the things I'd imagined, all of which involved staying inside (cough cough kissing) but sure, okay. We could go look for office knick-knacks to give him some street cred. Or whatever kind of cred cool art gave to an upwardly mobile type like Paul. Fun.

I mean, not really. But making out was also not fun if you had to suggest it, so instead I grabbed my sneakers and we set off for the market. It ended up being fun for real, mostly because Paul grew more exasperated with every recommendation I made. He finally gave up altogether when I insisted he needed some blown glass grapes that looked more like stylized crystal poop emojis.

"Come on, you should totally get these grapes since we can't go to Napa for the real thing," I'd said.

And he'd pried them from my hands, hauled me from the gallery, and herded me into an ice cream shop to shut me up. Smart man.

Chapter 6

The week went fast even though each day felt sooooooo long. But work kept me busy non-stop, especially since I was trying to clear my desk for Saturday so Paul could sweep me off for whatever adventure he had in mind. He wouldn't tell me what it was, but knowing him, he'd plan it down to the tiniest detail, and each one would be perfect.

It actually made the long days more bearable as I sat through staff meetings or worked through the eighteen million emails that came in hourly from my team. Whenever I wanted to just bag it and go home and crash, I would think about having a full day of being spoiled, and I'd buckle down again. And when that didn't work...I found a second form of stress relief.

Jack's social media accounts.

I was slightly ashamed of my low-grade stalking, even though I knew I didn't have any reason to be. But I'd gotten in the habit of waiting until I hit what I was sure would be the most frustrating part of my day. Then, once I handled it, I'd check his Twitter to see what new absurdity he'd gotten up to.

Monday: Bryce in purchasing put a hold on my invoice because of a snafu in the system that didn't show I was authorized to order new tech for my team.

I checked Twitter to distract from the need to throttle Bryce in purchasing. I told myself I was looking for tech-related hashtags, but soon I found myself clicking on Jack's feed. He'd posted a picture of a frat-looking boy running across a city street, his face full of fear. The request read, "Can you make my friend look like he's running from something scary?" Jack had Photoshopped the weird, beady-eyed Dutch puppets from the Disneyland Small World ride behind him. It saved Bryce in purchasing's life.

Tuesday: the IT guy couldn't upgrade my status in the system without a help ticket request from Human Resources.

I checked Twitter to keep from winging my stapler at the wall. The request showed a twenty-something hipster alone on a stool and asked, "Can you put a bunch of people in so I look like I have a social life?" Jack had Photoshopped in a bunch of preschoolers with cake-smeared faces and made the hipster look like a balloon artist. It saved my stapler.

Wednesday: the Human Resources manager said she couldn't send a help ticket until my boss gave her a form she'd been nagging him for.

I checked Twitter to keep from flipping my desk over. Someone sent a photo of herself staring out at a beach sunset but there was a restaurant at the end of the pier in the background. "Take out the restaurant, ok," was all it said. Jack had replaced the restaurant with a pile of sardines.

Thursday: Everything went fine. My boss turned in the paperwork, and I got my system upgrade, which meant Bryce in purchasing approved my requisition.

Checking Twitter at the peak of my daily frustration had become a quick form of therapy. Well, checking Jack's clever posts had.

Once or twice it crossed my mind that Paul wouldn't be too happy if he knew about it, but there was zero contact between me and Jack. I pushed those nagging worries out of my head. I had an overdeveloped conscience that always tried to make me feel guilty for stuff I didn't need to feel guilty about. Like if I got home to discover that a cashier had accidentally given me an extra coupon, I'd have to talk myself out of making a forty minute trip to return it. Or when I smack-talked my brother's favorite NFL quarterback, I'd feel guilty for criticizing someone I didn't know. It got kind of ridiculous sometimes.

So I kept checking Twitter. Following a public humor account that I didn't interact with at all wasn't cheating. So even though Friday at work went well and nothing frustrated me at all, I checked Jack's account anyway—with a clear conscience. It was my reward for making it through my first full week as a boss.

A man had sent in a picture with his girlfriend flashing some serious red-eye and asked Jack to restore her "baby blues." So Jack Photoshopped some Mr. Magoo-style blue eyes onto her, all wild and bulgy behind thick glasses. It was disturbing. I laughed until I got the hiccups.

I arrived home in a good mood that only improved when Paul called to give me the time for our Saturday shenanigans.

Well, not shenanigans. He wasn't really a shenanigans kind of guy. He used the word "outing." And even though it meant setting the alarm for a time even a rooster would disavow, I was ready in "sailing clothes" when he knocked on the door

Saturday morning.

"Sailing clothes" were some layered J. Crew-style shirts and white capris that I settled on after googling images of "sailing clothes." It was either that, a jaunty nautical blazer and a captain's hat, or a string bikini. So I J. Crew-ed it.

Paul smiled when I answered the door. "You look perfect."

"Ah, thanks. I've always wanted to learn to sail."

"We're not learning. Sorry." A touch of anxiety dimmed his smile. "I hired a guy with a boat, and he's going to do the work. I thought it might be less stressful. I was watching YouTube tutorials to see if lessons made sense, but I kind of worried we'd spend more time being frustrated than relaxed."

I kept any disappointment out of my expression. I liked doing hands-on stuff. It was a good outlet for me to work out stress, but I could see how it would only increase Paul's. "That makes sense. Who wouldn't want someone else sailing them around for hours? We'll just lie back and enjoy it."

An hour and a half later we were out on the water with a grizzled old dude name Andrew piloting us around the bay. He didn't talk much, but I tried anyway.

"What kind of sailboat is this?"

"Sloop."

"You're kidding."

Grizzled Andrew stared at me and blinked.

"That's the best thing ever." I broke into a corny nineties dance move. I didn't trust the boat enough to stand yet, so it was mostly seated chest pumps. "Sloop, sloopy-doop, you make me want to sloop."

"Um, what?" Paul asked. He looked embarrassed for me.

"You know that nineties song, Shoop? Salt-n-Pepa, I think?"

This time it was Paul who blinked at me.

I stopped my choreography. "You're saying your mom never blasted this song in your house and danced like she was back in her college bar crawl days to torture you into cleaning faster?"

Blink. Blink. "My mother is a bookkeeper."

Like that somehow explained it…? My mother was a successful real estate agent, but it didn't stop her from Shoop-ing at my brother's wedding like she had no dignity. I used to hate it when she did that, and the madder I got, the more she did it. But now, watching how it made Paul squirm, I understood her devilish impulse.

Grizzled Andrew said, "This is why I hate telling people what kind of sailboat this is."

"You're saying I'm not even the first person to make that joke?" That bothered me even more than the fact that it had fallen flat.

"I make people want to sloop at least once a month."

"It was funnier when I said it."

Grizzled Andrew only lifted his eyebrows.

"I don't think he likes it," Paul said. He kept his voice low, as if Grizzled Andrew couldn't hear us from eight feet away.

"He loves it." But I didn't sing anymore. I looked out over the water instead. "This is beautiful." I leaned against Paul as we sat in the bow. The whole bay looked as if it had been sprinkled with crystals.

"Yeah?"

"Yeah." And it was. The warmth of being snuggled into Paul's side as the chilly breeze washed over us, the perfect blue sky, the skim of the sloop over water.

Sloop. Haha. But I resisted the urge to sing again.

It was nice for about an hour. But something wasn't right. I kept wanting to scoot away from Paul because he felt too warm despite the breeze. And I kept wanting to make sloop jokes even though no one else found them funny. And I kept wondering if this was...all?

Shouldn't it be enough to be sailing on a postcard-worthy day? Who got fidgety on a sailboat beneath a perfect sky?

Why was I so restless?

I wondered if I could convince Grizzled Andrew to take a picture of Paul and me doing the Titanic pose on the boat. Except I'd have to convince Paul first before I could even take a crack at Grizzled Andrew. Oooh, maybe I could convince ANDREW to do the Titanic pose with me. Yessss.

He wouldn't go for it. But maybe...I sat up and pulled my phone from my beach bag and snapped a few pictures of the bay, then the boat, then subtly worked it around to point it at Grizzled Andrew. If I could get a good shot of him, maybe Jack could do something—

Oh. Wait. Jack? Jack had no business on the boat with us. I deleted the picture of Grizzled Andrew and put my phone away.

For the next hour I did my best to be the poster girl for Most Relaxed Slooper Ever. I tried. But all I could think about was that Paul was crowding me and the shore was too far away and...

I recognized the feeling. It was the same feeling I had

when Josh Greeley invited me to his fifth grade birthday party, and it turned out I was the only guest because he wanted to proclaim his love for me.

Trapped.

I felt trapped.

As soon as I put a name to the feeling, a giant metaphor rose out of the bay in the near distance. We weren't far from one of the most famous islands on the West coast. "Hey, look," I said, straightening and pointing to it as an excuse to create some space between me and Paul. "That's Alcatraz."

Paul blinked back to the present and smiled. "That's where we're going next."

"Cool," I said, meaning it. *Anything* to get off this boat right now. "It's one of those things I've meant to get around to but just haven't yet."

Grizzled Andrew guided us into the dock and gave us simple instructions to help him tie up the boat. I stared at the prison where it squatted atop the highest point of the island, and a little buzz of energy hummed in my chest. It was the signal of an adventure to come, and I grinned. I loved poking around in history, and I couldn't believe I'd gone this long without poking around the history in my own backy—er, bay.

Paul helped me climb onto the dock then hefted out the picnic hamper he'd lugged onboard from his car, and we started up the main trail. It forked here and there, but the primary path to the empty prison was wide and paved with clearly marked signs, so when Paul took one of the forks, I stopped and pointed to the sign ahead.

"The prison's up that way."

"I know, but we're not going there."

"We're not?"

"No. I thought it was weird enough to bring you to a prison island. It'd be going a little far to drag you through it."

"I mean, sure, but only if you actually dragged me through it. I'm going willingly, and I'm sure there are tours."

"Yeah, but then we'd have to figure out what to do with the food. And I didn't book Andrew long enough for lunch and a tour. We'll come back and do the tour sometime, but I think you'll like this." Paul pointed further up the hillside toward a side trail. "A conservancy society restored the gardens the old wardens' wives planted over the years, and I heard it's a great photo op."

Photo op. You know what would make a great photo op? A prison. I could just imagine what Jack would do with a—

Ugh.

Dear self: you are not currently responsible for finding stuff for Jack to Photoshop. The whole internet does that for him already. You are on a date with Paul. Your boyfriend. Pay attention.

And I did. Paul had brought some of our favorite foods, and the botanical society had created an oasis of native plants and heirloom flowers on a bluff with a gorgeous view, and we took it all in as Paul looked up the different flowers.

A light cloud cover drifted over the sun, muting the colors of each blossom he named, but I felt it even more keenly in my mood. Little wisps of cloud collected in my chest and filled in a growing hollow in my stomach, and no matter how many words Paul said or flowers he told me about or times he asked me if I wanted more hummus, I couldn't clear the fog inside me.

Dang it.

No. Dang it wasn't a strong enough word for the disappointment that crept up the base of my neck on the way to forming a full-blown headache. All the while, I smiled at Paul as he gave me word after word about flowers and shrubs and Alcatraz.

And as I wondered how to find the words I would have to say to him next, I finally recognized the feeling, and what it meant.

I had to break up with Paul.

Chapter 7

"Hey, you okay? You're awfully quiet."

I glanced at Paul, softening at the concern that touched his question. Grizzled Andrew had maneuvered us out of the slip and sent us back across the bay.

Paul's question was an opportunity. Now was the time to say, "I'm just thinking," and when he asked me about what, I'd say, "Us," and he'd ask, "What about us?" and I'd tell him. I'd tell him we didn't fit anymore.

But when I opened my mouth and glanced over at him with the wind riffling his hair, his color up from the day of sun, the lines around his eyes relaxed, and his posture slouched in the way it only did when he'd left his worries behind...

I couldn't do it. Who could? Who could dump a perfectly nice guy in the middle of a sailboat ride because he wasn't...

Wasn't...

I didn't know. I wasn't even sure of my reasons, but he deserved one, and I couldn't break up with him without explaining it.

Also, who breaks up with someone halfway across a bay when neither of you can leave?

So instead of telling him the truth, I smiled at him and gestured at the water. "I'm taking it all in, that's all."

His eyes drifted half-shut again.

A small wave of seasickness washed over me.

No. Not seasickness. My conscience was talking to me, trying to warn me. *You're going to go from stressed to miserable if you don't find a way to say what you need to say.*

I stared into the slowly—so slowly—approaching dock. How was it possible for a boat to move so slowly? I stared up at the sail to make sure it had wind, but it billowed, full and happy, so I gave Grizzled Andrew a squint-eyed examination to make sure he wasn't putting the brakes on. Or something. Did boats have brakes?

Anchors. They had anchors. Had he thrown ours out? But no, it sat on the deck.

Hurry up, Grizzled Andrew. I focused all my attention on him, trying to sink the thought into his brain. He only squinted back at me. Then he yawned.

At last a small bump shook me out of my thoughts, and Grizzled Andrew tossed a rope around the dock cleat. He climbed from the boat to help us out while Paul and I gathered up our stuff.

"Ladies first," Paul said with a chivalrous wave.

Getting off the boat meant I'd have to break up with him. I stared at the dock and our skipper's impassive face. Finally, I took a deep breath and Grizzled Andrew's hand, and as I stepped onto the dock I muttered, "Why do you hate me, Grizzled

Andrew?"

For the first time, his blank mask cracked and a sound came out, a sound that from anyone else might have been a laugh. "If you can't be still on a boat, you got more noise inside you than is good for you."

I missed a step at the sound of so many words coming out of him, but when I straightened and looked at him again, his face was as blank as ever.

Paul stepped onto the dock with a light thump beside me and finished his business with Andrew, giving him a tip and shaking hands with him. Then Paul's hand slipped through mine as he dropped a light kiss on my hair. "I can't wait to show you what I have lined up next."

And as he led me down the dock, this time a very clear laugh from Grizzled Andrew followed us.

Great. I felt like I was being heckled by a salty wannabe pirate for not being able to do what needed doing with Paul.

And I deserved it.

"So I have something cool planned," Paul said as we walked into the parking lot while I tried to figure out how to say, "I don't want to do the thing you planned."

"I was thinking we'd go for a coast drive. I rented a convertible and had it delivered here while we were on the boat."

Ah, dannnnnnng it. At least he'd be able to drive me home in style after I dumped him.

He opened the door for me and then settled the picnic stuff into the cramped backseat while he explained his plan. "I calculated it all out, and with the average rate of flow for Saturday coastal traffic and based on the time of sunset, factoring in the best mid-range priced restaurant with the highest Yelp reviews, I figured out exactly where we can catch the best sunset."

You didn't go find perfect sunsets. They found you. It was a law of the universe. And I was sensing a pattern here. Paul gets good idea → Paul immediately sucks the life right out of it by planning and executing it perfectly.

But Paul had always been like this. It's part of why we made so much sense as a couple. So why now? Why did I suddenly feel so stifled by it? Had Ranée finally gotten into my head with all her complaints?

No...I didn't think so. Weirdly enough, this was about...well, Shoop.

Because whenever my mom would do that—crank the song and dance through the house while she dusted, or worse, lose her mind at a wedding and dance her face off when it came on—it used to embarrass me to no end. Like she'd be out there singing along at the top of her lungs and shaking her butt like she was still in college or something, and I'd just pray for the song to change. Or death.

But it wasn't just me that it embarrassed. My dad hated it too. It made him so uncomfortable. And once, when I was eight, she'd had an extra glass of wine at a wedding and realllly got down with her college girlfriends on the dance floor, he'd mumbled an excuse and escaped to the restroom. When my mom came back flushed with wine—or Shooping or both—I'd complained. Again. "Why do you have to do that? It makes Dad so uncomfortable. It's not nice."

Dad was more like me. He liked order and structure. And

decorum, for pity's sake. But Mom had only smiled and said, "I do it *for* him, honey. It reminds him of who he used to be before all the pressure."

I'd been so mad then, because I didn't really understand her answer. All I knew is that I never wanted my dad to look at me with the same anger and embarrassment he'd had on his face before he escaped from the wedding.

In the end, she refused to change. So did my dad. Which is how they ended up divorced two years later. And how my mom went through about four more serious relationships, another marriage, a divorce, and now a third husband. David. They were going on three years, probably because he took her out dancing whenever she wanted. Even still, they were doomed to sputter out soon.

I didn't love my mom's uninhibited approach to life sometimes. Most times. And certainly not the way her lack of inhibitions led her to fling herself into one failing relationship after another. But now, listening to Paul talk more about the metric he'd developed for making sure we found the perfect sunset, I realized that there was a tiny bit of merit in her playfulness—if it were dialed down—A TON. Paul needed more spontaneity in his life. Not "Shoop-even-if-your-spouse-hates-it" spontaneity. But a big step away from his spreadsheets.

I'd been so worried for months about making sure our experiences together were low-stress and perfectly executed, and it was the opposite of what we both needed.

Not until I Shooped like an idiot on the boat had I realized how much I'd needed an injection of silliness. And Paul was many, many good things, but he wasn't silly.

He'd looked at me, embarrassed. It hadn't felt good.

I took a deep breath. All right. Time to do the right thing. The only thing that made it doable was the knowledge that it was the right thing for him too.

"I don't think I'm up for a coast drive. Can we just drive to the bridge overlook?"

"But I have this whole thing planned. It'll be great."

"I think I'm worn out already. I'm sorry." *Chicken. Do the right thing*. I cleared my throat. "But also, I want to talk to you about something."

Paul smiled. "The overlook then." He handed me his phone. "Can you sync it? I made a playlist."

It was called "Sunset Playlist," and as we merged onto the harbor road, the first of several love songs played.

Oh, man. This was going to suck.

Chapter 8

Paul steered us into the pullout for the overlook, and even though we could have enjoyed the view from the car, I climbed out anyway and sat on a bench. It was conveniently placed to provide an ocean backdrop for dumping people who were in all ways perfectly acceptable and somehow still not right for you. I burrowed into my sweatshirt against the chilly breeze.

Paul sat beside me, and I drew a steadying breath before turning toward him with a gentle smile. "So I've been thinking—"

"Me too," he said, picking up one of my hands and lacing his fingers through it. He wasn't usually an interrupter, but now his eyes shone, and the words tumbled out of him like he couldn't help himself. "I know we've kept things casual for the last five months while we both focused on work, but now that you've got a promotion, and I'm about to get one, I was thinking we should—"

"Paul." I couldn't let him get the words out. I owed him that much. I slid my fingers from his, and the excitement in his eyes dimmed. He pressed his lips together and looked at my hand, the one I'd drawn away to resettle in my lap. "You're getting a promotion? That's great."

He was no dummy. "What's going on, Emily?"

My eyes wanted to drift away, to focus on the ocean or the clouds or anything but the confusion on his face. But that wasn't fair, so I returned his gaze while I searched for words. "The last few months with you have been so great. I honestly saw it going on like that indefinitely, maybe even growing into something else. And this is the point where it should feel like that, right? Like the point where it's time to take the next step. I'm worried that's what you were going to say we should do next, but I don't want you to. I'm not sure I understand why, but I don't think I'm ready for that."

He straightened so he was turned toward the water instead of me and rubbed his hands up and down his thighs in short, nervous movements. Finally, he said, "I'm surprised."

I sighed. "Me too."

A long silence fell between us before he broke it. "I'm fine with waiting. When you get the hang of your new job, we can revisit this."

He was taking it with so much grace, I hated what I had to say next. "I don't think this is going to change with time. I feel a restlessness I can't explain when we're together. I don't know what it means, but I think my instincts are trying to overpower my brain for once."

"And for once you're going to let them?" His tone was flat.

"For once I'm going to let them."

He nodded, not looking at me. He shuffled his feet in the

dirt, then leaned down to pick up a small pebble and throw it out toward the ocean. He didn't bother to see where it landed. "Why didn't you say something before we started this big day?"

"Because I didn't know. I think there's been something bubbling up for a little while, and being on that sailboat cleared my head. And then I couldn't unsee it. I'm really sorry."

He winced. "Don't apologize. It makes me feel pathetic."

"Sorry. For apologizing."

The corner of his lips quirked up the tiniest bit. "That's not funny."

"It's a little bit funny."

He looked at me at last. "All right. Maybe a little."

I reached down to scoop up another pebble and handed it to him. "Here. Throw that one."

He took it. "Why?"

"I don't know. That last one seemed to make you feel better."

"True." He chucked it toward the water, watching as it fell this time. "I don't know why that works."

"Are you imagining each one hitting a shark on the head?"

"What?"

"Nothing." But it's what I would've done, and it definitely would've improved my mood if my boyfriend had just dumped me for no reason.

He turned back to me. "I've still got the car all day, and I still know the best place to get fish and chips down the coast a little bit. Let's go. Let's just drive, and maybe I can find more rocks to throw."

"I don't know. That feels like it could get..."

"Awkward?" he finished. "For me, maybe. But I'm not planning to change your mind at all, so it shouldn't be awkward for you. I just hate the idea of wasting this rental."

Good old practical Paul.

"If I can stand to finish this drive, you probably can too," he added. "You already did the hard part, right?"

"True." He was being remarkably chill. "You really want to do this?"

He shrugged. "Sure. And it allows me to play this cool and save my dignity. But that playlist is toast."

I laughed. "I'm in."

It shouldn't have surprised me that Paul had taken it so well. I should've predicted it based on his practicality. But honestly, a little anger would be good for him. I'd have to ask Jack to Photoshop a shark getting bonked on the head with a rock so I could send it to Paul and title it, "Therapy."

Although...he'd probably realize it came from Jack. And that was probably the last person Paul wanted to think about.

Actually, Jack was the last person I should be thinking about either.

And yet it kept happening. Ah, dang.

Dang, dang, dang.

Chapter 9

By the time Paul dropped me off at home, it was full dark, and even though it was too early for bed, I climbed into my pajamas and dragged my comforter onto our sixth floor balcony. I wrapped myself up against the night air and stared out at the city lights, which for me constituted the sulfur lights on the apartment buildings across the street.

I hadn't left this morning meaning to break up with my boyfriend. I hadn't meant to spend the rest of the day with him after dumping him and have it be...fine. And it had been. He was quieter than usual, but his meticulous calculations had indeed found us good fish and chips and the perfect spot to watch the sunset. But he didn't pout or anything. Didn't even make one passive-aggressive remark, and if I'd had to carry a little bit more of the weight of keeping the conversation going, well...that seemed fair.

But I was super wiped. All that fresh air and boyfriend dumping. And really, I should be sitting here trying to figure it all out. Like why the impulse had come over me. But I didn't want to. And when Ranée came home an hour later, I yawned and told her I was going to sleep without mentioning the Paul thing. I wasn't in the mood for questions.

That didn't keep her from jerking me out of sleep at way-too-early-o'clock the next morning when she landed on my bed with a weird cannonball/ninja roll.

"Wake up," she said with her face an inch from mine. But considering the cannonball, it didn't need to be said.

I blinked at her. "Please move out."

She crawled under the covers instead and stared at me from the other pillow.

"That pillow is for decoration, not roommate invasions."

"Why does Paul's Facebook say 'single' now?"

I rubbed my eyes and tried to process what she was saying. "Why are you even paying attention to Paul's Facebook?" Then I sat up and gasped. "Ranée! Do you secretly love him?"

She bounced the pillow I'd just abandoned off my head. "Shut up. No. But that Tyler guy just posted something on your wall asking what happened so then I looked at Paul's, and I'm incredibly smart so I kind of already know, but tell me what happened anyway."

"Wait, what?" Tyler was an old co-worker who'd switched over to Paul's company. I'd met Paul at a party at Tyler's house. Tyler was the biggest gossip in the office, so it figured he'd be the first to sniff something out. "Break this down for me. I'm only halfway there."

"Well, working backward, I think Paul changed his relationship status to single, Tyler saw it and posted something on each of your walls asking what happened, and that's when I saw it. So what happened? If Tyler gets the story before I do, you're dead to me."

I rubbed more sleep from my eyes and glared at her. "I'm fine with that."

"Talk."

"This is going to be really anticlimactic for you. He planned an awesome day, and I should have loved it, but instead I broke up with him. He was nice about it, and we hung out the rest of the day anyway, but I don't think we're going to hang out ever again." I collapsed back on my pillow. "I'm an idiot. What was I thinking?"

"He wasn't good for you. He's all the things you already are. You need someone who is all the things you're not. So let's figure out who that is."

I turned over to look at her. "Did you just tell me that I need to think of the ways I'm lacking?"

"Yes! I mean, no," she amended when she saw my frown. "I meant that you need to think of the qualities someone should have to balance you. Balance. That's good."

"You must be in marketing."

"How'd you know? So let's think of some stuff. Like you're a total planner, so you need someone who's more spontaneous."

"I just got out of a relationship twelve hours ago. Maybe I need some 'me' time."

But she barreled on. "You're too serious sometimes, so you need someone with an excellent sense of humor. Like maybe someone who is Twitter-famous for his Photoshopping skills."

I rolled out of bed onto the floor. "Bye," I said, army crawling for the door.

She jumped in front of it and shut it. "Jack's great. You should date him."

I sat up, and then, because it hurt my neck to glare up at her, I stood up instead. "First of all, he lives in Portland. Or near it somewhere in a hipster cave where he sleeps in a nest of flannel. So no. But also, there's this whole thing about I don't want to date him. Which is kind of my main reason. Now move."

I tugged the door open and slid past her to spend quality time with my Cinnamon Toast Crunch, or as my dad called it, "Dessert for breakfast."

"Let's talk about this," she said across the breakfast bar.

I poured a bowl of cereal without turning around to look at her. "There is no 'us' talking about this. You're going to talk *at* me. I can feel it."

"Yes. Yes, I am. Did you love Paul?"

"No."

"Then you're not heartbroken and we can talk about this."

"Of course I'm not heartbroken. I'm also not made of time, and I don't have time for dating right now. It shouldn't have been so hard for Paul and me to find time for each other. I need to get this new job under control and then I'll think about it."

I turned around to move to the table and squeaked to find her right in front of me, her phone up like a stop sign in her outstretched hand. "Before you say that, check this out."

I blinked and focused on the picture. I recognized her brother, Sean, and another guy in a beanie. They were hanging from climbing ropes, obviously near the top of a cliff that whoever was taking the shot was standing on. The other guy had an electric smile, one you couldn't help but return, even in a photo, and the corner of my mouth twitched up. "You want to hook me up with another one of your brother's friends?"

"You think he's hot?"

"He's more my speed than Man Bun Jack."

"That *is* Jack." She looked as satisfied as if she'd eaten all my Cinnamon Toast Crunch herself. Then she took the bowl out of my hands and began to do exactly that.

Somehow I now had her phone in my hands instead. I sighed and looked down at the picture, enlarging it for a better view. Either this was before Jack had grown his hair out or maybe it was pulled back, but now I could see the strong jaw and high cheekbones I recognized from his other pictures. It's just that in those, he had these faux-expressions, like over the top Handsome Man Smiles or Hot Guy Smolders. Here, he was just a really cute guy hanging out with his friend, no irony at all.

I set the phone down and poured another bowl of cereal. "Nope."

"I'm going to change your mind."

"You're really not."

"I am. Because there's no way you can say no to what I'm about to suggest."

"No."

"Stop being boring and listen to me. Here's the plan. You're going to start leaving funny comments on all of Jack's pictures, and he's going to find you irresistible. So then you guys will start DM-ing, leading to a delicious flirting affair. And then he's going to be so impressed with your sense of humor because you'll be the only woman who could ever keep up with him that he's going to fall madly in love with you, and you'll finally lure him out of his flannel cave nest, and Sean will get off my back."

"No." I blinked at her. "Wait. What do you mean Sean will get off your back?"

"I didn't say that. Let's stick with the plan. Write something funny on his Facebook. Or better yet, his Twitter."

"No way. You're not getting off the hook. What do you mean Sean will get off your back? About what?"

"Nothing." She waved at the phone in my hand. "Write the funny things."

I shrugged. "Sure," I said, tapping the screen. "I'll write all the funny things, but this is your phone, so it's you who's going to be flirting with him."

"What? Stop." She sloshed the milk from her bowl as she plunked it on the table and raced to snatch back her phone. "Now go do it on your own account."

"That's the least compelling suggestion anyone has ever made to me." I settled back into my chair to enjoy my cereal.

"You have to."

"I will. Right after you tell me what Sean has to do with this." I knew Sean well enough from previous appearances on our couch when he visited Ranée, so now my curiosity was way up about why he was involved. But Ranée only sent me a sulky look and hunkered back down over her cereal bowl. There was no way I was dropping that Sean comment, but I let it go for the moment. I'd find a different way to drag it out of her.

She left a while later, yelling something about tai-chi in the park on her way out. I had a whole Sunday stretching in front of me now, and no commitments to keep. Suddenly I didn't know what to do with all that time.

I opened Facebook to look at Paul's profile for myself, but he wasn't in my friends list anymore. When I typed in his name in the search bar, it offered me the option to add him as a friend. Which meant that I'd been unfriended.

It stung a little, like when someone said they couldn't go to lunch with you because they had a meeting. And even though you saw them walk right into the meeting, you still felt sort of dumb for having asked and been told no.

It was stupid to feel that way, considering Paul probably felt way worse, but I had thought we'd stay friends, or at least politely ignore each other on social media while still kind of keeping tabs on each other. Because of curiosity. Was that weird?

I wished Ranée were home so I could ask her, but then remembered her regular ex-boyfriend stalking and realized she'd tell me not only was it not weird, it was pretty much my right and duty as an American to keep track and make sure his next girlfriend wasn't as cute as me.

For sure I wanted Paul to move on. He could even move on to someone prettier and it wouldn't bother me. I just wanted her to be less successful or have weird habits.

Annoyed, I clicked to my own profile and changed it to "single" and uploaded a picture I'd taken from the boat yesterday, a shot of my bare feet, the bow stretched past them, the water glinting off the bay in the background. I captioned it "Lazy Saturday." I knew Paul wouldn't see it now, but it finally made me feel better to post about the day without any mention of him. Why not? He wasn't part of my landscape anymore. It seemed like a fair trade for Paul's unfriending, a passive-aggressive way to feel like I hadn't given him the last word.

But I didn't feel better. He'd straight dropped me from Facebook after we'd spent a good afternoon as friends. Rude.

I tagged Ranée in it and added a comment. "You should come with me next time."

I used the rest of the morning to re-organize the pantry, throwing out stuff that was past its expiration date and making grand plans to cook more and eat out less. I'd never stick to it, but the planning made me feel better anyway, pushed back the slight ickiness that came from breakup aftermath. Sometimes I felt relief when a relationship ended, that feeling of breathing a little better. This breakup with Paul was like that. Still, there was a bit of sadness when something you started with a spark ended with a fizzle.

My phone sent me an alert around lunch. "Jack Dobson has tagged you in a picture."

Chapter 10

Jack. Jack had tagged me.

Jack had tagged me because—since I was still in the 24-Hour Super Honesty Cycle—I had tagged Ranée with the sneaking suspicion that he might see it since she was a mutual Facebook friend.

Even though I hadn't done anything more strenuous than toss stale pasta in the garbage, my pulse suddenly jumped to mid-workout speed.

I pulled up the photo. It was the boat picture, but now it had a seagull the size of a Buick hovering in the air in front of it in an oddly regal pose, like an ancient thunderbird, and Jack captioned it, "When you're trying to hang out but things get transcendent."

I burst out laughing. I wanted to type back something funny, but that seemed too...I don't know. Like I'd just been sitting and waiting for him to say something about it. Which I had.

My thumbs hovered over my keys, twitchy to type

something smart-alecky, but instead I hit "like" and set the phone down. I didn't want to play games, but at the same time, I wasn't sure why I'd wanted him to see it. I felt the way I did before I dipped into my grandparents' lake for the first time each summer. Why had I opened my timeline to him?

Because I needed a good laugh this post-breakup morning and thought he might deliver, that's why. And he had. So that was good. Hitting "like" was a way to acknowledge him without turning it all into A Thing. This wasn't A Thing. I pushed him out of my head for the rest of the day.

Monday morning on my coffee break, I put up a new picture of the view from my office window. It was a cruddy view of half the facing building and a giant billboard advertising bail bonds. I captioned it, "Fancy executive suite."

After lunch, Jack tagged me in a photo. It was my office window, only it had the transcendent seagull outside of it again, blocking the billboard. His caption read, "Am I being...followed?"

We were one step away from a DM flirtation. I was kinda sorta doing exactly what I had told Ranée I refused to do. And I didn't care.

Tuesday morning I lined up my action figures along the window ledge. Jane Austen, General Leia, my Amelia Earhart Barbie, and Wonder Woman now looked back at me. I took a new picture captioned, "There. I fixed it. The view is 100% better."

Tuesday at lunch, I had a comment on it from Jack. "This picture can't be improved."

Oh, man. That's the one thing he could have said that I had no defense against.

Then another comment popped up. “But I’ll try.”

Of course he would.

I tried not to refresh my notifications obsessively all afternoon. I failed. Just before I was ready to pack up for home, Jack tagged me. This time, the seagull was floating in front of my office window, bowing to the action figures. It said, “Transcendent Seagull salutes you.”

I thought about the picture all the way home. Half the time I was smiling at Jack, and the other half I was frowning at myself. What was I doing? I mean, really? I was setting out pictures as deliberate bait for Jack to Photoshop because...why? Did I want the attention?

No. I wasn’t an attention seeker. And I’d had attention from Paul, so it’s not like I’d lacked it. Maybe...I...

I couldn’t come up with a good reason. I liked the way he turned the ordinary into the absurd. That was it. Everything about him was absurdity: his long hair and the way he made it the butt of his jokes, the way he introduced transcendent seagulls into ordinary photos. Something about it appealed to me.

Not the hair, to be clear. The hair was ridiculous.

But the other stuff...I didn’t remember the last time that I’d had so many laughs startled out of me. Ranée was funny, but not in a laugh out loud kind of way. More of a subtle, dry way. Jack...

At home, I headed straight for my bed and turned on my laptop so I could send him a DM. Why not? I mean, besides the obvious drawback of listening to Ranée say “I told you so”? It had been a cruddy few days in the post-Paul breakup funk, and I liked how Jack breathed a little life into—

Oh. No. Nope. Lots of nope.

I shut the computer off again. What I did NOT need to do was get caught up in flirting with Jack just because I was at a romantic low point. That was dumb. I'd never been the kind of girl who needed or wanted to get over one guy with another one. I preferred the old-fashioned method of ice cream and Hallmark movies.

I picked up my phone and opened Jack's profile. I scrolled through the transcendent seagull in front of the boat, appearing again in front of my office window, then again bowing to my girl power action figures. That was gold. And suddenly I was laughing again. I couldn't help it.

I flipped over to his Twitter feed. Today some smug-looking bro-dude had sent him a picture of himself standing in front of an old, tired Volvo and asked Jack to Photoshop him in front of an exotic sportscar. Now the bro-dude stood smugly in front of Lightning McQueen.

Ha. Pretty good, Jack. Pretty good.

I scrolled through a few more of his tweets and stopped on one that didn't look funny at first glance. It was a tween girl with an adorable wash of freckles on her pale skin. Her request broke my heart. "Can you get rid of the freckles so I look prettier?"

My hand crept up to my throat. The world of social media could be brutal for kids seeking validation. Unless she was lucky enough to ask Jack, who'd posted the exact same photo as the before and after with a simple message. "I never mess with perfection."

I mean…COME ON.

I dropped my phone and jabbed my laptop power button. It would be stupid not to talk to Jack just because I'd broken up with a sweet, boring boyfriend recently. It's not like I'd broken up with Paul *for* Jack or anything. And it wasn't like Jack was in any danger of becoming a rebound, especially not when he lived ten hours away in Portland. Really, it was overstating it to call my current situation a romantic low point. It was maaaaybe a slightly-below-average point. It would be no big deal to say hi.

Still, I couldn't help taking a deep breath before I opened our old chat and typed, "Hi."

He answered in less than a minute, with "Hey, stranger."

EMILY: You're never going to believe this but…

JACK: But…?

EMILY: I've been seeing these seagulls everywhere.

JACK: It's strange that you think that's strange. You're in San Francisco, right? Isn't that by the sea? What kind of gulls were you expecting?

EMILY: That's the thing. These are no ordinary seagulls.

JACK: Tell me more. How would you describe these birds?

EMILY: It's just one, actually. The same one.

JACK: Uh, how can you tell? I've seen a few seagulls. They're all the same. They can't even tell each other apart.

EMILY: I don't think that's science.

JACK: Sure it is. I just looked it up on Seagullpedia.

EMILY: Did you also just make up Seagullpedia?

JACK: Yes, I did. But tell me more about this seagull that

follows you. Does it have a name?

EMILY: I don't feel safe telling you about this anymore. It's almost like you're making fun of me.

JACK: Never. But I know a little bit about brains. I'm checking to make sure yours is firing on all cylinders.

EMILY: Ha. Brains don't have cylinders. I think you don't know anything about brains.

JACK: Busted. I'm just super curious. I promise I'm not judging. Anymore. Tell me about this seagull that follows you.

EMILY: It does have a name. It's called…

JACK: Larry?

EMILY: Transcendent Seagull.

JACK: Oh, I get it. These aren't hallucinations. They're spiritual manifestations?

EMILY: Yes, exactly. See? I'm not crazy.

JACK: No, not at all.

EMILY: It would definitely be weird if I thought just one seagull was following me, like a regular one. But when you find out that it's a giant seagull, as big as a car, and that it's bowing to my Shrine of Powerful Women then it doesn't sound so crazy anymore, huh?

JACK: Um, no. Definitely not crazy. But a point of clarification: it's closer to the size of a small house.

EMILY: YOU'VE SEEN IT.

JACK: Busted again.

EMILY: Do you know why this seagull is following me?

JACK: No. Why?

EMILY: I meant that as the kind of question you're supposed to answer. Do you actually know?

JACK: No idea. Here's a theory: Transcendent Seagull has a message for you.

EMILY: What do you think it's trying to tell me?

JACK: Google says that seagulls symbolize that you're about to win the lottery.

EMILY: Google just told me that seagulls symbolize freedom. Wait…

EMILY: …

EMILY: …

JACK: hi…?

EMILY: Why would you pick a symbol of freedom?

JACK: Real talk: that was pure dumb luck.

EMILY: So this isn't some comment on my recent breakup?

JACK: You're single now?

EMILY: Did you just type that in a suspiciously innocent tone?

JACK: Of course.

EMILY: Yeah. I'm single.

JACK: …

JACK: …

JACK: …

JACK: Are you okay with that?

EMILY: I chose it.

JACK: That doesn't always mean things are okay.

EMILY: They're okay.

JACK: Better than okay? Or just okay?

EMILY: They're…fine. I feel weird talking about this.

JACK: Let's talk about the seagull some more. Tell me more about its magnificence.

EMILY: I didn't say it was magnificent.

JACK: I saw it, remember? It was magnificent.

EMILY: You *made* it, you mean.

JACK: That's a filthy accusation. But it was magnificent. Admit it.

EMILY: FINE. It was pretty good.

JACK: That cuts deep.

EMILY: Are you always this insecure?

JACK: Only about my seagulls and maybe one or two other things that I can't

remember right now.

EMILY: If it means that much to you, then yes, it was magnificent.

JACK: You're just saying that to make me feel better.

EMILY: Brb, just gonna throw my laptop out the window now.

JACK: Do you have anger management issues?

EMILY: Not usually. You seem to be a special case.

JACK: If I had a nickel for every time I heard that…

EMILY: What could you buy?

JACK; Nothing. I never hear that. I'm the least upsetting human on the planet.

EMILY: I feel like that might not be true.

JACK: On what evidence?

EMILY: Your Twitter account, for one.

JACK: Oh, you follow that, hm?

EMILY: Why are you saying that like you just caught me riding past your house on my bike to see if you're home?

JACK: Because this is the digital equivalent.

EMILY: Is not.

JACK: Is too.

EMILY: So what's the analog equivalent of a guy who Photoshopped himself into my pictures then Photoshopped in a stalking seagull? Is that you waving at me from your window as I ride by on my bike? No. That's you hiding in my bushes and peeking through the window.

JACK: That seagull was not me hiding in the bushes. That was me standing in your yard, throwing pennies at your window.

EMILY: Pennies?

JACK: Rocks would break it, probably.

EMILY: Fair enough. Just got home. Gotta go eat.

JACK: We cool?

EMILY: …

EMILY: …

EMILY: …

EMILY: I asked my WINGman, Transcendent Seagull, if we're cool.

JACK: Ugh. I can't talk to you anymore.

EMILY: Then you'll never know what he said.

JACK: What did he say?

EMILY: He said we're cool.

JACK: I can only speak for myself here, but I'm not cool.

EMILY: Duh.

JACK: That hurts.

EMILY: I doubt it.

JACK: Smart woman.

EMILY: I really do have to go.

JACK: I'm glad we're cool.

EMILY: …

EMILY: …

EMILY: Me too.

Chapter 11

Ranée came home after dinner. She had a piece of straw in her hair and another one stuck to the bottom of her Vans. I almost asked, then decided I didn't want to know the answer. A different question popped out. "Why is Sean all up in Jack's business?"

She was opening the washing machine lid but paused and stuck her head out of the tiny utility closet at the end of our galley kitchen.

"Pardonnez-soy?"

"Moi."

"What about you?"

"No, you're mixing languages. The expression is 'pardonnez—never mind. You mentioned that Sean is the one who wanted you to make me talk to Jack again."

"I never said that." She disappeared into the laundry closet again.

"It's what you meant."

"You read minds now?" Her voice was muffled as she stuck her head almost into the machine.

"You said you wanted Sean to get off your back and it had something to do with me talking to Jack."

"I guess if you're reaching you could connect those dots."

"I'm connecting them." There was a loud thump as the washer lid clanged shut followed by a curse. Ranée knew a lot of good curses. I made a mental note of this one for the next time the network went down at work.

I waited until she rustled around in the laundry closet for long enough that there was not possibly anything else she could be doing in there, even if she decided to separate and fold all her clothes before she reappeared. When she finally walked out, she had a big old piece of lint from the dryer guard clinging to her hair on the opposite side from the straw. I almost told her. Then I decided she deserved it.

"Are you ready to talk about this now?" I asked as she veered toward the hallway and her bedroom.

"I didn't know there was anything to discuss."

"Ranée. Stop being weird. Why does Sean care if I talk to Jack?"

"I don't know."

"Then why not just say that?"

"I don't know." She ran her fingers through her hair and caught the lint, holding it in front of her to glare at it with slightly crossed eyes before she changed direction to drop it in the kitchen garbage can.

"Seriously. Something about this smells funny."

She immediately checked the bottom of her shoes, discovered the piece of straw, and sent it after the lint into the trash.

"Not literally smells funny. I mean about this whole you/Sean/Jack situation."

"There's no situation."

"Then why do you keep pushing the issue?"

She narrowed her eyes at me. "Why do you suddenly have so many questions about Sean?" Then they shot wide open. "Wait, are you crushing on my brother now?"

I snorted. "Am I sixteen? No. Stop deflecting."

"Then it's Jack. This is about him. Why so many questions?" She gave the same gasp she gave every time she found a new carton of ice cream in the freezer like it had been delivered by magical freezer elves instead of me. "Have you been talking to Jack? Do you love him now? Isn't he way better than Paul?"

It was my turn to examine her face, trying to figure out why she was being deliberately obtuse. I wouldn't mention that I'd been talking to him yet, mostly because I didn't want her to think she'd succeeded in bossing me into it. But also because I'd thought of another angle to get the information I wanted.

"I don't actually even know anything about your brother. He's older, right?"

"Five years."

That would make him in his early thirties. "So if you're both from Nevada, how'd you both end up on the west coast?"

She walked back into the living room and kicked off her shoes before settling on the couch. "School and then work for both of us."

"You didn't like Nevada?"

"It's Nevada." She said it like it explained everything. I'd only driven through it on the way to other places, and based on what I'd seen from the interstate, maybe it did.

"What does Sean do? I know he's outdoors a lot." Maybe it would give me some insight into how he knew Jack.

"He is. That's his job."

"What does that mean?" I remembered the flannel shirt she'd bought him. "Whoa. Is he an actual lumberjack?"

"No. He's an outdoor nature guide. He works in the national forest outside of Portland."

"So pretty much a lumberjack."

She rolled her eyes. "Actually, he was a nurse, but he burnt out and had a career change."

"Isn't he kind of young to have burned out of one career already?"

"He worked in a pretty intense unit. There's a million things you can do in nursing, but he wanted a total change, and he moved to the woods. Well, near them. I think he can't get enough of them right now because of growing up in the desert. I don't know if he'll ever get tired of the rain and the green."

I glanced out our window, and even though my view was another building I smiled. Even on the sixth floor I could still hear faint snatches of sound from the street. "I get that. I don't think I'll ever get tired of the city." I'd grown up north of LA in the most stereotypical suburban neighborhood imaginable, where all the houses and shopping centers and schools looked the same as they bowed to the power of the HOA.

I loved the chaos and constant change of the city, the way millionaires lived next to condemned buildings, and half the walls of both places were covered with spray paint, and sometimes it was graffiti and sometimes it evolved into art.

"Me either," she said. She rose and stretched. "I've had a long day. I'm going to go hit the hay."

I pointed to the spot in her hair where the straw had made itself at home. "Looks like you already did. What were you up to today?"

She smirked and plucked it from her hair. "Wouldn't you like to know?" she asked as she dropped it in the trash can.

"I think I really, really wouldn't. But I'll tell you what I would like to know. How Sean knows Jack and why he's on your case to connect me to him. If Jack's so great, why not hook you two up?"

"This is how I'd know you don't have a brother even if that was the only thing I'd ever heard you say. Brothers don't set their sisters up with anyone, ever. And Sean is overprotective."

"So…Jack's not good enough for you but he's good enough for me?"

"No. It's that Sean still doesn't think I'm old enough to date."

"Does he know you're twenty-seven?"

"No. He still thinks I'm fourteen. But he knows you're thirty-one, and he knows I think you're all right, and that's good enough for him."

"You think I'm all right? Aw, you love me."

"You're fine. Good enough for Jack."

We'd been joking again until she said that. My eyebrows went up. What an interesting way for her to put it. "It's your job as my friend to make sure he's good enough for me, isn't it?"

She smiled. "Jack's a special case. You should get to know

him."

"I kind of have been," I admitted finally and waited for the interrogation to start.

"Well, well, well," she said, but softly, and with a smile she slipped into her bedroom and shut the door.

Chapter 12

JACK DOBSON HAS SENT YOU A FRIEND REQUEST.

It didn't show up in my notifications in all caps. But it felt like an all caps kind of announcement.

I was about to click accept, but the tingle of anticipation that swept up from my stomach stopped me. I set my phone down and turned to stare out of my office window. The bail bondsman billboard showed a suave-looking dude trying to guarantee me a bail bond, but it was old and peeling. Part of the paper with his right eye printed on it had come loose and it fluttered, turning him from a one-eyed pirate to a James Bond wannabe and back to a pirate again.

I should not be so excited to see Jack's friend request in my inbox. I should only feel a pleasant little ripple of recognition, like, "Oh, that Jack guy sent me a friend request."

This was not a big deal. So why was I staring at my phone and experiencing an existential crisis about whether to pick it up and press "Accept"?

It was honestly bizarre. I didn't have a history of bad

romantic relationships. Yeah, my parents had divorced, but I didn't carry much baggage over it. They were happier apart and got along well enough. I didn't have a problem committing. Not really.

I mean, maybe a little. But not for any deep reasons, like past trauma. I dated nice guys. Nice, normal, well-adjusted guys. But I never felt that…thing. That thing they showed in romance movies and books where I needed another person as much as I needed to breathe. That thing where time apart felt like years and time together sped by like seconds.

I'd also never felt the electric current that had run up from my center because some guy had sent me a Facebook friend request.

And Jack was just some guy. A funny guy, yeah. But just some guy. Some guy with bad hair and good Photoshopping skills.

Just some guy. Yes. And a friend request was no big deal.

I picked up my phone and accepted it. Less than a minute later, it vibrated with a DM from Jack.

I refused to overthink it and opened my messages.

JACK: Good morning.

EMILY: Not really.

JACK: Uh-oh. What's wrong?

I couldn't remember for a hazy second. A few minutes ago work had been terrible, and then he'd sent a friend request, and then I forgot that I'd been in the middle of a work crisis about…oh, yeah.

EMILY: The breakroom has no coffee.

JACK: Don't you work at a tech company?

EMILY: How did you know that?

JACK: It's in your profile.

It was, but we were a startup, one that didn't have a lot of name recognition. Very few people besides our direct clients even knew us by name. And all I'd put was our name. So that meant…

EMILY: Did you research my company?

JACK: No.

EMILY: Then how'd you know I'm at a tech company?

JACK: You're in San Francisco. That's what everyone does.

EMILY: No. That's what everyone in Silicon Valley does. San Francisco is a whole lot of everything. Confess: you looked it up.

JACK: …

JACK: …

JACK: I didn't. But…

EMILY: ???

JACK: Sean told me what you do.

Which meant Sean had found out from Ranée. But…why? I didn't mind that Jack knew. My job wasn't by any means top secret. I just didn't get why Sean was so invested in trying to connect Jack with someone who lived six hundred miles away.

JACK: Is it a problem that I know?

EMILY: No. But turnabout is fair play. What do you do?

JACK: You didn't tell me. It's not really even if I tell you, is it?

EMILY: So I'll ask Ranée. Ooh, or Google you.

JACK: Good luck with that. But we're off subject.

EMILY: We were on a subject?

JACK: Yes. Your tragic coffee situation. I thought tech companies ran on coffee.

Isn't that GROUNDS for a strike?

EMILY: That joke is.

JACK: That's fair. But honestly, it's not right for a tech company to be out of coffee. Do you work in one of those buildings with a lobby café? Do you have a minion you can send to fetch some for you?

EMILY: No café. And I do have an assistant, but I need her too much for actual work to send her on coffee runs. I'm gonna sit here and suffer.

JACK: I'm going to make you the perfect digital cup of coffee. How do you take it up there in your fancy skyscraper penthouse executive suite?

EMILY: You mean my eighth-floor not-even-corner-office?

JACK: Fine, how do you take your coffee in your glorified cubicle?

EMILY: Venti, black.

JACK: I'll be honest, I wouldn't have guessed that.

EMILY: Was I supposed to say something frou-frou because I'm a woman?

JACK: No. Because straight coffee is gross.

EMILY: You're right. It's gross. I actually like a latte.

JACK: Hang on…

Five minutes later a picture popped up. It was a coffee cup bristling with enough tropical drink umbrellas to supply a sorority house. It was funny, but I'd expected something a little more for the time it had taken him.

EMILY: I thought maybe Transcendent Seagull was going to make an appearance.

JACK: That's ridiculous. Seagulls don't drink coffee.

EMILY: Are you sure? Because they eat Cheetos. I see them do it every time I'm at the beach.

JACK: Transcendent Seagull isn't a Cheeto eater. That's offensive.

EMILY: I love Cheetos.

JACK: That's fine for you. You're not Transcendent Seagull.

EMILY: What does he eat?

JACK: Prophecies and karma. But you have a latte now. Are you happy?

EMILY: Yes. I'm amazed you knew exactly how frou-frou I like it.

JACK: You seemed like a fifty-three umbrella kind of person. I know these things.

EMILY: Clearly. I'm going to go enjoy this latte. Have a

good day.

JACK: Later.

I saved the coffee mug picture. I didn't think too hard about why, and I definitely didn't think too hard about why I made it my phone's wallpaper. Then I turned my phone off completely and set to work reading the latest email chain dealing with a bug in our newest software, determined to put Jack out of mind until work was done.

Which would have worked if my assistant Hailey hadn't poked her head in through my door fifteen minutes later, a stress pucker wrinkling her forehead. "You know you can ask me to go get you coffee, right?"

"I know."

"Then why…" She stepped out of the way and a guy carrying a to-go cup printed with the logo of a nearby café walked in. "I would fetch it just because I like you. Now you're going to have to tip him."

"The tip was already taken care of," the delivery guy said. "You're Emily?"

"Yes. I didn't order any coffee though."

He shrugged. "All I know is that someone said to bring a latte here. I'm sorry I'm late, but I had to track down a couple of things." He set the latte on my desk and then reached into his delivery basket to pull out a bright yellow drink umbrella and a small bag of Cheetos. "I'm supposed to tell you it's from—"

"Let me guess. Jack?"

"No, some guy named T. Seagull. Have a good day." He tucked the umbrella into the lid and left with a polite nod.

I grinned. I couldn't help it. "This is ridiculous." This is what he'd been up to when he took so long to Photoshop the latte.

Hailey eyed the umbrella. "A little bit ridiculous. Who's Jack?"

"Nobody. Go back to using your valuable time doing valuable things."

She cast one more confused glance at the yellow drink umbrella then closed the door behind her. She popped her head right back in. "Nobody? Really?"

"Back to work, Hailey."

But the door hadn't even clicked shut before I had Google open to figure out who my nobody really was.

Chapter 13

The search for "Jack Dobson" returned almost seven million results. Several in the first few pages linked back to his Twitter account, but that was about it. There were lots of Jack Dobsons, from a prominent entrepreneur to a British gardener. Mostly it was ancestral records and obituaries for other men named Jack Dobson. Outside of his Twitter feed, nothing much came up for him.

I didn't need to check his Twitter and Facebook. I'd already prowled those. Each of the accounts only went back about two years, and neither of them gave me much beyond his usual Photoshop requests. He didn't have personal pictures or information. No snaps from vacations or adventures. No snaps of his food, even.

As far as the internet was concerned, Jack Dobson was essentially two years' worth of funny pictures and that was it.

Which meant, of course, that there was much, much more to the story.

He'd said, "Good luck with that," when I told him I was

going to Google him. I'd taken it as a throwaway comment, but now it took on added meaning. He'd known I wouldn't find anything.

I thought about that all day, wondering why. There could be a hundred reasons from sensible to sinister. I had a few friends who didn't put their real names on their public profiles, mainly to deter creepers like…well, me, currently. But what was weirder was the two year thing. There was another version of Jack somewhere, with a rich and informative digital life story.

When Ranée got home, I waited until she was curled up on the sofa and browsing through Netflix before pouncing. "So I've been chatting with Jack. And I've got questions."

She set down the remote. "Define chatting."

"We connected on social, and long story short, he had coffee and a bag of Cheetos delivered to my office today."

She turned the TV off. "No long story short. I want all the story."

I told her about the seagull pictures all the way up to the coffee delivery.

I expected her to gloat that she'd succeeded in connecting us, but she only nodded. "He's cool, right?"

"He seems to be. Funny, surprising. But secretive. And I want to know if that translates to shady."

She shook her head. "I've only met him once, but he made an impression. I've asked Sean more about him since getting him involved with the whole Photoshopping joke. Jack has an interesting story. You should get him to tell it to you."

"But if you know it, why don't you just tell it to me?"

"Don't you want the thrill of discovery?"

I rolled my eyes. “This from the girl who’s first to creep on any guy’s social if I so much as smile at him. Why are you being so cagey about this now?”

“Fair point.” She drummed her fingers against the arm of the sofa. “I know he had a career change a couple of years ago. I know he keeps to himself a lot. He’ll hang out with Sean, but Sean gets the impression he doesn’t hang out with too many other people. Sean actually doesn’t talk about him that much. Says he’s a cool guy, and he likes the idea of you and Jack talking. He wouldn’t suggest anyone shady. That much I can promise.”

“I’m so confused. You’re almost weirdly loyal to someone you’ve only met once instead of to me, your most favorite roommate of all time.”

“I *am* loyal to you, which is why I told you to get rid of Paul and to talk to Jack. No dumb boys for you.”

“Paul’s not dumb.” It was a reflex to defend him even though it wasn’t my job anymore.

She grimaced. “You’re right. He’s not dumb.”

Huh. Any kind of concession toward Paul was new. “You feel sorry for him now?”

“No. It’s a respect-for-the-dead thing. He’s dead to you now, right?”

“No. Dang, Ranée. We didn’t end on bad terms. I’d say hi if I saw him again.”

“But the relationship is dead?”

“Yeah.”

“Okay. Then out of respect for the dead relationship. But with Jack, it’s not loyalty. It’s more like I’m protective of him.”

“Protective?” It was an interesting word choice. “Why

does he need protecting? Is something wrong with him?"

"I'm not sure he does. It's almost a…I guess it's more like respect. Some people deserve to have stories told on them. But some people deserve to tell their own stories. He's more like that."

"You're freaking me out, being all deep and stuff. Stop it."

She grinned at me. "You got it. Can we talk about how insanely hot Jack is?"

"I appreciate him for his mind."

"And his fine-looking face."

"And his fine-looking face." And then I remembered something. "You never even told me what Jack does. I asked you before and you ducked the question."

"I don't think I was trying to. I don't actually know what he does now. I know what he used to do. He and Sean worked together. They don't work together now, although Jack found his new job because of Sean. He went out to visit him and he says the area 'spoke' to him."

"Portland?"

"Outside of it, yeah." She yawned. "Ugh, I need a nap before I go out. I'm so tired."

"You can always just not go out." She raised her eyebrows at me, and we both burst out laughing. "I forgot who I was talking to. You're right. Take your nap." I got my argument ready for when she tried to convince me to go out with her. I already had big plans for the night. I'd come up with a new strategy to do some Jack research, and I was itchy to get to it, but she didn't say anything, just went back to her room.

The door shut behind her, and I opened my laptop. I'd no

sooner logged in than a DM popped up.

JACK: Hey.

EMILY: Hey. I don't have time to talk right now. I'm trying to do some research on you.

JACK: On me? You can just ask.

EMILY: I have. You don't answer.

JACK: Oh yeah.

EMILY: Are you going to answer now?

JACK: Probably not.

EMILY: Why not?

JACK: I guess it depends on the question. Maybe you want me to answer boring stuff.

EMILY: It would be interesting to me. Doesn't that count?

JACK: Wait. You set that question up so that I can only say yes or I look like a jerk, and if I say yes, it implies I'm willing to answer your other questions.

EMILY:

JACK: Okay, I'll answer. But there are ground rules. No asking boring work cocktail party questions, like where are you from and what do you do. Do you accept?

EMILY: I accept.

JACK: And for every question you ask, I get to ask you one too.

EMILY: Any other rules?

JACK: We can choose not to answer any questions we want.

EMILY: This isn't turning out to be a very high stakes

game.

JACK: Them's the rules.

EMILY: Fine. Me first.

I took my hands off the keyboard so I could think about how to ask the questions that would get me all the answers I wanted. What could I ask Jack that wasn't "cocktail small talk" but would still help me get to know him?

EMILY: What are the best and worst purchases you've ever made?

JACK: 8 inch chef's knife. That was the best thing.

EMILY: You like to cook!

JACK: No. I like knives.

EMILY: That's not disturbing at all.

JACK: Yeah, I like to cook. I think this is where I'm supposed to impress you by telling you that I like making my own pasta from scratch.

EMILY: I'm impressed.

JACK: Don't be. I don't actually do that. But I do cook a lot.

EMILY: Is it small talk to ask you what your favorite thing to cook is?

JACK: Hmmm. Yes.

EMILY: Okay, then what's the biggest kitchen disaster you've ever had?

JACK: That's a good one. That I don't want to answer.

EMILY: Too revealing? Will I be able to psychoanalyze

you too well? Does it involve fava beans and nice Chianti?

JACK: Nicely done with the Hannibal Lechter reference, but maybe I'm the one that should be nervous you had that just sitting in your back pocket.

EMILY: If I can overlook your knife obsession, you can overlook this.

JACK: Fair. And I don't want to tell you because it's embarrassing, not revealing.

EMILY: I know I agreed to you vetoing questions, but I get to add a rule now: you can decline to answer on the grounds that something is too revealing because it would allow an internet stranger to track you down at your place of employment, but not because it's too embarrassing.

JACK: But what if I don't agree to that rule?

EMILY: Then I log off, and we don't play anymore.

JACK: I'll agree to the rule.

EMILY: Then you're up. Tell me the kitchen disaster.

JACK: My brother and I had a double date for the winter formal one year. To save money, we decided to make dinner at home. We decided to make pasta but not from scratch. From chefs Barilla and Ragu. That's already embarrassing.

EMILY: Better than Chef Boyardee. But you were saying how you're a total cheapskate and wouldn't take your dates out?

JACK: Rude.

EMILY: I kid. I'm sure you were trying to be fun.

JACK: No. We were being cheap. Anyway, our dates were sitting at the breakfast bar watching us and I decided to showboat. I plopped the noodles in the sauce pan and tried to get fancy with the tossing. It landed in my hair and ruined my white shirt, so then I had to borrow one of my dad's and it was way too big and I looked like a slob for the rest of the night.

EMILY: ...

EMILY: ...

EMILY: ...

JACK: You're trying to stop laughing long enough to type, aren't you?

EMILY: 😁

JACK: My turn. Best thing you ever bought?

EMILY: Some shoes.

JACK: ARE THEY MAGIC?

EMILY: Not exactly.

JACK: Then how can they be the best purchase ever?

I snapped a shot of the red stilettos I'd bought with Ranée to celebrate my promotion and sent it. It wasn't a fancy picture, just them sitting on my closet shelf, but I felt they spoke for themselves even without telling the whole story: that buying those shoes had indirectly led to us having this conversation at all.

JACK: I get it now. Without seeing anything else you've ever purchased, I'm positive you're right.

EMILY: I am. So it was a two part question. Worst thing you ever purchased?

JACK: I saved up a bunch of Fruity-O's box tops so I could trade them for x-ray

specs. It turns out that x-ray specs don't work.

EMILY: But that's not really buying anything.

JACK: I had to buy all the boxes myself because my mom said she wouldn't buy us sugar cereal. In six months I had twenty boxes and two cavities. I could have bought them at a local store for the price of four boxes. That…is the most 90's story ever. Do they even still do contests like that?

EMILY: Ranée lives on cold cereal. Let me check…nope. Five different brands, no contests. Although any time McDonald's does Monopoly my dad goes crazy and eats there three times a day while he tries to collect all the pieces. He doesn't even like McDonald's.

JACK: I mean, the burgers are bad. I get it. But can anyone truly not like McDonald's? Because the fries.

EMILY: The fries. 🙏

JACK: Your turn. Worst thing you ever bought?

EMILY: Easy. Tickets on a discount airline to Mexico.

JACK: Without any further details, that already sounds bad.

EMILY: So, so bad. But you're just repeating my questions. You need to come up with some of your own.

JACK: Uh…worst place you've had to bury a body.

EMILY: …

EMILY: …

EMILY: …

JACK: HAHAHA why would anyone ask that no reason next question

EMILY: Sorry. It's just that I'm a planner so I pick pretty convenient locations to bury bodies.

JACK: Understood. Then let's go with…an expression you would ban from English forever.

EMILY: "At the end of the day."

JACK: Amen.

EMILY: You would ban amen?

JACK: No, I meant at the end of the day, I agree with you.

EMILY: You're not funny.

JACK: I am.

EMILY: FINE. A little bit.

I stretched my fingers and yawned, realizing I'd been sitting so long that I had a trigger spot throbbing near my shoulder blade. I flicked a glance down to the time. It was almost eleven. Holy…

EMILY: Didn't realize it was so late. I have to go, but not until you tell me your answer. What phrase would you ban forever?

JACK: "I have to go."

My heart turned a tiny bit melty. Well-played, Jack Dobson. Well-played.

Chapter 14

It was weird to wake up and grab my phone first thing not to check my work email but to see if Jack had messaged me. But that's what happened the rest of the week. Every single morning. And every single morning, he had. And I'd smile and write back.

I didn't have time for any long exchanges so mostly I sent gifs of people drowning in paperwork, fighting tornados, anthills in crisis, and anything else to represent job chaos and Jack sent seagull gifs.

We'd picked up a new client that meant a massive amount of overtime for my team as we worked like said ants to integrate our software with their systems. I got home late every night, worked some more, and fell asleep exhausted, but it was funny how fast those morning exchanges became a part of my routine. They were almost better than coffee for waking me up.

Fine. They were better than coffee.

On Saturday morning, I slept in a whole hour and had my phone in my hand before I was even fully awake. Jack had sent a picture of a seagull doing a yoga child's pose to the sun and a message: "Good morning, sunshine."

EMILY: A yoga seagull? Mad talent.
JACK: Don't know if I can explain how hard that was. I know I make this look easy, but imagine a weightlifter doing lifts with popped out veins and bulging eyes and that was pretty much me with Photoshop last night.
EMILY: I'm honored.
JACK: I just realized how pathetic I made my Friday night sound. Please say you did something better.
EMILY: Is falling asleep at 8:00 and waking to this on my nightstand "better"?

I sent him a picture of a Haagen-Dazs pint I had only half finished before nodding off. Now it was a melted and congealed chocolate mess.

JACK:
EMILY:
JACK: But how is it possible that this is your Friday night? I thought maybe you went out and had wild nights on the town with Ranée, or…
EMILY: Or…?
JACK: …dates?

I held the phone against my chest and grinned like an idiot. He was fishing, and that meant I could too.

EMILY: You must be confusing me with yourself.

JACK: You think I'm going out for wild nights on the town with Ranée?

EMILY: Or…?

JACK: No dates.

I hugged my phone again. I was fine if he was dating people. Not seriously, or it would make him sketchy for messaging me. But it wouldn't surprise me if lots of women were interested in such a smart man.

Fine. And a hot one.

EMILY: Same here. No date.

JACK: Because?

There were several options here, like the truth. Or a version of it.

EMILY: Too tired. I was asleep an hour after I got home from work.

JACK: I feel you. I used to work a lot of long hours.

EMILY: On the railroad?

JACK: All the livelong day.

EMILY: I have an earworm now.

JACK: You started it.

EMILY: Quick, give me a chaser, something to knock it out with.

A minute later a YouTube link appeared for "Who Let the

Dogs Out?"

EMILY: I thought we were friends.
JACK: Do you remember the other earworm?
EMILY: I guess not. Am I really about to thank you for "Who Let the Dogs Out?"
JACK:
EMILY:
JACK: But no work today. So, plans tonight?
EMILY: Why are you forcing me to tell the truth and sound like a loser?
JACK: So that's a no. Me either. Which is normal, so judge away. But that doesn't seem right for you. Are there no smart men there? A smart man would take you out.
EMILY: Maybe I don't want to be taken out. My prerogative, right?
JACK: A smart man would say yes. And I'm a smart man, so now I'm torn. Because a smart man would both ask if you'd like to go out this evening but also recognize that it's your prerogative not to want to go out.

Wait. Did that mean he'd been about to ask me out for tonight? What the…

EMILY: Before I try to pick through all of that, let me start with: are you in San Francisco now or planning to be sometime today?
JACK: No.

Well. I was glad I'd asked before jumping to an embarrassing conclusion. I wasn't sure what to say next though. Umm, funny cat gif? It was always time for a funny cat gif. I was searching for one when his typing dots appeared.

JACK: …

JACK: …

JACK: I take it back. I'm dumb. I meant to ask you out but it came out wrong. So I'll try again.

JACK: Hey, Emily. Are you available for a virtual date tonight?

EMILY: Let me check my calen—yes. Yes, I am.

EMILY: Except I don't know what I just said yes to.

Jack sent a gif of a woman diving from a sheer cliff into the ocean.

EMILY: Pretty much.

JACK: I…like that.

EMILY:

JACK: I can guarantee you a Cheeto-free evening.

EMILY: Swoon.

JACK: If I was in San Francisco, I'd see if you wanted to grab lunch some time. I think the equivalent here is a phone call? How about I call you and we can chat with our actual voices. Is that called a conversation? But not Skype or anything. Just a regular phone. Then we don't have to do our hair. Conditioning is such a pain, amirite?

EMILY: I...

JACK: I'm only half kidding. I've only come to appreciate how true that is over the last two years. Now I feel bad for making fun of how long my sister took in the shower. But I'm not kidding about calling. In case you don't want to do that, in which case I was definitely kidding.

EMILY: Sorry, I was just really stunned that you would even half-joke about something as serious as conditioner. Okay. Let's not do our hair and talk on the phone tonight.

JACK: Does this feel like middle school? Getting on the phone and talking forever to a girl you like?

EMILY: I didn't really like girls that way.

JACK: Fine. To a boy you liked?

EMILY: No. I punched them and ran away.

JACK: I'm talking about when you were a teenager.

EMILY: I am too.

JACK: I deserve this.

EMILY: Transcendent Seagull agrees. But in all seriousness, no. I didn't get a cell phone until high school, and by then, it was mostly texting or IM-ing with boys I liked.

JACK: YOU'RE SAYING YOU LIKE ME?

EMILY: I'm saying if you want to call me around 7:00, I'll answer.

JACK: Cool. I'm just going to calmly saunter out of this conversation and go look up "Interesting Discussion

Questions for Phone Conversations."

EMILY: I'll prepare some in-depth descriptions of our current weather.

And I signed off from the chat with the dumbest smile ever and went to condition my hair anyway.

Chapter 15

At 6:55 I was next to the balcony sliding glass door with my phone in my lap. That was where we got the best cell reception.

Would Jack call right at 7:00? Or would he wait a few minutes to try to play it cool? What would I do?

Call at 7:00. Definitely.

6:56.

6:57.

The door opened and Ranée walked in wearing her scrubby clothes and increasingly tattered Vans. Was that…? I squinted. “Why do you have straw on the bottom of your shoe again?”

She glanced down, plucked it off, and threw it in the trash on her way to the fridge. “That’s a boring story.”

6:58.

I held up my phone. “There’s an interesting story about why I’m sitting here waiting for my phone to ring. I’ll trade you my interesting story for your boring one.”

She cracked open a can of sparkling water and took a few

huge guzzles. It was like watching a beer commercial parody. I half expected her to belch and smash her sparkling lime La Croix can on her head when she finished.

6:59.

"I'll take that trade," she said. "I've been volunteering at a horse barn."

Whatever I expected, it wasn't that. "In San Francisco."

She nodded. "Yeah. It's small, but there's a stable near the equestrian course by Golden Gate Park. I help out."

"With the horses?" I knew she'd ridden growing up in Nevada, but I hadn't heard her talk much about it.

"No, with underprivileged kids."

I couldn't figure out why she hadn't wanted to tell me about that. "Were you afraid I'd recognize you as the good person you are if you told me that's what you're up to?"

"No, of course not."

7:00.

My phone rang with a Portland area code. I'd looked it up.

I held it up. "Sorry, but my interesting story is that Jack and I are going on a phone date right this second, and I need to take this."

She grinned, and I turned away from her before I picked up the call so that my sudden nervous energy didn't make me giggle.

"Hi," I said. And then cursed myself for not thinking through the greeting first. "Hi" is what you said when your roommate or mom's number came up, not when a number you didn't know came up. Maybe I should have said, "This is Emily." But no, that was too business-y. Or maybe, "Hello?" like—

Before I could spiral into any more self-doubt, a warm male voice said, "Emily? This is Jack."

"Hi, Jack." His voice was the perfect pitch, which I didn't know I had an opinion about until I heard it. It wasn't too deep or high, just a middle tone with…I didn't know how to explain it. His voice was a perfect summer night. Or caramel apple dip.

"Are you someone who likes to have a guy show up with a date planned or do you like to be involved in choosing?" he asked.

His voice was both, I decided before considering the question. His voice was perfect summer nights *and* caramel apple dip. "First time out, I like a man with a plan."

"Glad I have one then," he said. "Do you prefer Rome or Mumbai?"

I had no idea what he was talking about, but I'd begun to figure out that it was entertaining to just go with it. "I'll be a cliché and say that since I've been to neither, I pick Rome."

"That was a trick question where both choices were right. Next question: do you have easy access to a laptop?"

"I'll get it," I said, climbing up to fetch it from my bed. "It's my work laptop. I'm curious whether your plans will make me forget that."

"I'll try," he answered. "Also, you're going to hear a knock on your door in about twenty minutes. Sorry, but I got your address from Sean, so I hope that doesn't freak you out. He had it because he and Ranée send each other cat T-shirts. Did you know that?"

"I definitely knew that." She'd worn one to bed last night picturing a gangster cat pouring out a glass of milk on the ground. It was captioned, "For the homies."

"Anyway, you should get a delivery soonish. You okay with that?"

"I'm okay with that."

"You are very chill," he said. "I can't believe you aren't asking me a million questions or trying to get the details out of me."

I considered this. "True. I'm a project manager, and I like planning and knowing what's going on, but recently I've figured out that maybe I need to be more focused on the journey than the destination. You know, all that fortune cookie wisdom kind of stuff."

"Maybe I should've picked China," he said.

"I have no opinion on that since I don't know what we're doing, but I'll go ahead and say I've heard Rome is nice this time of year, so that's still fine with me."

"I'm going to send you a link."

A second later it popped up in my chat box, a long string of gibberish my coders would've deciphered without even clicking. Not me. I had to open it. "I've got a picture of the Colosseum."

"Not a picture, exactly. It's the street view from Google Earth. I thought maybe we could walk around and talk."

A laugh bubbled out of me as I noticed the compass and dashboard on the lower right of the screen. "I can't believe it. You actually took me to Rome. This is a little bit genius."

"Ah, thanks. Glad you like it. See that guy straight ahead in the red shirt? I thought maybe we'd start there and see what we can see. Too bad I didn't book a tour guide."

"That's okay. I know a lot about the Colosseum. More than you'd guess," I said, tapping some keys as I talked. "Like for instance, did you know that this is built from travertine, tuff, and brick-faced concrete?"

"I didn't, but did you know that it was begun in 72 AD and completed only eight years later?" he said, reading the next line of the Wikipedia article I'd opened on "Colosseum."

"I think I read that somewhere," I said, smiling.

"Should we look around some more?"

We did, exploring sections of the building inside and out. Jack took over as tour guide, and I provided color commentary for several minutes until he suggested we step outside and stroll over to a restaurant for some fresh pasta.

"Do you like gnocchi?" he asked.

"I don't know. I don't think I've had it."

"Are you an adventurous eater?"

"I think so."

"Then I say we take a picnic dinner over to this Pamphili Park I heard about."

"Sure. Let me grab my gnocchi. It may look and smell like Cup 'o Noodles but—" I broke off as a knock sounded at the door, forgetting he'd warned me but simultaneously realizing what had happened. "You didn't."

"I definitely did."

I checked the peephole and opened the door to a delivery guy with a sack of food for me. "Let me guess," I asked him. "This has already been paid for, including the tip?"

"You got it," he said.

"Thank you," I said, closing the door behind him and

nestling the phone between my ear and shoulder as I carried the bag to the counter. “And thank you, Jack. Whatever this is smells delicious.”

“I gambled on gnocchi and Yelp told me where to find the highest rated in the city,” he said.

“Well, that’s lucky for me, but what are you having?”

“Pizza.”

“That doesn’t seem fair.”

“It’s not your fault there’s no Italian restaurant scene miles and miles outside of Portland. But I did make this myself, from scratch—and no kidding this time—I’m a good cook.”

I opened one of the containers and scents of garlic and pesto rose up. I took a bite. “I think I might die. This is so good. It’s so different from regular pasta.”

“It’s a potato pasta. I’m glad Yelp didn’t lie about it.”

“No, it told deep truth. But I’m sad you don’t get to try this.”

“Don’t be sad for me. I…I promise that’s the least correct way to describe my mood right now.”

It was the first touch of awkwardness I’d heard from him, and as much as I’d been having fun exploring the Colosseum with him, that slight hesitation was the first moment I felt total ease.

“Hey, Jack?”

“Yeah, Emily?”

“I know we’re only a half hour into this, but this is my best first virtual date ever.”

“Hey, Emily?”

“Yeah, Jack?”

“I know we’re only a half hour into this, but me too.”

We "strolled" through Pamphili Park while we ate. It was green and lovely until Jack said, "Check out that bird."

"I don't see a bird," I said, scrolling around my end of the street view. "What kind is it?"

"I'm not sure. It's right in that tree with the weird knot on the side."

"I don't see that either. Wait. This whole time I thought we were taking a walk together but now I'm thinking we haven't been in the same park at all. I'm so confused."

"Try this," Jack said, pinging me with a link, and when I opened it, I could see the knotted tree and the bird.

"Okay, I'm with you again."

"Whew," he said. "I don't know what happened. Maybe I was walking too fast. How tall are you?"

"5'7, with long legs." I cringed as soon as the words were out of my mouth. I'd only meant that I could keep up, but it sounded kind of flirtatious.

Jack let it go. "I'm 6'1, so I guess I didn't outpace you. I'm glad. That would be rude."

"Maybe," I said, now distracted by the fact that this hot man was deliciously tall. "But just so you know, I would never run to catch up. I'm full of dignity and stuff."

"I respect that since I'm full of dignity and stuff too. But also good manners, so I'd never make you catch up."

"There's a solution," I said, thinking about a tool we used at work. "We could share screens so we're both looking at the same thing."

"I don't know what to say. That feels so…forward of you."

My cheeks went hot, and I was grateful he couldn't see it.

"Right, I guess it sounded that way. It's not what I meant."

A warm laugh came over the line. "Sorry, I was teasing. I used to screenshare at work all the time. It's a good idea, but I don't have the app."

"I'll send you a link if you're okay with me driving."

"I have less than zero problem with you taking control."

My cheeks heated again because I was giving his words a subtext that his tone didn't seem to imply, but I sent him a link, and a minute later we were sharing my screen.

"You ready for a walk?" I asked.

"I'm done with my pizza, so yeah. Good to go."

"Want to go anywhere in particular?"

"Nah. Let's wander through the park and work off some of this dinner."

I laughed and navigated along the path that ran down the middle of the park. It was quiet and green. "There's not much to see here," I said.

"Sorry. I picked a boring park."

"I didn't mean it as a criticism, I promise." I rotated the view completely but that only gave us a view of the street parking. "But now I feel the pressure to come up with something to say because these trees are exactly alike, so if you comment on one, you've commented on them all."

"Sort of like castles and cathedrals." He pauses, then laughs. "That sounded fancy. It's just that I did a study abroad in England, and the castles and cathedrals all look like each other after a while. I had the exact same thought."

"England," I said on a sigh. "I loved London. My mom and I went there for my college graduation trip."

“Let’s go back,” he said. “Let’s skip this park and go hang out in Hyde Park.”

“I did really like Hyde Park. Okay. You talked me into it.” And within a minute we were in the middle of Hyde Park.

“Kind of chilly all of a sudden,” Jack said as the Google Earth photos filled the screen. They’d been taken during autumn, obviously, as several of the towering trees were turning colors and the ground was half green lawn, half fallen yellow leaves.

“I hardly noticed. It’s pretty much that temperature here in San Francisco most of the year.” I slowly rotated the view to show an empty paved path stretching in both directions. “Sorry I dragged you out into a deserted wood on our first date. I hope you’re not too nervous.”

“I’m carrying pepper spray, but I’ll be honest: you don’t really give off a scary vibe.”

“I resent that,” I said, sending us down the path toward more trees. “I’m super intimidating and fierce.”

“I don’t believe you for a second. I’ve seen your smile.”

Oh. Oh, swoon again. This was getting ridiculous.

“Still, you’re in the woods with a relative stranger,” he said. “I wouldn’t blame you for feeling nervous. I’m going to distract you by smoothly asking you some conversational questions to put you more at ease.”

I smiled. “Go ahead. I already made awkward small talk about the weather as promised.”

He cleared his throat. “Would you rather live without the internet or give up heating and air conditioning?”

“Whoa. You’re starting with trick questions right out of the gate?”

"I am?"

I knew he hadn't meant to, but the truth in that moment would put me in a very awkward position. "Pass."

"Seriously?"

"Seriously."

"All right." He was quiet for a minute. "Okay, would you rather go back in time five hundred years, or into the future five hundred years?"

"Ooh. Tough one. Can't we talk about our favorite colors?"

"Blue. And no."

"Also blue, and fine. I think I'd rather go to the future. What about you?"

"The past for sure."

"Wait, really? That's what history books are for. And so many bad things happened in the past."

"Yeah, but in the past, I'd know how everything turns out. I'd know that there's going to be hard things over the next five hundred years, but also mind-blowing advancements. You could watch it all happen and know that it works out okay. That we figure out better medicine and technology and nutrition. So it wouldn't be as depressing."

"But maybe going to the future means that you could see how all the stuff we're doing wrong now works out too."

"Or maybe I'd see that it doesn't. That there's nothing five hundred years in the future because we're screwing it up so much now."

We both fell quiet. He broke in with a rueful laugh. "Sorry. That was grim."

"Maybe. But your reasoning about seeing the past was

weirdly optimistic, so it balances out."

"Good. Next question. Would you rather donate your body to science or your organs to someone who can use them?"

"Jack? Aren't these questions supposed to make me forget I'm alone in the woods with a relative stranger?"

"Oh, right. Sorry. Job hazard. I'll think of something else."

Job hazard? "What kind of job makes you ask questions about what to do with dead bodies?"

"I'm a mortician. Didn't Sean tell you?"

"Um, no?"

"Probably because it's not true. And I guess it's not really a job hazard anymore. But that's all boring talk. New question: what do you think is the closest thing to real magic?"

"That's a good one. Let me think." I wouldn't let him avoid the job question forever, but I'd leave it alone for now. I clicked on the screen to send us along our path while I considered magic. The trees grew thinner as the path opened to the bank of the Serpentine River. "Closest thing to real magic? Google Earth maps."

"Agreed." I heard the smile in his voice, and maybe just the creeping edge of a yawn. The voice of my high school drama teacher echoed in my head for a minute. *Always leave them wanting more.*

"Hey, it's getting late and I should go, but thanks for taking me out this evening."

"Thanks for coming. Can I take you out again some time?"

I smiled. "Let me put it this way: after a night like this, you can have my central air. There's no way I'd give up the internet."

And I heard the smile in his voice again as he said

goodnight.

Chapter 16

I woke up the next morning, and my whole body felt like a smile. I lay there remembering every detail of the date, scrolling back over our route through Hyde Park on my phone.

It was honestly the best first date I could remember. I'm sure my grandmother would be appalled that I'd even call it a date, much less a first one. My parents were social media literate enough for the Age of Tinder Dating to be a logical progression, but they probably wouldn't have considered last night a real date either.

But it was. Very real.

That knowledge settled somewhere in my belly and fluttered, and I pressed my hands to my stomach, trying to identify the reason for the sudden onset of nerves. I wasn't a flutterer.

I'd had a few medium-range relationships. At thirty-one, I wasn't opposed to the idea of finding "the" right guy. In fact, I'd been open to it, choosing guys like Paul who were steady, committed, ready to settle. But Paul had been my second solid relationship to fizzle in two years, and I hadn't been nearly as upset as I should have been about either failure.

They didn't even feel like failures, honestly. I had a sense of escape.

That was the flutter, I realized. A little instinct urging me to run from Jack.

What? I sat up and forced myself to check in with each part of my body. Feet, arms, legs, back, and neck all reported in for regular duty. But my hands, head, chest, and stomach weren't quite right. But neither did they feel wrong, exactly.

Hands…slight tingle, like how they felt when I was at the beach and they were sandy and I plunged them into the cold Pacific to rinse them. It wasn't unpleasant. It was more like they were putting me on notice. "Hi. We're extra here today."

Head was easy. My brain had been replaced by a bunch of balloons, all bright and bobbing.

Chest…hmm. That was less cheerful. A tightness occupied its center. What was that? Was it the contraction around something that had gone missing? Or the presence of something new trying to make space?

I narrowed my focus to my stomach, the noisiest part of the neighborhood at the moment. It was telling me to run, but why? I turned the feeling over, poked at it.

My chest, I realized. My stomach was fluttering because it knew what that feeling in my chest was: I'd given up real estate inside it for the first time. Ever.

Jack had carved out a little room for himself.

I took a deep breath. Okay. This would be okay. I'd figure this out.

Right?

Yes, I would figure this out. But for now, I'd shut up the flutter with some food.

Ranée was already at the table eating cereal. She was dressed in her horse barn clothes. "Volunteering again today?" She nodded and pushed a piece of cereal around with her spoon. "You don't like it?" I asked, trying to make sense of her mood. Maybe she wasn't totally awake yet?

"I like it a lot." She pushed another marshmallow around her bowl and set her spoon down. Then she stared off into the distance.

Okayyyy. I went to the fridge to decide what would make my stomach stop fluttering. Not yogurt. Not eggs. A muffin? Maybe. Bacon? My stomach gurgled. Of course bacon. I pulled out the package and rattled around in the cupboards looking for the skillet and a plate for draining the strips.

I glanced over at Ranée while the skillet heated. She hadn't moved. "Ranée?"

She sighed. "I'm going to the horse barn. Did you know Paul volunteers there?"

Whatever I'd expected, it wasn't that. "Paul? Like Proper Paul? My Paul?"

"I mean, he's not really your Paul, right? I thought you were interested in Jack."

"I am. And no, he's not my Paul. But I had no idea he rode horses."

"I guess he used to do it at summer camp a lot. Seems he was recently dumped and he was trying to cheer himself up by going back to a happy time in his life and that meant riding horses, I guess."

I winced at the word "dumped." "I broke up with him. I didn't dump him."

"What's the difference?"

"I'm too nice to dump anyone."

"Maybe I was wrong to tell you to dump him."

"Are you high?"

"I'm not high."

"Then maybe you're having a stroke? I bet that's it. You're having a stroke that's wiping out your short-term memory of the five months you spent nagging me to cut him loose."

She shrugged. "I admit that I'm rarely wrong about people, but I got Paul wrong. He's all right. I'm saying I wouldn't give you a hard time if you date him again."

"I'm not dating him again. This is why I don't like to tell you stuff sometimes. I didn't break up with Paul because you told me to. I didn't start talking to Jack because you told me to. I have never made a single decision in my life to do anything because you told me to."

"You should start that bacon."

I got up and laid some strips in the skillet. "I'm not doing this because you told me to."

"Understood." The sizzle of cooking bacon filled the silence for a few minutes. "So is it weird for you if Paul and I both volunteer at the barn?"

"Weird in the sense that it's a bizarre coincidence, but it doesn't bother me at all. Wait," I said, almost running to plop down in front of her again. "Are you trying to tell me you want to date Paul?"

She looked at me like I'd just suggested she go for a naked jog. "Definitely not."

"Then why are you so stressed?"

"I really like this volunteering thing and I didn't want it to be awkward for you that he's there."

"Nope. That's it? That's what you were stressed about?"

She muttered something, but I could make it out plain as day. I made her repeat it anyway. "Sorry, a little louder, please."

She scowled at me. "I *said* I was worried I had maybe ruined your dating life because I was wrong about Paul."

"That last part one more time?"

She rolled her eyes and rose to take her bowl to the sink. "You're the worst."

"Just so we're clear, Paul was nice, but you're right. He was too boring for me."

"I'm glad it's not a big deal if we end up having overlapping hours. I love riding, and the kids aren't so bad either."

"I'm sure they'd be honored to hear you say so."

She flashed a grin in answer then changed the subject. "So you had a date last night. How's Jack?"

"Fine." So very fine.

"When are you going to meet him?"

I'd thought about it. Of course I thought about it. That's why I had an answer ready. "I'm not."

"Um. What."

"That's not what this is. Ten-hour car rides are bad for relationships."

"But one-hour flights are good for them. Of course you

have to meet him."

"If he lived here, or even kind of close to here, yeah, of course I'd go out with him. But he doesn't. It's a moot point."

"If moot means not meeting him is totally stupid, then sure. Moot point."

"It's a fun distraction," I said. "Joking around with him definitely helped me see why Paul and I were a bad fit. But this isn't about a relationship. It's about entertainment."

"I accept that you believe that right this moment. But is that how he's seeing this too? We all watch the same movies. I think ten out of ten people in this exact situation would meet sooner than later."

"I don't know," I said. "You know I'm not big into defining relationships."

"No," she agreed. "You roll with it until the guy refers to you as his girlfriend and then suddenly you're in a relationship, and then you roll with it a little longer until you break up with him. I know your M.O., girlfriend. It's a weird personality tic for such a—ahem." She fake coughed.

"Such a what? Control freak?"

"You said it."

"That's not true." Except it totally was.

Ranée didn't even bother to call me on it. "Either quit talking to him or start talking about what this thing is."

"I don't get this," I said. "You're the most commitment-phobic person I know. Why are you pushing me toward this when you can't stand relationships either?"

"I'm honest about it. I don't think you know you're a commitment-phobe too, but you're as bad as I am."

"That's not fair. We've been roommates for what, three years? And I've had two boyfriends to your zero."

"I'm straight with every guy I go out with. They know I'm just there for the party. You, however, honestly think you're open to relationships. It's what makes you dangerous."

Ranée was always a direct talker. It was one of my favorite things about her, but this conversation was not my favorite thing right now. But she wasn't done.

"You pick guys you know you can't fall for, and then—surprise—you don't."

"I know the type of girl you're talking about. I had friends like that in college, but those girls picked guys who were in relationships and were happy as the side chick because they got all of the perks with none of the work, or they got involved with professors, or dudes in their last year of law school who were going to be gone by the end of the semester so they could break it off. This Jack thing is the first time I've ever gotten involved with someone who I legitimately don't see a future with."

"Ah ha! You said you're involved."

"Oh for—look, haven't you ever heard of the analogy of the farmer's breakfast? He had bacon and eggs. The chicken was involved. The pig was committed."

She wanted to laugh. I could tell. But she wanted to win the argument more. "The whole reason I pushed you to talk to Jack is because he's exactly the kind of guy you need. He doesn't take himself seriously, and he doesn't let you take yourself too seriously either, does he?"

"I don't take myself too seriously."

She smacked her palm on the table. "Not with me. But you

never let guys see this side of you. You show them perfectly behaved Emily, highly successful Emily, and you never let them see that you are hands down the most ridiculous person I know." I frowned, and she snorted. "Don't even try to act offended. Your ridiculousness is my favorite thing about you. But that's exactly why you never let that side out for these guys. Because then it gives you a point in the relationship where you can say that he doesn't fully understand you, that you guys aren't clicking at some level, and then suddenly Paul's sitting on the curb."

I lifted an eyebrow. "Paul again?"

"Whoever. You know you do this," she said. "And it's exactly why you've let your real self out with Jack. Because you're counting on the distance to keep you safe, and that's not fair."

Irritation flickered through my chest and my palms started to tingle. It was a warning sign that the adrenaline of a temper tantrum wasn't far behind. "Why do you even care about my relationship dysfunction? I'm not hurting anyone. Let's talk about you and why every guy is a party and none of them ever gets a third date."

"Because I'm a total disaster. Disillusioned with men, heartbroken by a toxic relationship when I was too young, the whole bit. I'm not a mystery."

I took a calming breath. She wasn't trying to hurt me, even though it felt like I should be hunkering down in a foxhole right that second. "I don't want to talk about this anymore."

She shrugged. "You shouldn't talk to me about it. But you definitely should talk to Jack and make sure he knows that whatever this is now, that's all it's ever going to be."

She was repeating my words, but it gave me a hollow pang

inside to hear her say it.

"I'll say something to him the next time we talk."

"When is that going to be?"

"I don't know. We didn't make any plans or anything."

She got a knowing look on her face. "He will. *You* will. I saw your face last night while you were counting down the minutes until he called, and it said something very different than what your mouth is telling me right now." She jumped up and gave me a drive-by hug before she pulled a U-turn and sped for the door. "Gotta muck some stalls!"

And then the door closed behind her, and I was alone with my thoughts, which was the last place I wanted to be.

Chapter 17

I tried not to think too hard about Ranée's criticism over the next few days, but flashes of it returned every time I caught myself grinning at every text from Jack, or when we spent an hour Tuesday night flirting over Messenger.

Ranée was wrong. I knew she had my best interests at heart, but mostly Ranée just liked to fix things while remaining a hot mess. Working on me meant she didn't have to work on herself.

I tried to ignore her when Jack texted me Wednesday morning to ask if I wanted to go out again.

Yeah. Yes. So much yes. But...what if this wasn't play time for him too?

Gah. Stupid Ranée.

I texted back with a short, `Sure.`

`Cool. Call you tonight to figure something out.`

I blinked down at his text to me. Call me tonight? If he was calling me tonight, then what was the date? Wasn't the call the date?

I hurried home from work and scarfed down some phở before I turned on Netflix and tried to pretend my phone didn't exist. I was halfway through an episode of *Jane the Virgin* when Jack called.

"Hi," I said. At least I didn't have to go through a shame spiral from answering the phone this time.

"Hey," he said. "Is now a good time?"

"I mean, I was busy improving my mind with some highbrow television, but I can pause it."

"I'm impressed. I was watching *Storage Wars*."

"That one guy who drives the old fifties car always overbids."

He laughed. "He does. So, are you free on Friday night?"

I nestled down in the sofa. "Friday works. But when one goes to Rome and London on a first date, how does one top that?"

"One doesn't," he said. "One changes directions completely. One upgrades the format and downgrades the activity."

"I don't follow, but you've got me very curious."

"How about a low-key night of board games?"

That didn't sound nearly as exciting as a stroll through Hyde Park, but I kept my voice light as I said, "Sure."

He cleared his throat. "But over FaceTime."

So that's what "upgrading the format" meant. "Sure," I said again, but I wasn't sure I'd kept it quite as light this time. "So I have to find my conditioner?"

"Nah," he said, and I could hear the smile in his voice. "But I'm definitely buying the good kind tomorrow."

Man, he was smooth in the dorkiest possible way. "I'll pencil in a tangle-free date for Friday." We chatted a few more minutes and hung up.

For the rest of the week, the stomach-flipping and flutters recurred every time I thought about our first face-to-face date. Or "face to face," I guess. But every time that happened, I also heard Ranée in my head. *Make sure he knows this is all it will ever be.* I imagined all the different ways I could shut her up when her voice intruded. Hand over her mouth. Duct tape. Or if it intruded a lot, maybe a pillow over her face.

That was the most annoying thing about Ranée. Once she planted an idea like that, I had to deal with it completely before I could dismiss it. So I tried.

The most uncomfortable part of her argument was that Jack's expectations might be different than mine. Even planning dates suggested a deeper investment than goofing off in chats and texts all week.

Gah. Stupid Ranée. I was going to have to deal with this.

I could not feel any stupider about having a "define the relationship" talk with my online playmate. And yet it didn't make me look forward any less to our game night.

Friday afternoon I rushed straight home from work and ransacked my closet trying to figure out what to wear. It all looked lame. I gave up and Googled "best colors to wear on camera." It was more like a list of all the things not to wear on camera, which could be summed up as "everything." Except blue. Blue was "safe" on camera, which was good because heaven knows tight patterns, dangly earrings, and above all STRIPES would make the camera explode, probably.

Google could only boss me up to a point, then I rebelled in very Emily-esque style by only kind of obeying but also not NOT obeying and pulled on a teal shirt because it wasn't exactly blue but wasn't NOT blue. Other famous Emily rebellions included high school spirit days when all the student government kids were required to wear our student council T-shirts. As the Club Coordinator, that meant me. I hated those boring gray shirts, so every Friday I cheered myself up by wearing a neon green bra underneath. No Google list was going to make me wear straight blue even though it's my favorite color.

I'd have fastened in some dangly earrings too except I didn't want Jack to think I was trying too hard. I put in a pair of tiny silver hoops instead. Then I sat. And then I started freaking out about the apartment being on camera too. I'd planned to stay in my room so Ranée wouldn't get nosy and holler something like "Emily thinks you're hot," because truths like that didn't need to be told aloud, but suddenly my bedroom seemed like a bad idea. Like, "Here I am on my bed."

Nope.

I figured the living room was safe enough. I fluffed the throw pillows and filled my water bottle in case talking parched me.

I practiced all the ways to ask Jack if I was stringing him along.

So, what are your expectations for this thing we're doing? Because I'm just killing time.

Do you plan on us ever meeting in real life? Because I don't.

You know we're not a thing, right? But can we still just

do all this flirting all the time anyway?

None of those seemed…good.

Instead I decided to think about how Jack was going to look. I mean, I knew how he looked from pictures and how he sounded from our European trip. But there was something different about seeing someone's expression and movement, from picking up the cues they didn't realize they gave away in their face.

On the phone, he'd seemed shy but not insecure. Insecure guys, they always had that touch of bluster. Sometimes it was arrogance, talking about their cars or their gym routines. Usually it was quieter than that, even. Paul hadn't bragged about being able to afford a decent apartment in the San Francisco housing market, but he'd find ways to mention compliments from his boss or refer to "his" employees to emphasize that he was successful enough to manage a team. I'd dated other guys who brought up their vegetarianism every so often, like, "Look at my virtue! Do you see me eating this lentil stuff? How about now? And now?"

It was all a way to highlight their best attributes, as if they were afraid I couldn't figure them out myself. Or maybe because they didn't want anyone to notice their flaws, so they trotted out their accomplishments like a personality combover.

Shy guys didn't lean on any of that stuff. They started slower, watching and waiting before they let you see parts of themselves rather than just plunking them down for display. Jack was more that way. How would talking on camera affect that?

My phone buzzed with the FaceTime alert, and I took a

deep breath as I pressed “Accept” to find out.

Chapter 18

There he was.

His head and shoulders appeared on camera. I half expected him to be in flannel due to my man bun prejudices, but he was wearing a dark gray thermal.

Here is the thing about men wearing thermals: they are so hot. I do not mean temperature.

How was that even fair? Guys can pull out their comfiest shirt and put it on, and immediately it gives them amazing shoulders and sex appeal. Meanwhile, one internet search on "what to wear on camera" later, and I'm sporting an adequate teal shirt and a FEMA situation in my closet.

His hair was pulled back, but a tendril had escaped and hung by his eye. I wanted to reach through the screen and brush it back. I had underestimated how hard it would be to keep a straight face. Not even a straight face, just not one of those pop-eyed, slack-jawed cartoon faces.

He waved. It was so much cuter than saying hi.

I waved back. Then I realized it was awkward when I did

it because now no one had spoken, so I said, “Hi.”

“How’s San Francisco?” he asked.

“Foggy. It’s a good night to be inside playing a board game. How’s the hermit house?”

“Small and Oregony.”

“What does Oregony mean? Is everything made of hemp? Do all the throw pillows get their tassels dreadlocked?”

“No, I think that’s a San Francisco thing. I need to specify that this place is rural Oregony which means it looks like an LL Bean catalog in here, except if it was decorated by two old guys sloshed on Budweiser who dragged in all the furniture their wives wouldn’t let them keep and then shoved it wherever it fit.”

“I’m going to need to see this.”

He reversed the camera, and I cursed myself for making the demand because there couldn’t be anything more interesting in his house than his face. “This is something else,” he said, panning around the room. Faux wood paneling covered the walls, which seemed like an odd choice for a cabin in the actual woods. I spotted an old TV, a tweedy brown sofa, and a kitchenette with avocado green counters. The only modern touch was a large, sleek computer monitor on a card table in the corner that I glimpsed before he flipped the camera again.

“In my defense, I’ve made none of these choices.”

“You’re forgiven. How long have you lived there?”

“Couple years, I guess.”

The answer startled me. I’d expect to see his own style in there somewhere after so long. Not that I knew what his style was, but he’d already said it wasn’t this.

“What about you?” he asked. “How long have you been in

San Francisco?"

"I've been in the Bay Area for about ten years. I came up for college, and I've been around ever since."

"Up? San Francisco is not up. Oregon is up."

"Up from the suburbs of LA. Everything is relative."

"Should we have a deep discussion about that? Relativism?"

"I mean, sure. Is this because we've veered into boring cocktail party talk?" It bothered me a little that he wanted to shift the conversation so quickly, but I couldn't figure out why. It had definitely been small talk. People always say "small talk" like it was a bad thing, but at the same time, those things added together gave a true picture of a person, not walks through London and Rome.

"It is," he said. "But it's a me thing, not a you thing. I'd love to know all of this stuff about you, but it's not fair to ask you to share all that stuff when I'm not willing to."

For a minute, I wanted to blurt, "Let's play Scrabble!" because here we were, three minutes into this conversation and already I had the perfect opening to bring up the most premature and awkward define-the-relationship talk EVER. And I didn't want to do it. I'd rather just goof off, but Ranée's words were sticking with me. Stupid Ranée.

"Why is that uncomfortable for you?" I asked instead of taking the easy road. I waited for some internal glow of satisfaction at having done the "grown-up" thing. It didn't come, unless it felt like my stomach clenching while I waited for his answer. This whole situation was suddenly a thousand percent less fun than the clever DMs and texts we'd been exchanging.

"Shady past? Problems with emotional intimacy? Desperate need to project an air of mystery to hide how boring I am? Which one of those answers is good enough to get me off the hook and keep this conversation going?" He gave me a tight smile, the kind that said he knew none of the answers were good enough.

I rested my chin in my palm and studied him. After a few seconds, he imitated me, only he crossed his eyes, and I laughed.

"This is a weird situation," I said, deciding to stick with the grown-up thing. "We're not dating, but—"

"Wait, isn't that exactly what we're doing right now? We're on a date, and unless I'm way off, we're about to have a talk about definitions." His expression and tone were mellow, maybe slightly amused.

"It sounds dumb when you say it like that," I said.

"What? No." Now he looked as if I'd told him we needed to speak only in Swahili. "It's good. Why not talk about it? If we lived in the same town and went on these dates in person, we probably wouldn't need to discuss any of this stuff for a while. But we're not, and so it makes sense that we have this conversation in a different order too."

"I guess I just want to be sure we're…" I stopped.

"We're what?" He leaned toward the camera slightly, as if it would put us closer.

"This is fun. The texts and DMs and now this." I pointed back and forth between us to indicate the video call. "And it could be this forever and ever and I'd be happy with it."

"Forever and ever?" He held up his hands in a "settle down" gesture. "I don't know you well enough for forever and ever."

It made me laugh again. "I mean that I'm fine with us just having a virtual friendship."

"*Friendship?* Come on, this is at least a flirtation."

"All right, flirtation. I'm fine with a virtual flirtation indefinitely." It was true. Going back and forth with him in any medium had become a bright spot in each day, but I wasn't into the idea of a long-distance relationship with a person I hadn't met, would never meet, and even if I did meet…what was the point? I wasn't moving. I didn't expect him to, either.

"Indefinitely." He scratched his nose. It was adorable. "All right. I accept your terms. An indefinite virtual flirtation."

I nodded. I wasn't sure what else to do. It was so official sounding that it seemed like we should shake hands.

I held up my hand to the camera. "High five to seal it?"

He held up his hand too and we high-fived.

Okay. So we were in agreement. It was exactly what I wanted.

So how come I felt disappointed?

I pulled myself together and tried to figure out where to go next after opening the date with basically, "I know we've never met, but let's define this thing." I glanced around the room, trying to find something I could seize on for conversation. There was nothing. Unless I wanted to talk about throw pillows or indoor lighting. Which I didn't.

"I'd like to destroy you in Scrabble now," Jack said.

It was pretty effective as changes of subject went. "You wish. You should probably tell me now if you're one of those types who hates losing to a woman."

"What if I am?"

"It'll make beating you even more fun."

He grinned, and I had a full-blown pitter-patter of the heart. Man, he was gorgeous.

"It's on," he said as a link for an online match pinged in my DMs.

I opened the game and examined my tiles. I got first play and I made it bloody. As in I literally spelled out the word "bloody" and scored 24 points.

"I see how it's going to be," he said.

"From start to finish." I flashed a return grin at him.

"That looks less a smile and more like what a shark looks like before it eats you. People are friends, not food, Em."

I liked the way he used my nickname instinctively, like he'd said it that way forever. But all I said was, "Chomp, chomp."

It was a bruising game, and even though I led the whole time, he always stayed within twenty points, not something a lot of people could do when I played. And for sure no one had ever made me laugh as much during a match. At least, not until he wiped the smile off my face by playing "zambuck" on a triple word score for his final play and destroying me.

"*Zambuck*?" I said.

"You want to challenge it?"

"Obviously not." The program didn't let you make up words. If it was on the board, it was a real word.

"That's one of the downsides to the online games."

"That it keeps you honest?"

He laughed. "No. That I can't lure you into challenging a word that ends up backfiring on you."

"So ruthless, Jack."

"Only because I've discovered you really are a shark."

"Sharks don't go from winning the entire game to losing by thirty in one play."

"You know how it is. Sometimes letters just line up exactly right."

"It's not luck that lets you come up with a word like zambuck."

"Could be. Maybe I put letters on the board until I guessed a real word that the game let me play."

"I doubt that's what you did." He didn't seem the type, and I liked that.

"You're right. A zambuck is a slang term for a paramedic in Australia."

My jaw dropped, and he laughed.

"You didn't even have to Google that, did you?"

"Nope."

I almost wanted to give him another fifty Scrabble points for that answer. "Why would you know that?"

He shrugged. It drew attention to the many favors his soft cotton thermal did for his broad shoulders, so much so that I almost missed his explanation.

"I knew a guy."

"You knew a zambuck?"

"I did. Play again?"

"Wait, I feel like this requires more investigation. How did you meet a zambuck? Did you go on vacation to Australia and stumble across one?"

He shifted and rubbed his eyes. "Not exactly. It was kind

of a work thing."

I wanted to ask what kind of work thing requires you to cross paths with a zambuck, but he didn't look like he wanted to get into it any further, so I let it go. Instead, I clicked to start a new game. "Play again."

I beat him by ten points that I had to work really hard for. Somehow, at the end of two hours, we were tied at one win each, but he was about a hundred points ahead in the making-me-laugh category.

"You're really funny," he said. "I like that."

"I was literally just thinking the same thing about you," I admitted. "You're even funnier than you are on Twitter."

"Thanks," he said. His focus shifted for a second, blinking at something on his screen that wasn't on the camera. "I should probably call it a night. But I've never had so much fun being a loser before."

I gave him a mock frown. "If we're talking total points, this is a murder scene and I'm dead."

"Dark. I like it."

I liked how often he said he liked things about me. It was a nice change from Paul's earnest but constant suggestions for improvements I could make. "That's me. Pitch black soul."

"On that note…"

I smiled at him. "I'll 'see' you around."

"Definitely."

We cut the connection, and I stood up and stretched, enjoying the prickle of every nerve ending coming alive.

Wait.

I sat back down as the adrenaline washed over me. How

could I feel this tingly and alive after playing Scrabble for two hours?

I almost wished Ranée were here to help me work through that. Because this wasn't as simple as, "You feel tingly because you like him." There was something else at play, but I wasn't sure I could explain it to her. Besides, she would most likely be out for hours still. It was only ten at night.

For a second, I paused to wonder why Jack had needed to go. It looked like he'd gotten a call or text while we were talking. But I refused to jump to fretting that maybe he had another virtual flirtation going on. So what if he did? It was none of my business. I wasn't the jealous type, and I wasn't going to become so now.

I was a whole ball of things at once. Energized, worried, slightly smitten, a little stressed. All of it made my insides itchy, like when I was a kid and I'd watched too much TV, and I'd suddenly need to be outside doing pretty much anything as long as it got me moving.

I headed back to my room to do my FEMA work. Imposing order on chaos always cleared my head, but as I plucked some workout clothes from the floor to fold, I realized what I really wanted was to be OUT. Out of my house, out of my head.

I changed into the workout clothes instead of putting them away, grabbed my keys and phone, and headed out the door to the gym. There was nothing like several miles on a punishing treadmill course to burn off the restlessness. It hummed in my chest and over my scalp, like I could flick my fingers and strike a spark with the excess energy buzzing through me.

If that didn't work out the strangeness cresting inside me…

Well, I needed the run to work. That was all. I just did.

Chapter 19

The gym was deserted. That was no surprise late on a Friday night. I was glad for the empty line of treadmills and jumped on the middle one, setting the course for hills.

I raced up them, digging hard, trying to outrun the unsettled feeling. It began to work, and my muscles loosened into the easy rhythm they usually found around the three-mile mark. But I forgot what also happened around the three-mile mark: mental clarity.

As I turned the situation with Jack over in my head, one truth bubbled up, even when I tried to flip the problem and look at it another way: I liked Jack. *Really* liked him. Liked him in the way that made me care whether he'd ended our date to talk to another woman. That made me care about why he'd invested so little of himself in a place he'd been living in for two years. That made me care about why he held so much of himself back from our conversations.

Yes, he was funny, creative in our dates, generous in the way he sent me treats tailored to make me smile. And he'd resisted the idea of classifying us as "Just friends." But there were little details I didn't know about his life, and even though I'd pressed only very lightly, he'd thrown up fortress-like defenses when I tried to ask about the simple things.

Something wasn't right here. Something wasn't right at all.

Ranée said he was a good guy. My instincts told me the same thing. But they were also telling me that he was hiding something. What could he be working so hard to avoid talking about?

Did it matter? There was nothing I could do about it. I couldn't make him tell me a thing. My choices were to quit talking to him, or to let this stay what it was—a "virtual flirtation"—or to press him until he quit talking to me.

I didn't want to quit talking to him.

I started mile five and reset the course to stay flat so I could think. Why was it important to me to keep talking to him? I'd gone from being furious with him two months before for his ninja photoshopping to dumping Paul when I realized I wanted someone more like...Jack.

But Jack wasn't possible. Jack was hundreds of miles away. Jack was funny and handsome and thoughtful. But he was also secretive and elusive.

So what was the draw?

The mystery?

That was part of it. No one could resist a good mystery. But it wasn't like me to become wrapped up in it to the exclusion of everything else, to pause during my work day to check in on his Twitter feed, or wait impatiently for his next IM. I'd never been that girl. And yet here I was.

By mile six, I was chasing down a new realization. I was thirty-one, excelling in my career, and some part of me was ready for a relationship. But Ranée was right: there was a part of my brain somewhere that kept choosing guys I knew I wouldn't really commit to.

I hadn't been willing to be "distracted" while I established myself professionally. But now I was firmly on the path up to the executive suite. I was good at what I did, and there would only be more promotions in my future. And now that I had what I'd worked toward, I felt a hole somewhere. Obviously I'd sensed that even when I was with Paul, or we'd still be dating.

Was my subconscious trying to tell me that JACK was the answer?

No. That made no sense. I had spent my whole adult life avoiding a relationship like my parents', where my dad's focus and my mom's free-spiritedness had been oil and water. I was an urban-dwelling corporate ladder climber. Jack was a flannel-loving rural Oregon tree dweller.

I finished mile seven and slowed the treadmill, walking to cool down and crystallize my next step in my own mind.

By the time I headed to the locker room, I knew what I had to do: this pull I felt toward Jack was trying to tell me that it was time to find The One, a real relationship, one I could commit to as I entered the next phase of growing up: finding and keeping true love.

I already had the glimmer of a plan I couldn't wait to put into action.

Chapter 20

Ranée rolled in a little after midnight and grinned when she saw me on the couch with my phone. "Date is going that well, huh? Tell Jack I said hi."

"It's not Jack."

She stopped in the process of pulling off a boot. They were tall and black and definitely not for riding horses. "You're cheating on him already?"

"It's not cheating."

"How could you?" she demanded. But she'd been standing on one leg, half-crouched, and now she toppled over.

"That's what happens to people who get on their high horse," I said.

She grunted and pulled her boot off the rest of the way. "You're a cold woman."

"Am not. And you were totally right about me being commitment-phobic. But not anymore. I'm ready for a relationship."

"Yay, Jack!"

"Not with Jack."

The boot sailed toward me and landed near my feet.

"What do you mean not with Jack? Of course with Jack."

"No. Don't get me wrong, he's awesome. But also far away. So." I waved my phone at her. "I'm on Flash Match. I already have a coffee date and a lunch date set up for next week."

"Flash Match? What? No. Don't swipe right. Don't even swipe left. Here, just let me swipe that right out of your hand." She climbed to her feet and hobbled over in her single boot to grab for my cell.

I held it out of her reach. "Bad Ranée. No-no."

She plopped on the carpet in front of me and worked at her other boot. "Why are you going on other dates?"

"I made real choices. I picked profiles for guys I could really go for. I'm going to start putting the same effort into these dates that I've put into hanging out with Jack. He's great, but he's made me realize that I want the real thing, not someone I can keep at an emotional distance because he's at a physical distance."

She dropped her head to her knees and groaned. "Why are you getting this so wrong?"

"I feel good about this." I stood and stepped over her. "Night-night."

"You can't sleep with a guilty conscience."

"Good thing I don't have one." I laughed as her other boot thumped behind me in the hall.

Nothing made me feel better than having a goal to work toward, and I went to sleep with the next phase of my plan running through my head.

Tuesday morning I threw my new black heels into my gym bag before I headed into the office. I'd wear them to my coffee date with a programmer named Jeff. I'd dressed in a conservative top and slacks, but the shoes would keep things interesting.

Mid-morning I slid them on and sent a picture of my feet propped on my desk to Ranée captioned, "Good choice?"

Really good.

I'll tell you how it goes, I typed.

I got back a puke emoji. I hope it sucks.

I laughed and grabbed my handbag, then let Hailey know I'd be out for a while.

It turned out to be a short while. Because Jeff turned out to be short. Really short. Even shorter when I had on four-inch heels. He'd opened with, "You lied about your height." Well, one of us had, or my heels wouldn't have mattered. The conversation hadn't improved, and when Ranée texted ten minutes in to demand, "WELL?" I said it was a work emergency and bailed.

I texted her on the way back to the office. Fail. I don't care if you're short. I care if you lie about being short.

Her reply was succinct:

That about covered it.

Jack and I had still been texting every day, but he hadn't mentioned another date. I wasn't sure what to think about that. It was good, probably. Better to spend that time on real dates. But I wondered if he hadn't asked because he was waiting for me to make the next move. Or maybe I'd said something during our Scrabble date that made him want to step back.

That was all fine. Good, even. It was one less conversation to have. But when his name flashed on my phone after dinner, my heart did the corniest possible stutter step. It happened every time he texted. I was a walking Hallmark movie character.

I plucked my shirt away from my chest and stared down at my heart. "Knock it off."

"Do I even want to know?" Ranée asked, walking into the kitchen.

"No. Going riding?" She'd been at the stables almost every day.

"Volunteering. Gotta balance my karma after getting up to no good all weekend."

"Please don't give me any details. I don't think I'm woman enough for it. My hot date was playing Scrabble, remember?"

"But it was a hot date, wasn't it?"

My phone buzzed again. Another text from Jack. "Yeah. It was. But I'm lining up other ones. Got lunch with an architect soon."

She shook her head as she dug through the fruit bowl.

I opened the text and blinked at it. "Ranée? How did Jack get this picture?"

She froze. "I don't know what you're talking about."

The fact that she hadn't even turned around to see what I meant told me she knew exactly what I was talking about. It was the "Good choice?" picture I'd sent her of my shoes before the coffee date, only Jack had Photoshopped an ankle bracelet of Scrabble tiles onto it. The tiles spelled, "Great choice."

I got up and set it on top of the fruit bowl in front of her. She studied it, then moved it to the counter and plucked out an apple.

“You don’t have anything to say for yourself?” I asked.

She took a loud bite of her apple.

“What am I supposed to think about this? Is it supposed to be charming? Or stalkerish?”

Her eyes widened and she spit her mouthful of apple in the sink. “Not stalkerish. I sent it to him to motivate him. I said you were going on a date, and he should Photoshop it so you would know he didn’t care. It was supposed to make him care enough to tell you not to go.”

I groaned. “We’ve reached an uncomfortable level of weirdness.”

She winced. “I know. That’s my fault. But that’s on me again, not him. I swear I’ll stay out of it.” And then she slunk out of the door.

Now I had to figure out what I was supposed to say to Jack. It wasn’t any of his business whether I was going on other dates, but if I didn’t answer it would turn into an awkward text silence. Yet it bugged me that he was so chill about me going on another date. It felt like a dig.

I made no sense. I knew it. But I also knew what I wanted to say back.

`Thanks!` 😁

There. Boundaries enforced.

Chapter 21

Thursday I set out for a lunch date with an architect named Reza. He spent half the meal talking about how much he liked women in high heels. And sandals. And wedges. And flats. I declined dessert and deleted his profile on the grounds that I suspected he'd picked me for the wrong reasons.

Saturday I ended up getting coffee and bagels with a physical therapist named Martin. The only red flag was that we kept having long silences that neither of us could fill. It maybe wouldn't have been such a big deal except I had conversations with Jack to compare it to.

Jack.

The one thing I did not have over the weekend was a date with him, and when I got home from boring coffee, Ranée had something to say about it. She was stretched out on the living room floor, flipping through a recipe magazine, but she sat up when I walked in.

"Coffee Martin is too quiet." I hung up my handbag and debated whether to get some work done next or do some cleaning.

Netflix. Netflix was obviously the correct answer.

"Please tell me you're doing something with Jack tonight."

"I'm not."

"Ugh. Why are you being so stubborn?"

I glared at her. "I'm not."

"You are, or you wouldn't be going on lame dates."

I plopped down on the sofa. "I'm not being stubborn. Jack just hasn't asked me out."

"Did my grandmother burn her bra in the Elko courthouse so you could wait for a guy to ask you out? *You* ask *him* out."

"No."

"Stubborn."

"For the third time, I'm not. I'm realistic. Jack is whatever. A bonus. If we fake hang out, we fake hang out. If we don't, we don't."

"He's 'whatever'?" She repeated the word with the exact skepticism she'd had when I announced I was going off coffee. I'd lasted a day-and-a-half. She'd been right then. And she was right now.

"There's no point, that's all. So that's why it's just gravy if we talk. That's all it's going to be."

"You act like airplanes don't exist. This is a solvable problem."

"You act like there's some simple end to this road somewhere off in the sunset of Happily Ever After Land." I waved my hands to indicate some serious airy-fairyness. "Let's say Jack and I meet in person. Let's say it goes perfectly, and we have amazing chemistry, and we fall in crazy love. Then what?"

"Then you're in love and it all works out."

"In the sunset of Happily Ever After Land. Not in real life, where one of us has to uproot entirely to make this work. It requires a one-sided sacrifice that neither of us is willing to make."

"You aren't, it sounds like. But how are you so sure he isn't?"

"Because he won't even tell me boring details about himself. I don't think he's hiding any deep dark secrets, but he's also not willing to open up all the way. And you know what? That's fair. He doesn't have to, not when this road ends in a fork, one leading to Portland and one to San Francisco, and that's that."

She sighed. "You know I try not to mind anyone else's business except yours, which is why I haven't said much about why Jack is kind of touchy about that stuff. It's not like I know his whole life history, but I know him well enough to know you guys are perfect for each other. I was trying to be all protective of his privacy and let him tell you things in his own time, but he's being an idiot, so I'm going to give this a little nudge. I know you googled him, but did you try an image search? That might get you somewhere."

I narrowed my eyes. "What do you know?"

"I know that people need to tell their own stories. Try that and see where it gets you."

"No. He needs to tell me himself. You just said so."

She rolled her eyes. "Don't act like you're not dying to google his picture now."

I crossed my arms. "Nope."

She didn't say anything. We stared at each other for about thirty seconds before I hopped up to get my laptop. "I'm image googling him."

"Dig," she called after me. "It may not be front page news."

What was "it"? Some sort of incident I should know about? I mean, obviously yes, or she wouldn't be pushing me to search.

I couldn't believe I hadn't thought to google images. It was the kind of thing I did when I wanted to know what kind of bird or flower I'd just seen, so it should have occurred to me. I went through our old DMs to find the pictures Jack had sent me of himself when we first started talking, the absurd Photoshop creations of him on the back of a unicorn, or the ones I'd made of him to tease him.

The first surprise was exactly how many old messages I had to scroll through. We'd had dozens of conversations, long and short, but always daily for over a month now.

Finally I found a picture that would make a good candidate if I cropped out the fake wreath of Cheetos he'd made around himself.

I pasted it into the image search and Google gave me some results. On the first page, half of the results were him. That gave me hope that the search might work. But all of them were photos he'd posted as part of his social media alter ego. They were on par with his riding-a-unicorn masterpiece. That made me despair that I'd never find anything besides the persona, but I clicked through the next page, and the one after. All of them were reposts of the same handful of pictures.

How deep was I supposed to dive? I decided to go twenty

pages. After that, I'd march into the living room and beat Ranée with a pillow until she spit out whatever information she was dying to tell me anyway.

But it didn't take twenty pages. It took fourteen, and there, on the second to last result, was a picture of Jack I hadn't seen yet. It looked like a formal picture, the kind people sometimes had to take for work if management wanted everyone's headshot on a lobby wall or something. Jack had short hair in the picture, but it was definitely him. His cheekbones and jawline would have given him away even if his smile hadn't. I'd memorized it during our Scrabble session on FaceTime.

It was a shock to see him there, smiling back from the screen, clean cut and so very Jack. Except that when I clicked it open to view it more closely, the name in the caption didn't read, "Jack Dobson." The guy in the picture was Dr. Jack D. Hazlett.

What was going on?

I immediately Googled the full name Jack D. Hazlett. More images popped up, including one linking back to the online version of his old high school newspaper in Bend, OR. It was his senior portrait, showing him in a suit and tie, his hair a little shaggy over his ears and hanging down to his eyebrows, his cheekbones and jawline already showing the promise of the handsome man he would become.

He'd graduated five years before me, which made him around thirty-six now. The article was an interview with the class salutatorian. No surprise that someone who went on to become a doctor was a high school brainiac. He was also a two-sport athlete lettering in cross-country and swimming, and he was his senior class president.

The article listed other accomplishments, but the two that caught my attention most were his superlatives: Class Clown and Most Likely to Succeed. Well. Those were two you didn't necessarily expect to see together.

I, on the other hand, had been on drill team and voted as "Best Sneeze." Look, I couldn't help it. I always sneeze three times in a row. The first two sounded like a Chihuahua and the third big sneeze sounded like an old grandpa. It wasn't intentional, and it also wasn't avoidable. If I sneezed while a teacher was talking, they would stop and wait for the third one and then pick up where they left off. I had everyone in my grade trained. I was weirdly proud of it. But it was no "Most Likely to Succeed."

I went back several pages to the oldest references I could find on Jack. He'd gone to Princeton for his undergrad and then the University of California, San Francisco medical school. That sent my eyebrows up. People knew about Harvard and Johns-Hopkins, but few people outside of the Bay Area or medical field realized UC San Francisco was just as highly respected. How long ago had that been? Had we overlapped time in the city? Why had he never mentioned he'd done med school here?

He'd done an oncology residency in Boston and then, working forward, I dug up a link to a spotlight feature from a newsletter for a children's hospital in Oregon announcing his arrival to the oncology department.

Pediatric oncology? Wow. That was like a cop choosing SWAT or a soldier choosing Special Forces.

There were research articles co-written by him and other

people with long strings of credentials after their names, articles with fancy titles like "Rhabdomyosarcoma complicating multiple neurofibromatosis," and others I understood even less.

Then the mentions began to dry up, and by the time I pulled up the first page of his most recent results, the last mention of him was dated two years prior. He wasn't listed on the hospital's web page. There were no more scientific articles.

I sat back and stared at the results, trying to make sense of what I was seeing. Obviously, something had happened to make him leave medicine. I almost walked out to ask Ranée about it. This is obviously what she'd wanted me to find. She probably knew why he wasn't practicing anymore.

But as I considered the possibilities, I began to understand why she kept insisting it wasn't her story to tell. It was a big enough deal that he'd left behind a career as a cancer doctor for kids. But he'd gone far out of his way to bury that part of his history. Did he have something painful he didn't want to talk about? Was he hiding the wounds from working in a tough career?

Or was he hiding a secret?

I hadn't heard from Jack since the previous afternoon before I left work. He'd asked how I was feeling at the end of my work week. I sent him an exhausted emoji. He sent me a Photoshopped picture of me wearing a snorkel and diving into a giant cup of coffee.

I'd been telling myself that I was fine with him not asking for a date this weekend. I'd been busy enough that I thought I believed it. But not anymore. I almost went out and asked Ranée her advice on what I should do next, but I heard it in my head before I even climbed off my bed. *Cowgirl up and ask him out yourself.*

I texted him. `Hi. Are you free tonight?`

He answered right away. `Could be. Are you asking for yourself?`

`Yes,` I answered.

`Then I'm definitely free.`

I was glad he wasn't there to see how big my smile was. It was a stupid response to someone who wasn't a real presence in my life. But it was an honest response. I could admit that. But only to myself.

I hesitated before sending my next message. `How about a date? My treat.`

His response was slower this time. `Wow. I feel so honored you can squeeze me in. I didn't think you had room on your social calendar.`

I rolled my eyes. `Yes, yes. You're very lucky. I'll be sure to remind you of it when we hang out.`

😁 `What's the plan?`

I wanted to get him talking, but I wasn't sure how to pull it off yet. I needed to buy some time while I figured out what I even wanted to know, and how I wanted to find it out. `I'll surprise you. Facetime, 7:00?`

He sent back a thumbs up emoji, and I set my phone down. I had five hours to figure out how to crack Jack.

Chapter 22

This was going to take a visit to the toy store. And a costume shop. Obviously.

I had no idea where to find a toy store, but I grabbed my purse and set Siri to looking for the nearest one on the way out the door.

An hour later, I was back with a bag of loot, and then it was on to the next phase. I dug through all the magazines under our coffee table and created a stack that leaned more than Pisa.

I sat back to study the effect. I had all the right pieces. I had them in the right order.

But did I have the right?

Was it my place to push him like this? An uneasy flutter in my stomach had me reaching out to sweep everything off the table and shove it out of sight. But…

But we needed to talk. I needed to know who he was beneath the pretty hair and the jokes. I needed to find the real parts of Jack, and this was all designed to make it easier for him to share that with me. This would be fine. Right?

I drew my hand back. Right. This was right.

Finally, I grabbed a quick shower, pulled on a plain white tank top and jeans, and did my hair and makeup with more drama than usual to balance the understated outfit. I'd spent my whole college sophomore year learning to do perfect winged eyeliner, and I smiled at the effect in the mirror. Some soft pink lip stain and Jack would be putty in my hands. I blew my reflection a kiss. Nailed it.

With fifteen minutes to go, I double-checked the coffee table to make sure I had all my supplies. I opened my laptop to make sure the camera was the right height while keeping my surprises out of view. I was rearranging a few items when Ranée walked through the door.

She stopped short and peered at the large syringe in my hand. "Do I even want to know?"

"It's for my date with Jack."

"Well, sure. That was my first guess."

"Are you going to be home tonight? If so, I'm doing this in my room."

"I have a feeling whatever *this* is, I'm going to prefer that you do it in your room anyway. But no, I'm going out again. I'm grabbing drinks with the accounting girls. I'll be out of your way in a few minutes."

I nodded and went back to figuring out where the syringe should go in the lineup. Ranée continued down the hallway. I didn't even hear her bedroom door open before she marched back into the living room.

"I can't take it. Just tell me. What are you up to?"

"Ha. You're such a know-it-all that it's nice to have you in the dark for once. I'm keeping it that way."

"I hate you."

"Do not."

"Fine. I hate secrets. It's very important for me to sit here until I get it out of you, but I like going out with friends on the weekend more than I like dragging your nonsense out of you, so I'm letting this go for now."

I wiggled my fingers at her in a "shoo" gesture. "You didn't hurt my feelings even a little bit. I know your tricks. Go away."

She growled but checked her watch and retreated to her room again.

At 7:00 exactly, I FaceTimed Jack. He answered immediately. He wore a plain dark blue T-shirt, and his hair was in a messy topknot.

Dang. I wished *my* hair looked that good in a messy topknot. I really needed to get the name of his conditioner.

"Hi." He smiled, and I lost my train of thought. I'd thought that I remembered how hot he was, but somehow the picture in my head—as vivid as it was—didn't match up to the living, breathing Jack. Wow.

"Hi," I said back.

His smile widened. "You look nice."

Ah, guys. Sometimes they were so simple. A basic white tank top had the same effect as a little black dress on them. At least Jack was predictable this way even if I couldn't predict much else about him.

"Thanks," I answered. "You do too."

"Yeah, well, I put a lot of thought into whether I should choose one of my five T-shirts or one of my six flannels. Glad I picked right."

He had to know it would be impossible for him to choose wrong. But I let it go and started Phase One of Operation Crack Jack.

"So I feel like I know you so well and yet not at all," I said. "Does that sound crazy?"

He pressed his lips together and tilted his head for a minute. It was his thinking face. How cute. See? I'd already learned something new about him: his pondering expression. This was going to be a productive night.

Finally he said, "No, it's not crazy. I think in some ways you know me better than a lot of people in my life right now."

I was very glad I was sitting down because I'd just discovered that "going weak in the knees" could actually happen in real life, not just Ranée's cheesy novels that I stole and devoured when she was gone.

"I thought tonight could be about getting to know each other better," I said, "but I was trying to figure out how to still respect your rules for no cocktail party talk. The answer is obviously that I have to psychologically profile you using the most cutting edge tools available."

His eyebrows went up. "Obviously."

"I've assembled the finest personality assessments available. Look." I angled the laptop so he could see the precarious pile of magazines. I picked *Cosmo* off the top and held it up to show him the page I'd left it open to. "Can you read that? It says, 'What Is Your True Age According to Your Social Media Habits?' I figured this would be a good one to start with considering how we spend most of our time talking."

"I don't need to take it. The answer is thirteen. Maybe fourteen. Next."

"Fine. We'll find out which Backstreet Boy we're each meant to be with instead. Oh, but before we get started, I should warn you, I'm on my laptop because I'm running out of data on my phone plan, but the Wi-Fi is acting up, so it might cut out every now and then."

"It is?" Ranée said, choosing that moment to walk back in. "Weird. It's been fine for me." She leaned down to smile at the camera. "Hi, Jack," she said, squishing into the shot with me.

"Hi, Nay-Nay."

"Nay-Nay?" I couldn't help that it came out almost as a hoot.

Jack's eyebrows scrunched. "Yeah. Nay-Nay. That's what Sean always calls her, isn't it?"

"Who cares?" I asked. Okay, fine. I almost crowed it. "That's definitely what she'll be called from now on."

"Ugh." She straightened. "Everything was fine until that stupid dance and song came along. He's not allowed to call me that anymore. Neither are you and Jack."

"Okay, Nay-Nay," we said at the same time and then cracked up.

"When I said I hated you before, I was kidding. But now I mean it. I'm leaving," she said, heading for the door.

"Bye, Nay-Nay!" Jack called from the computer.

"I'm not on your team anymore," she yelled before shutting the door behind her. Hard. A magazine slid off my pile.

"Too far?" Jack asked.

"Definitely not. You've made me so happy."

He shook his head. "Cheetos and coffee and using a nickname your roommate hates. You're not exactly high maintenance, are you?"

"I don't know, but I have a quiz that will tell us." And then I started mouthing words without saying anything. After a couple of seconds, he cut in.

"Emily? I can't hear you?" He pointed at his ear and shook his head.

I mouthed, "You can't hear me?"

He pointed at his ear and shook his head again. I held up my finger in a "just a minute" sign and then disconnected the call.

I grabbed the first item from my arsenal, the shirt from a pair of scrubs I'd bought at the costume store and pulled it over on top of my tank top. Then I hit FaceTime again.

Phase Two was about to begin.

It had only been about thirty seconds since I disconnected the call, but if Jack was surprised to see me in hospital scrubs when he answered, he didn't show it.

"Sorry about the call dropping," I said.

"No problem. You were saying something about the Backstreet Boys?"

"We better start with a pre-quiz question: do you know who the Backstreet Boys are? I mean, I'm sure you know the band. But do you know each of the members? Because otherwise the results might not mean anything to you."

He looked at me like I'd just asked who the president was. Instead of answering, he stood up, backed away from the camera, and reached for a flannel shirt on the back of a nearby chair. He slid it on without buttoning it, then held each unbuttoned flap and shook it to make it look like the wind was blowing. He gazed back at me soulfully and sang, "Tell me why, ain't nothin' but a heartbreak," in a perfect imitation of the video for "I Want It That Way." I could practically see him on the airplane tarmac.

He sat back down and gazed at me expectantly.

"That came to you way too easily."

"I might have done a homecoming lip sync in high school with the swim team guys."

"With full choreography?"

He nodded. "And Speedos and flowy white shirts. So bring on the quiz."

I had a very important question I suddenly needed to ask him first. "What about 'Shoop? Do you know it? Do you like it? Can you do it?"

"I don't exactly have 'a body like Arnold with a Denzel face,' but yeah, I can Shoop."

I stared at him without speaking for so long that he tentatively said my name. "Em? Did I answer wrong?"

I swallowed. Hard. "No. That was the right answer. Um, back to this quiz. First question: you're going on a first date and it just happens to be their birthday. What gift do you get? A, I'm the gift. B, a bouquet of balloons. C, why do you have to get a gift if you don't even know them, D, chocolate never fails."

"All bad answers," he said. "E, flowers. I'd choose ones that make me think of her personality."

"Oooh. Nice answer. But I'm going to put you down for chocolate. Next, if you were on *The Voice*, who would be your coach?"

"Blake Shelton."

"It's because of the plaid shirts, isn't it?"

"Obviously. I would always know the dress code. I like dress codes that involve jeans for everything."

"Noted. But what if your date wanted to go somewhere that required a brand-new pair of red high heels?"

His eyebrows went up. "If they're the red heels I'm thinking of, then I would sew my own tux by hand if that's what it took to make it happen."

Oh, man. He was good. Very, very good. I cleared my throat and asked the next question. "Choose a cheesy nineties trend. Flannel, mood rings, "No Fear" shirts, golf visors, or starter jackets." I rolled my eyes and marked flannel. "Got it."

"It's like you know me."

I asked him a few more questions, pretended to tally the results, and read him the result I'd already written up ahead of time. "You got Brian Littrell." He scoffed, but I ignored him and continued. "You're an all-around good guy. You have a lot of patience, an even temper, and would probably work well in a profession with children." I set the magazine down and studied him. "Interesting."

He kept his expression neutral. "I thought this was supposed to tell me which Backstreet Boy I'm meant to be with."

I shrugged. "I must have misread the name of the title." Then I started mouthing words to him again. His forehead wrinkled then cleared. He folded his arms across his chest and sighed.

I disconnected the call and pulled my hair into a topknot of my own then slid a tongue depressor behind my ear like it was a pencil and called him back.

"Sorry again," I said when he answered. His eyes flickered to the tongue depressor, but he didn't say anything. "The Wi Fi is such a pain today. I have a bad feeling this call will drop a few more times."

"Me too."

I shot him a bright smile. By now he had to know what it would take to end this escalating nonsense. "Ready for the next quiz? We're going to figure out which Marvel superhero you are."

"Can't wait." A touch of amusement laced his voice.

"Would you pick to be part of The Avengers, S.H.I.E.L.D., The X-Men, or the Fantastic Four?"

"Avengers."

Of course. I got the answers to other questions such as what motivated him, whether he'd ever date another superhero, and what he'd want for his last meal. (Bacon. It was alarming how perfect he was.) I slowed down on the last one. None of the answers mattered in terms of the result I would give him, but I wanted to know his answer to the question for real. "Interesting," I said, reading it silently. Did I have the nerve to ask it? He leaned forward slightly. "Tonight's the night," I read aloud.

His eyebrows shot up again. "Are we going down this road?"

"Settle down and wait for the rest of the question. Tonight's the night: you're going on your third date with the most perfect person in the world. What makes them so attractive to you? Is it A, they have a—"

"Wicked sense of humor, quick mind, and a sense of adventure? A strong sense of herself and no fear in setting boundaries? Someone who is driven and ambitious? A killer smile and better hair than me?"

My mouth fell open a tiny bit. I didn't know what to say to that.

"Just put me for whichever option that is."

I nodded and marked something random. I wished I could record this conversation and play that bit back over and over. "Ready for your result? Oh, this is shocking. It's a tie."

"Can't be. I'm Thor, obviously." He pointed to his long hair. "Except his looks better down than mine does."

I loved Chris Hemsworth as much as the next girl. More, probably. But as a bonafide Chris Hemsworth lover, I wasn't so sure he had anything on Jack in the hair up OR hair down department. I kept that to myself and shook my head instead. "Sorry. Thor isn't even in the tie."

"Let me guess." He settled back and shot me a look of resignation. "It's a tie between Captain America and Bruce Banner."

He was exactly right. "How'd you know that?"

"Wild hunch."

"Good instincts. Let's see, if I read through both of these and sum it up, it sounds like you've got the excellent problem-solving scientific mind of Bruce Banner with the strong sense of duty like Captain America. It says here you'd be well-suited to a career that combines a fine diagnostic mind with a desire to help others."

"It says that, does it?"

"It does."

"And now that this quiz is done, are we about to have

another totally random Wi-Fi outage?"

"No, but here's the thing. I'm kind of hungry so I was thinking I'd make myself some avocado toast. Is it going to bug you if I eat while we're hanging out?"

"Of course not."

"Oh, good." Since he refused to take the bait on the scrubs and the tongue depressor, it was time to raise the stakes.

I reached for the syringe.

I'd already loaded it with guacamole, so when I held up a plate with a piece of toast on it and a syringe full of green paste, Jack looked even more confused than he probably would have by me holding up a giant syringe at all.

"I have a bad relationship with avocados," I said.

"Okay..."

"They're perfect for about two minutes. The rest of the time it goes hard, hard, hard, hard, two minutes of ripeness, mushy."

"If you feel that way about avocados in California, imagine our pain in Oregon."

"The thing is, if I were a Marvel superhero, I would probably be Iron Man because I came up with a brilliant invention to solve the problem."

"You did?"

Yeah, I did. About four hours ago when I was trying to figure out how I'd work a syringe into our conversation. But all I said was, "Watch this. I think I need a patent." And then I angled the camera so he could see me squish out enough guacamole to spread it around with the tongue depressor on the toast. I held up the syringe again, half empty now. "See? All this guac I didn't use will stay in here, no air, not turning brown."

Hmmm. Maybe I really did need a patent.

"I concede. Definitely genius."

"Glad you can see that. Now for another quiz."

"Oh good."

"It almost sounds like you don't mean that."

He dropped his head. "Can't imagine how you got that idea," he mumbled into his folded arms.

"Now we're going to figure out what our patronus is."

He lifted his head. "Mine's a sparkle unicorn."

I shook a magazine at him. "This quiz will decide that. All right, first question. What is your natural element?"

"Hermit cabin," he said before I could give him his choices.

"Earth, air, fire, or water?"

"Mud."

"Runny mud or thick mud?"

"Thick."

"So earth. Next: your significant other reveals she cheated on you, but she apologizes and promises never to do it again. Do you—"

"Wait, why are you cheating on me?"

I knew he was kidding, but the implication that I was his significant other made my cheeks heat. I ignored the interruption. "So do you dump her, try to work it out, follow your gut, or cheat in revenge?"

"Definitely dump her."

"What kind of dancing do you like to do? Slow and smooth, like a waltz? Fast and crazy? Free flowing? Never mind the answer. Let me figure out where 'hip-hop in a Speedo' fits."

He laughed, and I asked him a few more questions and then pretended to tally the results again before I read the answer I'd already written. "How interesting. You're a Caribbean flamingo. Apparently they're super nurturing, and they produce this natural concoction full of fat and protein to keep their flamingo kids healthy. That's fascinating."

"I'm riveted."

"Oops, I couldn't hear you. Wi-Fi connection must be going bad again. I better try reconnecting." I hung up, pulled on a surgical mask, and hung a toy stethoscope around my neck. Then I pressed "Call" and listened to the heightened sound of my heartbeat in my own ears. I didn't even need a stethoscope for that.

This was it. He *had* to crack now.

"Hi." I grinned at the sound of my muffled voice coming through the mask when he answered.

He blinked at me.

"Next quiz. What's your Hogwarts—"

He held up his hand in a "stop" gesture. "I'm sure whatever the result is, it will turn out to be the house that's produced the most wizard doctors." He sighed and rubbed his eyes. "I get it. You know I'm a doctor. Did Ranée tell you?"

"No. And I feel betrayed that she didn't." I removed the mask, using the excuse of setting it down to gather my thoughts. He didn't seem at all amused by my efforts to win that confession. "I found out the old-fashioned way. Relentless googling."

"Did you consider there might be a reason for that?" He

didn't sound angry, exactly. His voice sounded the way my eyelids used to feel after studying all night in college.

"Yes. But I hoped if you knew I knew, then we wouldn't have to talk around it anymore. That nothing in our conversations has to be off limits. We can discuss philosophy or small talk."

"It's not small talk. This is hugest-thing-in-my-life talk."

"I get that."

"I think you don't." His face slipped from pained to stony, a sudden shutdown of his emotions that left his expression blank.

He could have stabbed me with my hypodermic needle and it would have stung less. My whole point had been to get him to open up so I *could* understand him. Now my instinct was to close the laptop, crawl into bed, go to sleep, and wake up to a morning where I discovered I'd never started this conversation. But all the evidence that I'd opened a door I couldn't close now was scattered in its Fischer Price garishness before me.

"I'm sorry." His expression didn't change, but I soldiered on. "I shouldn't have pried. But we've had big and small talk for weeks. Now that I know about you being a doctor, can't it all just be real talk?"

The tiredness I'd heard in his voice crept into the tight lines around his eyes. "Haven't you been following my Twitter posts? You've seen the work I do. I don't do real."

"I think it's amazing that you're a doctor. I'm just trying to understand why this is so hard for you to talk about."

"Are you?" His voice was even, but all the warmth I'd grown used to hearing in it had leached away. "Or are you trying to solve a mystery to satisfy your own curiosity? Because that's what it feels like from where I'm sitting. Didn't I just say something about how much I respect that you set clear boundaries? Why does that only go one way?"

If the earlier comment had felt like a needle, this was a scalpel, slicing through all my layers of justification for prying, right to the heart of things. "Okay. Your life isn't a joke." I tugged the stethoscope from my neck. I was ashamed of its bright yellow and redness as it dangled from my hand. "I'm sorry." And then I didn't know what else to say, so I said, "I should go now."

He nodded. "Talk to you later." And he disconnected as I was reaching for the button to hang up. The FaceTime logo filled the screen, and I shut the laptop. The urge to crawl under my covers and hide washed over me again. Instead, I stood and gathered up all my props from the coffee table and dropped them into the trash can, returning for the pile of magazines and giving them the same treatment.

Then I crawled into bed and pulled the covers over my head to wallow.

What had I been thinking? People who went to those kinds of lengths to keep their pasts under wraps didn't want to talk about them for a reason.

Maybe the better question was *who* had I been thinking about?

Me.

I'd been thinking about my need to know. Why had I needed to know?

Because Ranée kept pushing me to find out. This was her fault somehow.

I flung down the covers so I could draw a breath of cool air.

But why had Ranée pushed me? And why had I let her? She couldn't talk me into anything I didn't want to do.

The first answer was easy. Ranée had pushed because not only did she know that Jack was a doctor, but because she must have some idea of why he'd quit practicing.

The second answer was harder. I'd let her push me into digging. Because…

I really wanted to know. That's why.

And if I really wanted to know it was because I cared. Curiosity alone would never have driven me to make such a ridiculous plan to make Jack tell me his secrets. Because this had been a secret. I'd known it when I was digging for it, but somehow I'd decided I was entitled to it.

Jack didn't owe me his secrets. And the fact that I'd worked so hard to uncover them said more than I wanted it to about how far I'd already fallen. Into this rabbit hole mystery.

And into him.

Chapter 23

I woke up to a gray dawn. I wasn't sure how long I'd lain there last night trying to figure out how to quit falling so hard for a guy I had no future with, but I didn't wake up with the answer.

I reached for my phone, but only email alerts from overnight business spam waited for me. No Jack. But I hadn't expected anything. Not really. I wasn't sure he would want to hear from me again, much less talk to me.

I pulled on some workout clothes, grabbed my keys, and headed to the gym for the early morning weight training class. I hated the instructor. He was way harder and barked much louder than the evening instructors did, but it felt like exactly what I needed to banish the fog that had followed me out of sleep.

An hour later, I racked my weights and toweled the sweat off my face and chest, and decided I was wrong; the fog was still with me.

I stopped at my favorite café on the way home to see if I could drown the fog with a big enough shot of espresso, or smother it under the weight of the largest possible banana nut muffin. Instead, when I got home, I only felt jittery, overstuffed, sore…and still bad. I wished jumping in the shower would wash off the feeling as easily as it did the sweat, but no. It didn't.

I collapsed on my bed and opened the notes on my phone, trying to tap out a list that would help.

How to Stop Feeling Bad

Apologize

Make it up to Jack

Accept that I broke this and I can't fix it and move on

Wait for Jack to cool off and contact me

The problem was that I'd apologized last night. I hadn't even tried to make excuses. I'd said a simple, heartfelt, "I'm sorry." Sometimes, continuing to apologize when the other person didn't want to hear it was a way for the apologizer to make herself feel better while it did nothing for the other person. Maybe it might even make it worse.

As for making it up to Jack…how? I couldn't turn back time and not do the internet search. Maybe this was time for a grand gesture, but what? And why? That was kind of at the heart of everything here. Why it mattered. Who I was doing it for. Because right now, a grand gesture still felt more about me than him. About taking control over a situation that was making me feel bad instead of sitting with it and letting it play out.

And that told me exactly why it mattered.

It was the epiphany I'd already had last night. It mattered because I cared. So. Much.

Which was why option three wouldn't work. I could accept that I had broken this. I could accept that I couldn't fix it. But I couldn't accept that I needed to move on.

How had this even happened to me? How did this man who I'd never met become the standard I measured my other dates against? How had we so quickly gotten to a point that a day without talking or texting made my insides feel the way I had when Ranée switched our coffeemaker to decaf without telling me? The day carried an extra weight without Jack to put some snap into it.

It was more than that. But I didn't want to wrap words around it. This was enough to process already. But no moving on.

The next option—waiting for Jack to cool down and contact me—was far more passive than I liked. Because what if he never reached out? What if I'd shut him down completely by pushing so hard for him to talk to me about his past?

I'd been so disrespectful. So very, very disrespectful.

I dropped my phone and considered crawling beneath the covers again as the full weight of my wrongdoing pressed me down flat, and I sank further into the mattress under the heaviness in my chest.

I closed my eyes and forced myself to play through the whole chain of events that had led us to this point. Ranée pulling Jack in on a joke, me telling him off, his genuine apology, the easy chemistry we found right away through our senses of humor, my increasing interest in him shining a light into the gaps I hadn't seen yawning between Paul and me. Me breaking up with Paul. Jack and I laughing. And talking more. And going on dates.

I hadn't understood it. That was the problem. Hadn't been able to see the way it would all play out. We had become a puzzle I couldn't solve, so I had gone looking for pieces. I thought if I understood him better, I could understand what we were. And then I would know how to feel about it.

So stupid. Because no one got to decide how to feel. The feelings showed up. Like warts. Or rainbows, if you were happy about them. Which I wasn't. So, warts.

Maybe not warts. These were feelings that appeared like freckles when I forgot industrial strength sunblock—and I never, ever forgot. I'd forgotten to apply my industrial strength feelings blocker. And now I had them, all pressing me deeper into the bed.

The heaviest was guilt. I had done so wrong by Jack. And shame. Because I'd done it out of a need to make myself feel better about something I didn't understand.

Except now I did. And sitting on top of everything else was the fear that I'd figured it all out too late.

Ranée popped her head in an hour later. I opened my eyes but kept them trained on the ceiling.

"Didn't see you last night. How did your date go?"

"I burned everything down with the match you handed me."

"Um, what?" She came in and climbed up to sit cross-legged on the foot of my bed.

I struggled upright and sighed. "I made this whole dumb plan to get Jack to tell me all about his past. It backfired. Now he's mad I went looking, and I don't think he's going to talk to me again."

She winced.

"And I'm kidding about you handing me the match. This is all on me. I just feel like spreading the misery around a little."

"No, you're right. I know Jack hates talking about the doctor thing. I was trying to walk this fine line of wanting you to know that your man-bun-wearing internet comedian had more layers than he was letting on, but..." Now it was her turn to sigh. "I guess that wasn't my call to make."

I plucked at the blanket. I should get up and do a bunch of work, get a jump on the week before it started tomorrow. I could keep myself busy enough that I didn't have to think about all of this. But I didn't make a move. I plucked up a new piece of lint instead.

"What's the plan?" Ranée asked.

I shook my head. "No plan."

"Of course there's a plan. You're the queen of planning."

"Not this time. I've run the scenarios and there's nothing that doesn't make it worse."

"Even an apology? Apologies make everything better."

"Except I already apologized. It was the last thing I said to him before he hung up. That I was sorry."

"Okay, but was it a sincere apology?"

I glared at her. "Ranée. Seriously? I know how to apologize. I learned in preschool, same as you."

"In my preschool, the teacher would make us say we were sorry, explain why what we did was wrong, and tell what we would change in the future, then ask for forgiveness. Did you do any of that? Like this. I'm sorry I ate all your peach vanilla yogurt. It was wrong because it didn't belong to me. Next time I'll ask first. Do you forgive me?"

"I guess I didn't get specific. But it was totally clear from the context that I meant I was sorry for snooping."

"What were your exact words?"

"I'm sorry."

She stared at me like I was dumb, but I felt the first sputters of purpose rumbling to life in my chest, and I didn't care.

"I need to be specific in my apology so he knows I really get it," I said.

She gave me two exaggerated thumbs up. "Good job. But also, you didn't answer the question."

"What question?"

"Do you forgive me?"

I blinked at her, waiting for my brain to catch up to her words. Then I got it. "The peach vanilla yogurt wasn't a hypothetical. You ate it all."

"In my defense, it was really good."

"You're right. That yogurt was just asking for it. How can you be held responsible for it sitting there in the fridge, just out in the open like that?"

"You get me." She hopped off the bed. "Next time I'll let you know before I eat it all. See? That's how an apology is done."

"I don't think you get it. You're supposed to apologize and say you'll buy me more."

"I'm teaching the apology lesson here, not you, and I went to the best preschool in Elko, so I'm sure I've got it right. I'm going to hit the shower."

Only now did I notice that she was in her riding clothes again. "How's it going with the horses?"

"The kids are great with them," she said. "It's amazing to me how the horses seem to get these kids and the kids know it. They feel it. And it knocks off one or two of their hard edges. I was mostly in it for the free riding, but the joke's on me."

"That sounds pretty awesome. How's Paul doing?"

"He's amazing with horses. Who would've thunk, huh?"

"I meant with life in general."

The tops of her cheekbones went pink, and my radar finally went off. That was interesting. Very interesting.

"He's fine, I guess," she said, heading for the door.

I let her get away with it. "Bye, yogurt thief. Thanks for listening."

"Sure." She shut the door behind her, and I picked up my phone and stared at it.

It stared back. I blinked first. It was still blank.

What to say? And how to say it?

I opened up my text messages and started drafting.

`Hey. Sorry about last night. I was out of line. I was trying to—`

I broke off typing and erased it all. What was I supposed to say? That I was trying to get Jack to spill some personal information he obviously didn't want out there? He already knew that.

The "why" mattered a lot more here than the "what" did.

I tried typing again. `I wanted to show you—`

I stopped and deleted. No.

I set the phone down. I didn't want to text. It was too easy to mistake tone, to get things wrong. This needed a more direct approach.

I ran my hands over my hair to tame any flyaways and thought about what I wanted to say. I'd give him the truth, but how much of it? Considering the twelve miserable hours I'd spent between last night and this morning, thinking and second-guessing everything, I didn't know what else I had to lose. At this point, I wasn't at all sure I would hear from Jack again. I couldn't make things any worse.

The whole truth, then.

I picked up the phone and opened my messaging app. Then I took a deep breath, activated the camera, and hit "record."

"Hi. I just want to say I'm sorry again for last night. The more I think about it, the worse I feel. You didn't owe me any explanation, and I shouldn't have pushed you for one. I definitely shouldn't have treated it all like a big joke. I'm not even sure why I pushed so I hard. I think it's because—" I broke off. I couldn't bring myself to put everything out there. "Anyway," I continued. "I'm sorry for digging into your past and bringing it up. It was wrong because it's your life and your story to tell. Next time I'll…" I trailed off. There wouldn't be a next time. So I said that. "Next time nothing. This isn't something I'll ever do again. I'm really, really sorry."

Then I ended the recording and sent it before I could talk myself out of it.

I half held my breath while I watched the screen, tapping it now and then to wake it up. A couple of minutes later, the little checkmark appeared next to my video telling me Jack had seen it. Another few minutes went by and the "…" thinking dots appeared.

Then they disappeared.

They reappeared.

It went on for a few more minutes until finally they disappeared, and I realized I'd been waiting for almost a half hour with no dots at all.

Jack had seen it. But he had nothing to say.

Chapter 24

For the next two days, I still didn't hear from him. What I should have done was blow it off.

Prime me: "Whatever. I don't have time for guys who get their feelings hurt that easily."

Current me: *Refreshes phone madly.*

I knew it didn't make sense. If I had heard the last of Jack, what had I lost, really? We weren't in a relationship. We didn't have a future. We didn't owe each other anything.

But at a bare minimum, we'd become friends. And when it came down to it, that was no small thing. Friends whose senses of humor were as out there as your own…those were four leaf clovers in the weed patches of life. I would feel just as bad if I had this kind of fight with Ranée.

It was cold comfort to know I'd at least offered up a sincere apology. I'd done the only thing I could do to make things right.

On the third day, I still didn't feel any better. I'd read a book recently where a character described the feeling of missing someone as losing a tooth and constantly poking at the hole in your mouth where it should be. That was how the silence felt between Jack and me.

It was absurd. And unsustainable. And I couldn't do a thing about it but suck it up and move on.

I decided to pour my frustration into work, and I kicked on my afterburners for the rest of the week, scheduling more meetings, running more efficiency diagnostics, checking in personally with more of my team than I had since my promotion.

On Thursday morning, my assistant Hailey chased me down the hall waving a message slip at me. "Peter called." I read over the message from my boss while she put her hands on her knees and caught her breath. "I've got four times as many steps as usual today, and we're only halfway through. Just tell me, are you trying to kill me? Because if you are, I need to go upgrade my healthcare plan."

"Peter wants to order lunch for the team tomorrow because we're two days ahead of deadline. I'll find out what everyone wants."

Hailey straightened. "Boss, that's my job. You have to let me do it. Go sit in your office and think management thoughts while I handle the details."

"But—"

"But that's my job. Half of which you've been doing for a few days. Let me. I enjoy the feeling of earning my paycheck."

Hailey was six years younger than me, but I felt like I'd just been schooled by someone twice my age and experience. I hesitated, then nodded. "Have I been micromanaging?"

"Um."

I waved her off. "Enough said. Go get the orders. I'll stay out of the way."

I returned to my office and looked at my list of tasks, trying to figure out which ones I was micromanaging. I had eight things on my list. Technically, I could cross off five and leave them for other people. And maybe now was a good time to read a few articles on effective leadership to remind myself not to be a giant pain in my team's collective backside.

I picked up my phone to pull up some bookmarked articles and froze.

I had a text from Jack.

I should set the phone down and do some deep breathing, manage my expectations before I opened it up.

I should.

But I fumbled it to the floor in my effort to swipe the message open as fast as possible.

In your message you said you weren't sure why you pushed so hard, but you thought it was because…and then you didn't finish. What were you going to say?

I set the phone down again. Whatever I had expected, it wasn't that. Maybe, "We're cool. Wanna FaceTime later?" Possibly, "Please don't contact me again." But not this.

I picked up the phone and opened our DMs to replay my message, trying to hear it from his perspective.

My face filled the screen. Even through my makeup I could see the slight circles under my eyes from the restless night I'd had the night before. Video Me started with a wobbly smile then cleared her throat. I fast forwarded to the part he asked about. "You didn't owe me any explanation," Video Me said. "And I shouldn't have pushed you for one. I definitely shouldn't have treated it all like a big joke. I'm not even sure why I pushed so hard. I think it's because—"

Video Me broke off, stared down at her hands, and her shoulder rose and fell as if she were brushing something off. Then she picked up again. "Anyway, I'm sorry for digging into your past and bringing it up."

I closed the message. It had been a two second pause, but even I could hear what he must have heard in it: a silence that spoke louder than words.

Why did he need me to fill it? What did he want? A true confession…of what? Feelings? But how was that supposed to play out? I dropped my head into my palms and tried to imagine it. Not how I wanted it to go, but how it would actually go.

ME: Well, Dr. Jack, it turns out that I feel something for you at an emotional level that I don't remember feeling before, and maybe there are names for this feeling, but I don't want to use any of those names because they all make me feel panicky. Do you have a prescription to fix this?

JACK: Sure. Let's meet and see where this thing between us goes and figure out if we've got what it takes to grow a relationship. Because I think you're right. We've got something.

ME: Is that crazy? We haven't even met for real.

JACK: Why would that be crazy? We've spent hours talking and making each other laugh.

ME: We haven't talked about our real things. About our hard things.

JACK: But we understand each other's personalities. As well as I've understood anyone's. Am I imagining that?

ME: No, but…

JACK: We already know we can talk for hours. That's a big cornerstone of a relationship, right? So we've got something. Let's build on it.

ME: Sounds good. The San Francisco housing market is rough, but I'll keep an eye out for a good situation. Even if we were within a couple of hours of each other, we could make that work, right?

JACK: Oh. I was thinking maybe you'd just move up here and make way less money at a job you may or may not find in our much smaller Portland tech market.

ME: I'm not doing that. There aren't tech jobs everywhere, but San Francisco needs doctors. Come on down!

JACK: I refuse to talk about being a doctor and my reasons are excellent, but I'm not going to tell you what they are.

Me: Well, I guess we tried. Bye.

JACK: Oh, well. Bye.

And I didn't want the conversation to end that way.

"Emily?"

I shot up, blinking at Hailey who poked her head into my office. "Hi."

"You okay?"

"Yeah, great. Just visualizing the week."

She looked a little uncertain, but she stepped into the office holding her hands behind her back. “Excuse me for saying so, but you don’t seem all right in that underneath way, if that makes any sense. And I can’t say this would do it for me, but it seemed to make you happy that one time, so here you go.” She held her hands out to reveal a bag of Cheetos and a large cup of coffee.

It was the treat Jack had sent to my office all those weeks ago, only now instead of making me smile, it sent a hairline fracture through my already failing composure. I wasn’t sure what showed up on my face, but Hailey’s eyes widened. “Oops. Looks like I made a bad call. I’m sorry. I hope you feel better!” She backed out, treats still with her.

“No, stay.” I waved her over to my desk. “This is the sweetest thing anyone’s done for me since…” I touched the bag, and it crackled. “Well, since the last time someone did this for me. Thank you. I mean it.” I handed her my credit card. “I’m sorry I’ve been a crazy person this week. Go load yourself up with something from the café on me.”

She plucked the card from my fingers. “If you insist.”

“I’m ordering you to.”

“Bye, boss.”

I turned around to examine my superheroes on the window ledge. I bent forward and looked General Leia in the eye. “What am I supposed to do here? Give my life to the resistance? To resisting? What is my cause?”

I swear she rolled her eyes at me. I turned her to face out of the window but studied the rest of my action figures. All of them would have said, “You don’t need a man. But they make things more fun." Except Jane Austen. Jane Austen would say to get the man.

Well, she would say to let the man come to me. And wasn't that what Jack was doing?

Wasn't he taking a step toward me by asking me to fill in that gap after "because..."?

I picked up Jane Austen and set her on the desk. Then I picked up my phone. It was time to give Jack an answer.

Chapter 25

I typed slowly, trying to pick my way through the words without hitting any landmines. "Hi. I pushed so hard because it matters to me to know. I don't know why I feel like I want to know everything about you. But I do. So."

I didn't push send. I read and re-read the message. Did it say too much? Or not enough? All I knew for sure was that if forced to choose between sending it or presenting to the company board in my laundry day underwear, it would be a toss-up.

That was an overstatement. I'd definitely rather present in my ratty underwear.

Jane Austen fell flat on her face. I picked her up and steadied her. "I guess I know what you think about all this."

I pushed send and bolted out of my office to do a million tasks that did *not* involve thinking about how Jack would take my text. By the time Hailey came back, I'd done about another half of her jobs for the day. She shot me an exasperated look when she intercepted me going to make copies. I stepped around her and promised her another coffee run the next day.

I hadn't heard back from Jack by the end of the day. I stopped at the gym on the way home and ran for miles on the treadmill. Still no message from him.

I took a long, scalding shower and checked my phone when I got out.

I blew my hair dry, flat ironed it, and filed my nails. And finally my phone dinged with a DM alert. I opened it.

Finally, a message from Jack. A *video* message.

"Hi. I guess I have to say what I need to say in a minute or less." His eyes darted toward the corner of his screen, and I knew he was watching the ring count down how much time he had left in his recording. "I figured since you sent me a video, it's the least I could do to answer back in one." He scrubbed his hands through his hair, which I realized was hanging loose. I'd never seen him wear it down outside of his ridiculous Photoshops of himself. Instead of softening the hard lines of his cheekbones and jaw, the contrast made them stand out more. "The thing is, my hard things are the heavy kind that try to sink whoever is carrying them. I don't want to do that to you. Because I like you. So much. So much that I won't put this on you. I'm sorry. I should have known better than to…I don't know, let my hair down, I guess."

Right then, a hank of his hair fell forward over his eyes. He brushed it away and laughed. "Wow. I wasn't trying to be literal. Anyway, sorry about all this. Just know I wish you all the good things. And also—"

But the recording cut off before he finished. He also wasn't online anymore.

That was it, no follow up video to expand on what he'd meant to say before it cut out.

I mulled the message and replayed it a few more times, but I didn't know what to say to him. "Give me your heavy things"? To what end? I'd played out that conversation to its logical conclusion where one or both of us upended our lives to gamble on a relationship that didn't have a deep enough foundation to support the emotional kind of weight Jack was hinting at.

And honestly, that was all on him. He wanted us to keep it at a level where we didn't dig too deep in the way you have to when you're building a strong foundation.

Also, if I made one more stupid building analogy, I was going to find the tallest one in San Francisco and push myself off it. Enough, already. Enough.

I set down my phone again. I would not be reading management articles. I would not be crossing anything off my to-do list. I would have to buy Hailey more coffee instead. She had a lot of chasing after me ahead of her because the second I slowed down, I would dwell on Jack. And I didn't want to do that anymore.

At work, there were two types of inefficiency: the kind that came from not working smart and the kind that happened when you didn't work at all. And when I got caught up too much in worrying about Jack, I got nothing done.

That wasn't me. That wasn't okay. And that wasn't going to happen anymore.

I attacked work again, examining any sections of my schedule that looked like they were unstructured enough to give me time to brood. Or sulk. Or whatever happened when I thought too hard about Jack. Then I stuffed them full of more work.

My new task list was a meditation, like the lists I made in my head at night to force out all the intrusive thoughts that tried to keep me awake. I'd done it for years, growing each list until I could get all the way from A to Z in a category before moving on to a new list. When I was trying to name a vegetable for every letter of the alphabet, I got too hung up on H to focus on any stress trying to creep into my brain and wake it back up.

When I had a solid week structured that allowed no head space for Jack, I poked my head out of my office door and smiled at Hailey. "I'll stop doing your work."

"Yeah, right." She held out her hand. "Should I go load myself up at the café now?"

I shook my head. "I mean it. I figured out a schedule for me that involves doing none of your work."

She clasped her hands and mouthed a "thank you" to the ceiling like we were in the cathedral of Our Lady of Administrative Assistant Sorrows.

It was a good first step toward imposing order on my emotional chaos. Of course, it didn't solve the problem of what to do when Jack intruded on my thoughts during non-work hours. I set up a strict policy of only checking my phone once an hour for alerts and removed all my social media apps until I could break the habit of checking his feeds.

Unfortunately, my mind still wandered his direction during any of my unstructured time and the urge to break all my protocols would grow stronger.

Is this what addicts felt like?

No, that was stupid. As best as I could understand, real addiction was a painful, debilitating illness. Trying not to think about Jack was more like…

Oh. It was exactly like the time when I'd gone to my friend's church camp when we were thirteen, and I got poison oak on my leg. The camp nurse told me not to scratch because it would make it worse, but in the endless hours between midnight and dawn, nothing could have convinced me that scratching wasn't exactly the cure I needed. So I scratched. And ended up spreading it over more of myself.

Jack was emotional poison oak. It wouldn't kill me, but this situation would only make me more miserable the more I poked at it. That meant drowning out the itch when I wasn't at work too.

If I found myself wondering what Jack was doing at the same moment, I spent time cleaning out old messages in my email folders. By the fourth day, I was already digging back to 2014. And that was after filtering thousands of emails. Based on how often I had to distract myself, biologists could conclude that wondering what Jack was doing was a reflex as instinctive as breathing.

If I caught myself reaching for the phone to see what he'd posted on Twitter, I immediately picked a spot in the house to reorganize instead, which is what Ranée found me doing on Friday afternoon when she walked in from work and called hello.

"Hi." I had my head inside one of our lower cupboards while I hunted for a container lid.

"What are you doing?" she asked.

I stayed in the cupboard, still sifting through the plastic in the farthest reaches of it, but I waved my other hand behind me, brandishing a medium sized round plastic container. “I’m solving the Tupperware problem.”

“We have a problem?”

“Yes. We have almost twice as many lids as containers and somehow only half of them still fit. I’m purging. We’re going to get on top of this thing once and for all.”

“Wow. I feel so safe with a hero like you policing the cabinets of San Francisco.”

I backed out and turned to face her, settling with my back against the cupboard and a pile of plastic in different colors and sizes in front of me. I rummaged through it. “You laugh, but you have no idea how satisfying this is.” I plucked one of the lids out and snapped it on the container in my hand. “Look. Chaos,” I pointed at the pile, “and order.” I waved the newly sealed container at her.

She pointed from the pile—“Sad,” to me. “Sadder.”

I plucked up another lid. “It makes me feel better.”

“Than what? A poke in the eye with a sharp stick?” She set her purse on the counter and dropped down cross-legged in front of me. “Is this working?”

I didn’t pretend not to know what she was talking about. “I like it better than moping.”

“But Tupperware, Em? Is that what you’ve come to?”

I went back to sifting lids. “I’m highly productive and functional at work. I need to be that way at home too, then it’ll be fine.”

“What’s ‘it’? Your life? Your heart? What are we talking

about here that's going to be fine?"

I tapped the lid against my knee, trying to think of what "it'll be fine" meant. "All of that. I'll go back to being me."

She pulled the lid away. "You've seemed less like you this week than I've ever seen you. You're a workbot. It's weird."

I dropped my head against the cabinet and squeezed my eyes shut. "My brain isn't cooperating right now. Giving it projects helps. I need to get back to a non-Jack habit."

"Why?"

My eyes popped open. "Are you kidding me?"

"It's not like he's bad for you. He makes you laugh. You guys have a good time. Just call him up and say hi. Or text him. Or whatever. But there's no reason for you to act like you don't exist to each other. He's a quality person, and those are the kind you keep around."

I scooped up a bunch of the plasticware and turned to shove it into the cabinet. "It's not my choice."

"It *is* your choice."

I shoved the rest of the plastic into the cabinet, heedless of any order, and climbed to my feet. "You're right. I *choose* common sense and respect for boundaries." I stepped over her and walked out of the kitchen, listening to the sounds of her scrambling to her feet to follow.

"Would you react like this if he didn't matter?" she asked, pausing in my doorway as I knelt beside my bed to pull out a storage bin that needed organizing. "You weren't even this upset when you and Paul split."

"I'm not upset." I yanked the bin out and tried to open the lid, but it was clamped on too tight.

"Wound up, then." She leaned against the wall and watched me trying to find a good grip on the bin.

"It's not Jack. Or not just Jack. It's not even about boys." I couldn't get my fingertips underneath the lid far enough for any leverage to pop it off.

"Then what's it about?"

I dug my fingertips in harder and felt a fingernail break. I pounded the lid in frustration. "It's about realizing that my life is out of balance and needing to find it."

She walked over and held her hand out to me. "You've always worked hard, but you found play time too. This workaholism started after Jack, not before, so I guess I don't follow your logic."

I looked from her hand to the bin and back again. Finally, I shoved the bin beneath the bed and accepted her hand up, but she didn't let go when I was on my feet, instead tugging me toward the kitchen.

"I'm putting on some tea, and we'll fix this."

"I'm not sleepy." Sometimes Ranée made me chamomile tea to help during my insomnia spells.

"No, but your brain is so wired I can almost see sparks flying out of your head. You need to relax. And I don't mean that in the condescending way. I mean you need to breathe or something, find a way to gear down your levels."

I sat at the table while she filled the electric kettle. "I'm not in love with him."

She immediately shut the water off and turned to stare at me. "No one said you were."

"I'm just making that clear."

She turned the water back on. “Why do you feel like you need to?”

“Because if I was in love with Jack, being this much of a nutcase would make more sense. I’m into him, yeah. But the more I date, the more I’m starting to realize that I’m more ready for a relationship than I thought I was. Like I want that in my life in a real way.” I sighed. “If I could just get a hybrid of Jack and Paul, I’d have the perfect guy.”

She dropped the kettle, and the clatter into the sink made me jump. “You thought Paul had qualities of the perfect guy?”

“Mainly that he lives in the same city. Maybe not the rest of him. But you add that to Jack, and we’d be getting somewhere.”

“So you didn’t like anything else about Paul?”

There was something odd in the way she asked. It reminded me of the way my mom used to ask me too-casual questions on lazy Sunday afternoons to get a sense of my weekend when I was a teenager. It was a way of trying to get info out of me, making sure I was on track, without asking things point-blank so that I clammed up.

“Paul was fine,” I said, trying to figure out what Ranée needed me to say. “I’m never going to be convinced that he was the personification of watching paint dry.” That had been one of her more memorable criticisms of him after an awkward double date when Ranée’s chatter had unnerved him enough that he barely spoke.

“I might have overstated that for dramatic effect,” she said, turning the water off.

“Duh.” But my eyes narrowed. From Ranée’s mouth, that

was a borderline defense of a guy she had once called her nemesis. Wait, no. Not *her* nemesis: the nemesis of all that was fun and interesting in the world. "Have you been seeing Paul around lately?"

She fumbled the kettle as she tried to settle it on its base. "Stupid kettle." She bent and glared at it like that would somehow make it fit.

"Ranée?"

"Hmm?"

"I asked if you've seen Paul around lately."

"Around? Yeah, sure."

"And how's he doing?"

"Fine."

"How do you know? Do you guys talk?"

"Sure."

This was getting interesting. The more vague her answers became, the more curious it made me. "About what?"

"You want to know what we talk about?" She shrugged. "Just whatever."

"Just whatever. I see. And how often do you guys talk?"

"He's at the barn a lot."

"And so are you. So you guys talk a lot at the barn?"

"Sure."

"Ranée?"

"Hold that thought. I'm going to change my clothes while the water heats. Efficiency. Aren't you proud of me?"

"So proud I can hardly stand it." It was hard not to laugh as she disappeared down the hall. She was obviously hiding something, and it equally obviously had to do with Paul. Those conversations must be going *really* well for her to want to avoid the subject. Not too long ago, she would have spent all the kettle-heating time making fun of him.

Ranée might drive me crazy in a dozen different ways, but for as much of a know-it-all as she could be, she was also quick to admit when she was wrong. She wouldn't normally have a problem saying she'd misjudged Paul and confessing that he was a pretty good guy. I didn't think that was what had sent her escaping into her room. Which meant…

Whoa. Ranée had a thing for Paul.

Chapter 26

It was the only thing that made sense of her behavior. I considered the facts. Ranée used to call Paul names and say he was the most boring guy in the world. Ranée bumped into him at the volunteer barn and got a different side of him. Ranée automatically gave anyone who knew horses a higher starting grade as a human. Ranée then had to revise her opinion of Paul. Ranée started seeing Paul around the barn regularly and her opinion kept improving. Ergo…

Ranée liked Paul.

How did I feel about that? On the one hand, it was a clear violation of girl code to date the guy she'd spent months convincing me to dump. On the other hand, I hadn't dumped him because of her. I'd dumped him because it was time. Our relationship had run its natural course. That was all.

When it came right down to it, I wasn't the jealous type. Never had been, really. It had been forever since I could even remember feeling jealous about a guy. Could I even remember being jealous about a guy?

Oh, wait. There was that one time a couple of weeks ago when I'd been jealous thinking about Jack going on dates with anyone else.

Which was stupid and irrational. He wasn't mine, yet that flash of envy had nearly turned my stomach inside out when I hadn't so much as held his hand. But somehow, examining the possibility of Ranée's interest in Paul only struck me as funny even after I'd made out with him for a few months. I didn't feel a hint of possessiveness.

It didn't take a therapy session to figure that out.

The kettle gave a loud but cheerful beep, and I considered how I should approach the subject with Ranée. The grown-up thing to do would be to discuss it like a rational adult.

But I owed Ranée payback. So. Much. Payback.

Ranée didn't seem to want to do the adult thing either because she stayed hidden in her room. You could hear the kettle anywhere in the apartment, so she knew it was ready.

"Ranée?" I called. "Are you going to make my tea?"

She answered with a muffled, "In a minute."

At least three more passed without any Ranée. Oh, this was going to be fun. The most fun I'd had since…

Since everything had gone wrong with Jack.

I cleared my throat. "Come out, come out, wherever you are."

It was another minute before she emerged from her room, dressed—no surprise—for the barn. Worn T-shirt. Ratty Vans. Guilty expression.

"So you were saying?" I prompted her, as she dug into a box of tea bags.

"I don't remember. I'm sure it wasn't important."

"I'm sure you're right. Going to the barn again?" She wasn't getting out of this so easily.

"Yeah. Working with one of my favorite kids tonight."

"Sounds good. Maybe that's what I need to do. Volunteer, take my mind off things."

"Totally. There's always a ton of places looking for help."

"No doubt. Will you see Paul at the barn tonight?"

"Probably. Give me a second, and I'll google some volunteer options for you while the tea steeps. Let me go get my laptop."

No way was she escaping into her room again. "I can handle the googling. Don't worry about it. So tell me about Paul. You said he's doing well?"

"I guess."

"How often do you guys end up volunteering at the same time?"

"I'm not sure."

"Guess."

She shot me a sharp look before her gaze slid away. "I don't know. Seems like we're always there at the same time."

"And you guys always talk when you're there together?"

"It would be rude not to."

I snorted. "You're right. I mean, you were rude right to his face so many times when he was over here, but a barn calls for better manners."

"I admitted that I was maybe too hard on him."

"Maybe?"

"I was. Happy now?"

"I think I'd feel happy for sure if I know Paul is happy. So is he?"

Ranée sighed. She picked up the two mugs of tea and set one in front of me before taking the seat across the table. "Is there something you'd like to say to me?"

"I don't know. Depends on if you have anything you want to tell me. Like about you. And Paul. And these conversations you have."

She stirred the tea bag around in her cup. "So…uh, I guess maybe I should tell you something."

I leaned forward. "I can't wait."

"So…" She dipped the tea bag a few times. "This is awkward."

I smiled at her, the most angelic smile I could muster, determined to make her spit out every bit of this without help.

She scowled when she saw it. "You know, don't you?"

"I don't *know* anything. But I have some real strong hunches."

"Paul and I have been talking." The words burst out of her like she was a shaken can of Coke.

"So you've said."

"This is real talking. Like when we're putting up the horses at the end of the night, and the conversation wanders. And somehow we're talking about state policies on adolescent mental health for urban teens. And then we're talking about how when you move to the city, your country roots always stay with you, and it makes you feel like you have extra wisdom, somehow. Because you understand stuff that city natives don't. And then we're talking about how you learn that wisdom, and what you do with it. He's got layers."

I'd always known he wasn't as bad as Ranée had thought he was, but this level of introspection from him surprised even me. "Those sound like good conversations."

"Yeah." She stirred her tea some more. Then, without warning, she dropped her head onto the table and buried it beneath her arms. "I don't know what to do." The words came out muffled, but her angst was clear.

I allowed myself one big grin before I decided to put her out of her misery. "Ranée? If you wanted to date Paul, I wouldn't be mad."

She hid beneath her arms for another minute. I sipped my tea and enjoyed the moment.

"Really?" The word finally floated out from her arm cave.

"Really."

She picked up her head. "I'm not saying I want to date him."

"Okay. Then talk to him. Ponder the mysteries of the universe together. It still won't bother me."

"I don't want to just talk."

"You don't want to date him. But you don't want to talk to him. What do you want?"

She picked at the edge of the table, not meeting my eyes. "Suddenly I have stuff you've said about him on replay in my head."

"Like what?"

"Um, I think you mentioned he's a good kisser? And now I can't stop thinking about that."

I spit out my tea. "Oh, man. That is so much better than

anything I thought you were going to say."

"It's not funny," she said, handing me a napkin so I could mop up the tea on my shirt.

"I'm living for this." I switched to Sandra Bullock's singsong taunt from *Miss Congeniality*. "You like him, you want to kiss him."

She disappeared into her arm cave again.

"You want him to corner you in a stable and smooch your face off."

Her head shot up. "No, I want him to ask me politely if I'm okay with him kissing me."

"All right, fair enough. Yay, consent."

"But then I want to drag him into the corner of the stable and kiss him."

I burst out laughing. "Not to make it weird or anything, but it's definitely worth it."

"You really don't mind?"

"No. You know I don't dwell on exes. When I move on, it's for a reason, so I'm fine with letting the past go. This one was even easier because you distracted me with Jack." I gasped. "Was this all a plot to steal Paul away from me?"

"Yes. Em. I somehow knew that Paul would show up at the barn where I volunteer and suddenly act and talk like a totally different person, so I plotted against you in the most genius romantic sabotage ever."

"You'd be smart enough to do something like that. And to, oh, say, put into motion a complicated plan involving a cheesy romance cover hero and a handsome Photoshop expert with a man bun."

"Fine. You caught me."

"I knew it."

She took a sip of her tea and glared at me over the cup rim before she banged it down again. "Two months ago, I really did think Paul was the personification of paint drying."

"I know. That's what makes this so fun. So, you're going to kiss him."

"Nooo," she wailed. "There's no way. He'll never do it. He's not the kind of guy who would ever jump from one girl to her roommate. He has this code of honor, I think."

I knew that. But I didn't point it out. "It means you have to make the first move, let him know you're okay with it."

"No, because then I'll look like the girl who would move in on her best friend's boyfriend."

"Ex-boyfriend."

"That's like the smallest possible improvement. And I'm not that girl. Except I am that girl."

"No, you'd be that girl if I cared, which I one thousand percent do not. So you should make the first move."

"Except you know that, and I know that, but he doesn't know that, so it's still going to look bad no matter what."

A new thought struck me, but I hesitated to express it. I didn't want to ruin the stirrings of this new thing—whatever it was—that she was feeling, but I also didn't want her going any further down the wrong road if it was going to dead end. "I guess I should ask you...do you think that's something Paul wants? Do you get a vibe from him?"

"I do. That's what makes this so hard. Like I'll catch him watching me, but then he looks away. And if we're slipping past each other to hang the tack or get a brush, I swear there's that heightened thing going on between us. You know that thing where the air kind of tingles?"

I held up my hands. "I don't want to hear about your tingling."

"You know what I mean!"

I did. "I can honestly say it was never like that between me and Paul. So your gut says he's feeling it?"

She hesitated then nodded. "Yeah. He is. I'd bet on it. That's why this is killing me. There's as much unsaid stuff floating in the air of that barn as there is stable dust."

"That's a super romantic image."

"And yet it doesn't change the fact that sometimes that stable is so full of electricity, it feels like the hay is going to catch on fire."

"Because of rolling in it?"

"Shut up."

"Look, suffer in silence if you want. Kiss Paul if you want. I support you."

She rose from the table and rinsed her mug. "I'm going to go get my jacket."

When she disappeared down the hall, I whipped out my cell phone. My revenge was almost complete. Almost.

Chapter 27

`There's no delicate way to put this: you should kiss Ranée.`

I pushed "send" on the text to Paul, and waited, curious to see what would happen.

It took a few minutes that I spent entertaining myself by imagining Paul's reaction to the text. Confusion? Relief? Curiosity? Embarrassment? That really cute mortification like high school kids get when word of their crush leaks out?

Is it possible that when my phone went off I was wearing an expression of impish glee?

YES. Yes, it was.

But honestly, how could I not be grinning like a fool? Ranée deserved a good guy, and Paul and I may have brought out the most boring parts of each other, but it sounded like he and Ranée were a potential fit. I wanted them to find out if it was a great fit.

I slid my messages open, but it wasn't a text from Paul. It was from Jack. `Can we talk? Maybe Facetime or` something?

What? Why now? I'd been putting him out of my thoughts for days. I had a cabinet of plasticware chaos behind me to prove it. But it's not like I was going to say no to that.

Sure, I typed. I didn't even hesitate to press send.

When? His response was just as fast.

Ranée walked past me, zipping up her hoodie. "I'm off to the barn."

"I want every detail when you get back."

She gave me a strange look. "There's not going to be anything to tell. There's never anything to tell." And she shut the front door behind her.

Now is good, I texted Jack. And I refuse to put on makeup for this.

Fair. This is a come-as-you-are kind of call.

Thirty seconds later the FaceTime ring sounded. I barely had time to feel anything but confusion. "Hi," I said. Then I burst out laughing at the sight of Jack's T-shirt. It was white with a kid's marker drawing of a stick figure with longish hair. It said, "Dr. Jack" in kid scrawl, the J backwards, and Jack's stick figure wore a pink cape. "Nice shirt."

He glanced down at it and gave me a tight smile. "I did promise a come-as-you-are call. This is one of my favorite shirts."

My own laughter fizzled away. Was it a good sign that he'd worn something in front of me referencing his doctor life? Or a bad sign that every part of him from his tired eyes to his forced smile spoke of stress? His hair was down again, but it looked like it hadn't seen a comb for a day or two.

"It looks comfortable," I said. But that felt awkward to leave hanging there, so I dove in. "Why did you want to talk?"

"Because not talking seems stupid?"

"Is that a question?"

He sighed. "No. Or if it is, I know the answer. It's pretty stupid that we haven't talked for a few days."

That wasn't on me, so I raised my eyebrows at him.

"We're not in a relationship, are we?" he asked.

That was a question I hadn't expected. "I don't know. No? No, we're not in a relationship."

"Because a relationship is where you date each other. But only each other, right? And don't see other people. And you make that decision because you've spent time together and you both agree you don't want to date anyone else. So you don't. And you hang out with each other and do couple stuff, like go to each other's boring work parties, or take bike rides, or fight over the remote."

"I don't fight over the remote. I don't care about the remote. That's why Ranée and I get along so well. She would marry the remote if she could." I threw out the joke because I didn't know how to process everything else he was saying. It sounded like he was working out something aloud, so I'd sit here and let him, to see where he went.

"See? I would know that if we were in a relationship. But we can't be. Because you're in San Francisco."

A faintly acid ripple burned through my stomach. I was having the exact conversation I'd played out in my mind a week ago and filed under, "Conversations Never to Have."

"You're on an Oregon mountain. Maybe that's the problem."

"It is. It's just as much of a problem. But I don't plan to change that any time soon. Do you?"

"No."

"I didn't think so, either. So why keep talking? All it does is make me want to come down off the mountain. Or talk you out of the city. I want to be sitting right across from you when you make me laugh. I want to make you laugh, and hear it myself. It kills me to hear it filtered through a screen. I want to…"

He trailed off. He wanted to...? Whatever he wasn't saying, I wanted it too.

He shoved his hands through his hair. I was learning this was a sign of his frustration. "It gets worse every time we talk, not better, so it made sense not to talk anymore. There is literally no point, is there?"

It was a hopeless question, but I felt a smile tickling the corners of my lips anyway, because…

He wanted to sit across from me and watch me laugh.

"There's no point," I agreed. "Not if the goal is for us to be in a relationship."

"And we can't be, right?"

I shook my head. "It doesn't make sense." But it was even harder to fight my smile. It felt so good to know I wasn't the only one who'd been driving myself crazy with this.

"It's not funny," he said, narrowing his eyes at me.

"No." But I realized the smile had won anyway.

"The thing is, it's kind of sucked for a few days without your texts. Everything is boring and stupid."

"Wow, Dr. Jack. I had no idea doctors were so articulate."

"Stop making fun of me." He leaned in until I got an extreme close up of his glare. "We should still talk."

"Okay."

He leaned back to a normal distance. "Okay?"

"Okay. But."

"But…?"

"I'm tired of off-limit topics. It's like trying to do the tango on eggshells except if the eggshells break, everything blows up. I'm over it."

"I'm tired of off-limit topics too. I get it. But we still need ground rules."

"Oh, yay. Ground rules." A text alert came in at the top of my screen. I didn't know who it was from, but suddenly I wanted to check that much more than I wanted to keep having this conversation.

"I think we both have to stay honest about what this is. That's my only ground rule."

The twitch to check the text disappeared. "That doesn't sound too bad. Explain that some more. Like, can we bring up whatever we want? I can ask you doctor questions?"

"Yeah. I mean, maybe don't ask me about any growths you have. But yeah, we can talk about whatever it feels normal to talk about. But since this isn't ever going to be a relationship, I think we should quit flirting. Just talk like friends."

"Friends." I considered the way the word felt in my mouth. How the idea felt in my chest. "Maybe I should feel bummed about that, but this doesn't feel like a downgrade."

"Right?" Relief flooded his face, the tight lines around his eyes finally softening. "Friends is good."

"Friends is good. But bad grammar."

"But a good thing to be."

"A good thing to be," I agreed. "But I would prefer not to be the friend you tell your dating stories to."

"Ditto. And tell Ranée not to send me pictures of any shoes you're wearing on dates. Especially not if they're high heels. And the higher they are, the less I want to see them."

I leaned forward, like that was somehow going to magnify his face on the screen. "You have a thing for high heels?"

"I'm pretty tall. I appreciate them for purely practical reasons." He drummed his fingers a couple of times. "Are we flirting?"

"You started it. Knock it off."

"I will. I'm being serious. It's weird not being able to send you something funny when it happens, or to go out of my way not to talk to you." I opened my mouth to respond, but he held his hands up. "I know. That was my fault. But we're good now?"

"We're good."

"So what should we talk about?"

How about how he wanted to sit across from me and listen to me laugh? That seemed like a pretty good start. But since I had agreed to the ground rules, I cleared my throat while I bought time to think of something else.

"Oh, I know. I finally figured out how to get revenge on Ranée for posting your Photoshopped pictures of us."

"I gotta hear this."

I recapped how she'd hated Paul then suddenly found herself volunteering alongside him at the barn and catching all the feels. "So in conclusion, neither of them is ever going to make a move on the other, and Paul especially is an overthinker, so I texted him and told him he should kiss her."

"Out of the blue? Tell me what you said."

"I said I knew there was no non-awkward way to say it, but that he should kiss her."

"So you haven't talked to this guy in a month—"

"Longer."

"And that's what you started with?" When I nodded, he burst out laughing. "Oh, man. Does she know?"

"No. She has no idea what she's walking into."

"Okay, but you have to tell me how this plays out. What did he say?"

"I don't know. It just barely happened. He might have texted me while we were talking, but I haven't looked at it yet."

"Are you kidding me? Look at it now. Go!"

I laughed and opened my texts. "It's from him. It says, 'I don't know what you're talking about.'"

"Is that possible?" Jack asked.

"Nope," I said. "Ranée is never wrong about this stuff. If she feels a vibe, she's right. I'm typing, 'Too bad. Because I happen to know she'd be into it.' There, I sent it."

"You really don't care?" Jack asked.

"I really don't. I move on, and I'm done. If I wanted to still be with Paul, I'd still be with Paul."

"But you don't."

There was a hint of wheedling about it, almost a question. "You're flirting. Ground rules, dude. And no, I don't."

"Because?"

He was fully aware of the reason why. I wouldn't give him the satisfaction of saying it. "Ground. Rules. Oh, I'm going to like this. It's like pleading the fifth when I don't want to answer anything."

"Sorry. Did he text back?"

It came in right as he asked. "It says, 'I don't want to be that guy.'" I rolled my eyes and read aloud as I typed back. "You're not that guy. This is me telling you: neither one of us will think you are."

"I'm trying to imagine how I'd feel about this if I were him," Jack said.

"Depends on whether you want to kiss Ranée."

"I do not."

"Then I guess we'll see what—ooh, he texted back. 'This is inappropriate for us to discuss.' Well, hot dang!"

"That doesn't sound good. Why do you sound happy? I thought you wanted him to kiss her."

"I'm not as invested in this as you're making me sound, but yeah, my gut says those two are going to be a weirdly good match, so I'm happy because I know Paul well enough to know that means he's going to kiss Ranée. He's got an old-school gentleman's code, so no kissing and telling."

Jack tucked his hair behind his ears and propped himself on his desk with crossed arms. "So let me get this straight: your revenge on Ranée is convincing your ex to kiss her, which is something they both want to happen?"

"Yeah."

He grinned. "You're not very good at revenge."

"Trust me, there's going to be a moment when she realizes

that I said something to Paul. She will be furious and mortified, and even though I'll never see that moment, it is completely satisfying just knowing she had it."

"I don't really understand women."

"I'll be your guide."

He scrunched his face. "That wouldn't bother you?"

"That would totally bother me. Never mind. Figure them out yourself."

"I'm glad it would bother you."

"GROUND RULES."

"Oh, yeah. So what else do we talk about now that we're done setting up your ex with your best friend? You're weird."

"You're weird, hermit. Let's talk about that. Tell me why you're a hermit."

"Because Oregon is nice."

I felt like one of the pigeons who thought it was out for a nice flight until it suddenly slammed into my office window. He was being flip. He was always flippant. I knew this about him, but I wanted to know the real answer.

He sighed. "Sorry. Okay, why I'm a hermit. It's a tale of woe, ridiculously tragic and melodramatic."

"Should I pop some corn? Grab a hanky?"

"Yes, and definitely. Or maybe I'll just give you the antiseptic version."

"Was that a doctor joke?"

"Of course." His hair had fallen from behind one of his ears, and he brushed it from his face in irritation, then reached for something off-camera as he started his story. "So I was a pediatric oncologist."

"Was? I thought you were still a doctor."

"I am. General practice right now." He'd grabbed an elastic and was pulling his hair back as he talked. I swallowed hard as he settled it into a sloppy bun. It looked so much better back than down. I was a dead woman if he ever cut it. He paused, staring out at me from the screen, a tiny twitch playing at the corner of his mouth. Did he realize the effect he'd had on me?

He picked up his story. "So I was a pediatric oncologist. In Portland. It was a hard job, but I thought I was good at it. Then I got it wrong one too many times, and I left the children's hospital. A friend of Sean's runs this rural clinic, but his wife got an assignment with her microchip firm in Germany, and when Sean told me about it, I said I'd take over for him while they were gone."

"How long are they going to be gone?"

"It was supposed to be an eighteen-month assignment, but they like it there, and I like it here, so it's worked out so far for me to stay longer."

There was more that he hadn't said. I could feel all the spaces in between his words. He'd handed me the bare bones, but I wanted the connective tissue. Still, it was far more than he'd offered before, so I accepted it. "How long has it been?"

"Two years."

I wanted to ask what had driven him out of the hospital and whether he was happy being a general practitioner after being a specialist. But I kept the questions to myself. Maybe it would come out over time. Maybe it wouldn't. I didn't have to decide right this second how I felt about that either way.

"How's work for you?" he asked.

It was such an ordinary request, and yet it felt new in our dynamic. This small talk stuff had been off-limits before, and as I told him about the shape of my day, it felt like I'd been let out of a box to stretch, finally, and breathe fresh air.

That was it. That was the whole conversation. Basically, "I missed talking to you. Let's at least be friends even though it won't go further than that. How was your day? This is how mine went."

So simple. But it felt so good.

A text alert went off on my phone. "Hang on," I said. "I might have a status update on the plot for revenge." I checked it and winced.

"Was it him?"

"No. It's Ranée."

"What did she say?"

"It says, 'I'm coming home. And I'm going to kill you.'"

Chapter 28

Jack had only laughed when I told him I had to go stock up on ammunition and get ready for Ranée, but I hadn't been kidding. I ran down to the corner liquor store to load up on candy. When Ranée charged through our front door a half hour later, I was waiting for her with three king-sized Snickers bars in front of me on the coffee table.

"What is wrong with you?" She slammed the door behind her.

I studied her closely and smiled. "You're welcome."

"What am I thanking you for? Humiliating me?"

"Honey, you have scruff burn and your lipstick is all gone. You have been kissed."

She glared at me for another second then sighed and plopped into an armchair. "Give me sugar."

"Didn't Paul already do that?"

"Emily, so help me..."

I threw her a Snickers. "I don't know why you're mad. You look like you had an excellent time in the barn."

"I can't believe you texted him. That was the single most humiliating thing that's ever happened to me."

"But then it was good?"

Finally, a grin broke through. "You were not lying about his skills."

"I demand details."

She wrinkled her nose at me.

"Not about the kissing! Tell me about how it got to that point."

"I walked into the barn. He wouldn't look at me, which is weird, because we have this energy that's hard to explain where it's like we're uncomfortably aware of each other but we're pretending like we aren't, and even with all of that, it's just easy to talk. But he wouldn't make eye contact with me, and if he did, he blushed. Like actually turned pink."

I grinned, imagining what must have been going through Paul's mind after getting my text and then coming face-to-face with Ranée.

"We normally work with the same three kids, but he volunteered to work with the kid the program director normally helps so that she could go catch up on some paperwork or something. And then he basically avoided me the whole night."

"Oh, Paul, you idiot."

"Paul nothing. That was *your* fault."

"Get to the good part. How did you get from that to this?" I waved at her beard rash and slightly puffy lips.

"We're supposed to supervise the kids while they brush the horses at the end of the night, but Paul said he wanted to take his horse—well, the one he rides the most—around the trail once, so he told his kids they could leave. I told my kids they could go too because I also wanted to ride. I wanted them out of there so I could ask him if something was wrong. I was having a mini panic attack, thinking maybe one of us had butt-dialed him while we were talking earlier, and he'd heard the whole conversation."

She was flustered. Ranée didn't get flustered. It was an adorable look for her.

"Get to the good stuff," I prompted her.

"I didn't really want to ride, so I started taking off Gert's saddle. She's the horse."

"I assumed."

"And he steps into the stall and says, 'I thought you wanted to ride.'"

I hooted. I couldn't help it.

She threw a pillow at me. I batted it to the floor. "Not like that. Get your mind out of the gutter."

"Sorry. Continue."

"Anyway, I say no, that I just want to feed and water the horse in peace and quiet after a long week. Then I ask him why he isn't riding." She took a deep breath, and I leaned forward. This was about to get good. "Then he holds up his phone and says you texted him. And that's when I knew I would kill you."

"Did he even tell you what the text said?"

"No! It didn't matter. There was not one thing you could have texted that I would have been okay with." She picked at her jeans for a second. "What *did* you say?"

"Like you said, doesn't matter. Here you are, all kissed and stuff. Fill in the blank after he said I texted him."

"So he says you texted him, and I say, 'oh, interesting,' like an idiot because I can't think of what else to say. Then he reaches over and takes the brush out of my hands and goes, 'It really was,' all kind of, um, sexy-like."

My eyebrow went up. "Wow. Paul has developed moves. Good job, Paul."

"That's the thing. He hasn't. He just said it quietly. Then he tosses the brush out of the way, and I'm standing there frozen, and he slides his hand around my neck and now I know what's up, and then he gets even quieter but he gives me this look like, 'Is this okay?' and I think I gulped." She got up and grabbed the pillow from the floor and hit me with it. "I gulped! Like a fish! I hate you."

I snatched the pillow from her and hit her back. "You're ruining the story. Tell me what happened next."

"What happened next is that he took that gulp as a yes and he was dead right and then he kissed me." She flopped back in her chair and closed her eyes, a small smile playing around her puffy lips.

"And?"

"And you're an idiot for breaking up with him."

"Hashtag no regrets."

She opened her eyes and straightened in her seat. "I heard you say that you don't care, and now I'm looking at you, and you truly don't seem like you care."

"Because I don't care. I mean, I care that you had a nice time rolling in the hay."

"I didn't roll in the hay. Shut up."

"Seriously. It's all good. If he's a good fit for you, then you have my blessing."

"Thanks," she said softly. "I wouldn't feel okay about this if I didn't."

"But you do, so how do you feel?"

"I feel good." She touched her lips, almost subconsciously, and I smothered a smile. She dropped her hand. "And also like I'm tired of talking about me. What did you do tonight?"

"Well…I talked to Jack."

"You called him? Yes!"

"Actually, no. He texted and wanted to FaceTime."

"Ooh, about what? Tell me everything."

"Not much to tell. We have ground rules now. We're just going to be friends, but this time there are no dumb restrictions on conversation. Except we agreed that neither of us wants to hear much about each other's dates. Other than that, we can have all the small talk we want. And real talk."

"Are you planning to date people?"

"If something comes up, I guess. But I haven't checked my app in a while. Maybe if I get bored or something." A funny expression flickered across her face. I couldn't quite decipher it. "What?"

"Did Jack say he wasn't going to talk about the people he dates either?"

"Yeah."

"He doesn't date anyone."

"Is that what Sean says? Do they see each other often enough for Sean to know?" I knew it sounded like I was arguing that Jack was probably dating regularly. But I wanted Ranée to prove me wrong.

She gave me a long look, like she wasn't fooled at all. "Sean works at the clinic as a nurse sometimes on his days off from doing guide stuff. He's in there at least once a week. They talk. He says Jack doesn't date. Not many options there, I guess, and if there were, he still doesn't think Jack would be into it."

"So he's living not just as a hermit but as a celibate hermit in his mountain cabin?"

She shrugged. "Basically. Sean has been worried about him for a while."

"Sean seems really into Jack's business."

"If it were me, wouldn't you be? Or was that someone else who texted my stable partner tonight?"

"Point taken."

She shrugged. "It's an interesting friendship. He says he and Jack lost enough patients together that it was like being in the trenches or something. I think they had a particularly bad case and lost a patient, and Sean quit. Pediatrics was too intense for him. I think he'll eventually get bored of playing mountain man and go back to nursing. That's why he likes helping Jack at the clinic. He says the patients are a lot more fixable."

A small pit opened in my stomach thinking about what it meant that pediatric cancer patients hadn't been as fixable. My mind didn't even want to wander down that path. I couldn't imagine what it had been like for Sean and Jack to live in that world, fighting losing battles day after day.

"Is he worried about Jack or just wanting to hook him up?"

She sighed. "He's worried. Sean is snapping out of it. He's getting restless. I don't think it'll be long before he's back in Portland or somewhere else in nursing full-time. But I don't think he's going to do pediatrics again. Jack…I don't know. Sean thought it would be so good for him to be outdoors more, reconnecting with the basics. Like unofficial therapy. And he says Jack is happy when he's outdoors, but that he's still not connecting with other people. Not even with his patients as much. And definitely not on dates."

"Okay. So Jack's not dating. Should I worry about that?"

"I'm saying…I don't know. Be gentle with him, I guess."

"There's nothing to worry about here. We're being honest about what this relationship is, which is platonic. We're not going to date, so no flirting in our conversations."

"Whose idea was it that you guys shouldn't talk about the other dates you go on?"

"His."

"That doesn't sound like a guy who doesn't care."

"I wouldn't like hearing about his other dates either. Not right now. But as we get into this friend groove, I think it won't be such a big deal. You make him sound like he has no idea how to handle women, and I'm liable to crush him or something."

"That's definitely not it." She shook her head. "He's not shy or inexperienced or whatever. I think he's had plenty of relationships. I just worry he's in a tough place right now."

"He was closed off before, and now he's open to talking about everything he didn't want to talk about. That sounds like progress to me."

She was only half-listening, running her fingers along her lips again. It was adorable. "What? Oh, right. Good point." She smiled. "Good, then. I like Jack. It's nice to think he's coming out of it."

I'd met Sean a few times when he came to visit Ranée, and he hadn't struck me as an over worrier then, but now I wondered. He almost acted more like Jack's mom than his friend. It must be those same nurturing instincts that had drawn him to nursing in the first place. I wondered how Jack felt about all the hovering. I'd have to ask him the next time we talked.

The next time we talked. I let that phrase sink in and enjoyed the shape of it for a minute. There would be a next time. Jack and I could talk whenever we wanted, about whatever we wanted. There would be no coy games over whose turn it was to call or text.

"You know what's great about this new balance Jack and I have now?"

"Tell me," Ranée said.

"I can text him as often as I text you without worrying about how he'll take it. We're friends now. Frequency of texts and calls don't mean anything, any more than it does when you and I text. Or don't."

"Speak for yourself. I pine for you when I don't hear from you often enough."

"Shut up. You don't. He won't. I won't. It's perfect."

"Glad you're happy." Then she rose and drifted off to her room, a jellyfish of twitterpation.

Well, well, well. File that under "Stuff I Wouldn't Have Predicted in a Million Years."

Chapter 29

By Monday I could predict that the week would be about a five thousand percent improvement over the previous one in terms of productivity and Jack. Not that he was the measure of whether a week was good or bad, but it made a noticeable difference when he wasn't a problem I had to solve. He was "around," and I didn't have to figure out how to distract myself from him.

I texted him a picture of a seagull hanging out on the ledge outside of my balcony. He responded, `Surrender your Cheetos and he'll leave you alone. He must take them to his leader.`

`Has Transcendent Seagull really transcended if he needs Cheetos for happiness?`

`Even swamis have to eat sometimes.`

He called after dinner. "What are you doing?"

"Trying to figure out what I want to eat. I'm out of Cheetos."

"You should have a salad. Mondays are always salad days."

"Is that what you're having?"

"Yeah. I make perfect salads on Monday when I'm motivated to eat well."

"Define 'perfect salad.' Does it have Cheeto croutons?"

"Mixed greens, protein, fruit, cheese, nuts, and probably a vinaigrette. Please don't think less of my masculinity because I said vinaigrette."

"Too late." I heard the sound of a plastic wrapper crinkling.

"I put Cheetos on it for croutons."

"All points restored. I'll make a salad too."

We chatted about work while I puttered in the kitchen. Well, about my work. He hadn't said much about his. I wished he would. I wanted to know more. And then I remembered that I could ask him. "How did it go at work today?"

He sighed, and I braced for a diversion of topics. But he said, "Fine. I'm having to become an expert in diabetes though. The obesity epidemic is no joke."

"Feeling bad about those Cheetos on your salad now?"

"I didn't actually put any on my salad."

"Duh. So clinic work is way different than your old gig?"

"Yeah. I do general practice now. The problem is that a lot of people need specialists, and I can't convince them to drive the hour into Portland to see them. So they depend on me for a 'good enough' Band-aid fix. But these aren't Band-aid problems."

We talked for an hour that passed like five minutes, and I learned about the life of a country doctor. He did pretty much everything from acting as his own receptionist and nurse to being a nutritionist and psychiatrist for the range of issues that walked through the clinic doors.

“Sounds tiring,” I said.

He yawned even though it wasn’t quite ten yet. “Yeah. It is. And I need to get in early tomorrow. Got the sheriff to agree to come in on the condition that I meet him at six a.m. when he’s on his way home from his shift.”

“Why do you have to work the weird hours to accommodate him?”

“Because it’s the only way to get him in, and for HIPAA reasons I can’t explain why, but the dude really needs to see a doctor. Even if it’s just me.”

“What do you mean ‘just you’? When I was stalking you to dig up your deepest secrets before, you seemed like kind of a big deal.”

“In my field. I was good at that until I wasn’t. I’m only average at this general practice stuff, but I’m all they’ve got here, so imagine how obvious the problem is if even I can tell by looking. If that means showing up at 6 a.m. then that’s how it goes.”

“Good luck.” We hung up, and I grinned. It had been such an ordinary conversation, but I felt like I already understood Jack twice as well as I had before.

Tuesday ended up being a garbage day at work, and I came home in a distracted frame of mind that even my workout endorphins couldn’t settle. My brain kept buzzing, irritation with my team flaring up every few minutes. I needed an even bigger distraction, something that would keep me so focused I couldn’t worry about work.

I texted Jack. “Scrabble?’

He texted back. “It’s on. I’ll FaceTime you in five minutes.”

“Hi,” he said, when I answered. “You ready to lose?”

I snorted. “Nah. I’ve been training.”

“How do you train for Scrabble?”

“Been eating dictionary pages for breakfast. Prepare to lose.”

“You okay?” he asked as he pinged me with an invitation to a new game.

I accepted. “Fine. Work was lame.”

“What happened?”

“There’s a bug in the new update that rolls out in two weeks, and my lead developer melted down which threw the rest of the team off their game. It’ll be fine. I’ll sit down with her tomorrow and talk it through, come up with a game plan, fix the issues.”

“Sounds like it’ll be okay.”

“It will. It’s just that we left work without any of that resolved and now I feel...” I shrugged, at a loss for how to explain it.

“Like you have an emotional pebble in your psychic shoe?”

That made me laugh. “Exactly like that. How did you think of that?”

“Easy. Watch.” He made his game play. It was “pebble” for 30 points.

“You’re supposed to be making me feel better. That doesn’t make me feel better.”

“Sorry, not sorry.”

"Then I'm not sorry for this," I said, playing from the end of "pebble" to make "pebbled" and "dryer" for 31 points. "But in other news, I feel better about work."

He gave me his best stank face. "That's it. No more Mr. Nice Guy. I was going to let you win by a little but now I'm going to crush you."

It only made it more satisfying when I squeaked out a win by twenty before we called it a night.

Wednesday night he texted, `Want to hate watch that new medical drama with me?`

`I saw the first two episodes. I liked it,` I texted back.

`You won't when I'm done with it.`

He was right. We watched it while on the phone, and he dismantled every unrealistic element of the show, making me laugh the whole time.

"Wow," I said when the end credits rolled. "Did they get anything right?"

He thought for a second. "The ER doctors do wear scrubs. That's about it."

I went to bed smiling again.

Thursday I texted him that my team worked out the bug. He sent me a picture of Transcendent Seagull eating a giant cockroach. When the doorbell rang about fifteen minutes after I got home that night, Ranée looked up at me in confusion. "Why is someone ringing our doorbell? Did you order take out? Can I have some?"

"I didn't order anything."

"It's obviously a murderer then. Don't answer it."

"How about I check the peephole?"

She shrugged. "It's your funeral."

There was a delivery guy on the other side. "Wrong address," I called through the door.

"Delivery for Emily Riker," he called back.

"Just so you know, it's a bad sign when you can't even remember ordering food for yourself. Do I need to put you in a home? Also, can I have some of whatever you got?"

I ignored her and opened the door. "I didn't order anything."

The delivery guy shrugged. "You got food. It's paid for."

"Was there any kind of note?"

He sighed like it was a massive imposition, but he fished his phone from his pocket and checked. "Oh. Yeah. It says, 'Congratulations on showing that bug who's boss."

I opened the plastic bag he'd been holding toward me. "Sushi!"

"I want!" Ranée called.

I tipped him and shut the door. "I'll share."

I set the tray of assorted pieces on the table and handed her a pair of chopsticks. She took a bite of a California roll, nodded her approval, and then kept eating while keeping her eyes fixed on me in an expression I knew well. It was her "solving a problem" look.

"What?"

She swallowed her current bite. "I don't see how you and Jack this week are any different than you and Jack in previous weeks. Tell me again what this is?"

"A friendship."

"You don't do this for any of your friends. None of your friends would do this for you."

"Of course you would. Remember when we celebrated my last big work victory with shoe shopping and sugar and TV bingeing?"

"All right, but I'm your best friend. That isn't what it means when a guy does this."

"It means exactly the same thing. That we're friends."

She leaned over and petted my hair. "You're so cute when you lie to yourself."

"I'm not lying to myself."

She ate a couple more bites of sushi. "Fine. You're not lying to yourself. You guys are just friends. This is in no way a substitute for a real dating life."

"No."

"Give me your phone."

"Are you going to text something stupid to Jack?"

"I could do that with my own phone, so no. I'm not going to talk to Jack at all. Give it to me."

"I don't know why I always obey you." I handed her my phone.

"Because I'm relentless in wearing you down, so you're saving yourself a headache by giving in up front."

"Oh, yeah."

She unlocked the screen and scanned it for a minute, then turned it around so I could see the icon for the dating app we both used sometimes. "This has seven notifications. When's the last time you checked it?"

"I don't know. I'm busy."

"You're no busier than you were three weeks ago when you were going on dates every day. And so far you've had enough time to hang out with Jack every night this week. And you guys are playing Scrabble and he's ordering you food and you text all day and watch TV shows together on the phone. He's your boyfriend."

"He's not my boyfriend."

"He's your something."

"Yes. My friend."

She squinted at me. "Is it hard to be you? With the whole not-living-in-reality thing, I mean?"

"Just because you don't understand the concept of guy friends doesn't mean I can't have one."

"I understand the concept. I have a ton. None of which order me dinners and spend hours on Facetime or the phone with me every night." She pushed her sushi away. "Look, I'm only worried about you. You've said you're ready for a relationship, and I think you are too. That's why I'm worried. This thing with Jack is filling all the emotional spaces any other relationship would need from you, so now you're not looking."

"I'm fine." I waved a piece of uni at her. "Know why? Because I'm a self-aware adult. I really am fine with this being a friendship with Jack. It's not a big deal. You have my full permission to jump in and pull me out of the deep end if you see me drowning, but I'm splashing around in the shallows and otherwise focusing on my career. It's fine. I'm fine," I repeated. "But thank you."

"You said you're fine a lot in that speech. You know, the way people repeat stuff when they're trying to convince someone? Like themselves, maybe."

"I. am. fine."

"Okay, great. So I'm imagining things, and there aren't so many red flags in this situation that it might as well be a 49ers home game?"

"That's what I'm saying."

"Good to know."

"Can we eat sushi in peace now?"

We did, talking about work instead. When she got up to take a shower, I texted Jack. `Excellent dinner. Thank you.`

He sent a thumbs up emoji, and just to prove to Ranée that it wasn't a big deal, I didn't answer him.

The next morning I got another text from him. `I've got a surprise for you this afternoon.`

`What is it?` I demanded.

`Oh, sorry. Wasn't clear. I have a S-U-R-P-R-I-S-E for you.`

`Is it a pony?`

`No. Don't bother guessing. You won't figure this out.`

Of course I spent the whole morning texting him pictures of my guesses. By lunch, I could confirm that it wasn't a monkey, Thighmaster, shave ice machine, or T-rex suit. `That was everything I wanted,` I texted. `Better return whatever it is.`

`Too late. Surprise in motion.`

Interesting.

Ranée might try to pin my good mood for the rest of the

day on her wrongheaded interpretation of our friendship, but I loved surprises. I would have been just as cheered by the promise of a surprise from my mom.

Ranée called me about an hour before I was supposed to get home. "Hey, so, uh...I want you to brace yourself. I just got a text from my brother. He says he's in town, he wants to know if he can stay at our place. And…he brought company."

I'd been standing at my office window, staring out while I took her call on a short break, but her announcement dropped me into my chair like she'd shoved me there. "Wait, what? Sean drove down from Oregon and he brought company? Who is it?"

Jack. It had to be. This was the surprise that must be "in motion."

"Your guess is as good as mine, but my guess is pretty good."

I cursed.

"You're not happy about this?"

"I wasn't prepped for this!"

"Doesn't matter, right? You guys are just friends?"

"Not now, Ranée." And I hung up on the sound of her laughing.

Jack was here? And coming to my house? How…what…why?

Chapter 30

I left work at 5:00 exactly. I had way too much work to be doing that. We had a huge software update rolling out in a week, but I left anyway and beat Ranée home. I didn't know what to do once I got there. Maybe get dinner ready? Or shower and do my hair? Or…

I texted her, panicked. "When are you getting here?"

"Leaving work in 15 minutes." So that meant she'd be here in closer to an hour. Great. That should be plenty of time to obsess about what to wear and make myself crazy.

I marched into my bathroom and stared at my reflection. "No," I told her firmly. "You have to quit freaking out."

It didn't work.

I beelined to my closet to figure out what to wear. It had to be something that looked like I'd actually wear it in my house but that was also cute without trying too hard. I settled on a gauzy tank top with a tiny floral print, cuffed jeans, and bare feet. There. I was practically an Anthropologie ad. I flat-ironed my hair and fixed my flaking mascara. Anything more than that would look too heavy-handed.

In between all the primping and closet-wrecking, I kept trying to figure out how I felt about it all. It should freak me out, shouldn't it, that a guy I'd never met had invited himself to crash at my house with no notice?

But he was coming with my best friend's brother. I knew Sean and trusted him, and I probably wouldn't have been fazed if he'd called and said he was bringing some random guy I'd never heard of to crash with him at our place for the weekend. And Jack was by no means random. We'd talked or FaceTimed for hours over the last couple of months.

The fact that he wasn't random might be the bigger problem. Was I supposed to think this was spontaneous and fun like I would if one of my old college roommates decided to surprise me? Probably, if Jack and I were friends.

That's not how I felt, though. I felt…I didn't know how to describe it, but I was dead certain my stomach had never done these gymnastics for any of my friends before.

I texted Jack and said, SEAN IS COMING TO MY HOUSE AND BRINGING COMPANY. WHAT IS GOING ON? But no matter how many times I shook my phone threateningly, it didn't dislodge any new texts from Jack.

I was in the middle of texting my fifth "HURRY UP" to Ranée from the couch when she walked through the door. I immediately tried to peer around her for company, but she only shut it behind her.

"Just me, myself, and I," she said, and I slumped back on the couch. "But Sean should be here any minute. And he's bringing pizza."

"And that's it?"

She sat at the other end of the couch. "Em, he's bringing—"

But right then the doorbell rang as the door opened and Sean poked his head through. "Hey, ladies," he said. "I brought a friend."

This was it.

I settled my hands into my lap and drew a calming breath while the truth washed over me. I couldn't wait to meet Jack. And now I didn't have to.

My phone vibrated just as Sean crouched down to pick something up. I checked the text to read, "It's not me. Still in Oregon," just as Sean backed through the door carrying a dog crate.

It felt like riding a roller coaster all the way to the top, starting the wild downward dive, and having it lurch to a stop mid-plunge. All of my adrenaline had spiked but now it had nowhere to go.

"Ladies, meet my new roommate, Shep." He opened the gate and an Australian Shepherd puppy scrambled out.

"Sean got a new dog," Ranée said, getting up to greet her brother with a hug. "I told him you like dogs."

"Is it okay if he hangs out with me here until Sunday? He's still so young that I didn't want to leave him with someone else. But he's housebroken, I swear."

"Of course he can stay here. Can I pet him?" I only asked to be polite. Normally I would love to meet a new dog. I adored them, and it wasn't Shep's fault that he felt like a bait-and-switch, a consolation prize instead of the person I most wanted to see.

Shep wasn't a large dog, and I could tell he still needed to grow into his paws a little, but he was more grown than not. He had a beautiful coat with patches of tan and white, but mostly it was gray with splotches of black. He raced over to Ranée and around her feet while she knelt and loved on him. "Oh my gosh, he looks just like Charlie Boy."

"That was our favorite dog growing up," Sean explained, grinning at his sister fawning over Shep.

This isn't the dog's fault, I told myself. *Don't be a jerk.* I mustered a smile. "I can see why. We always had black labs, but I love Australian Shepherds."

"So you really are cool with us crashing? A second ago you looked—"

I cut him off with a shake of my head. "Just didn't expect a dog, but you're both welcome, any time. It'll be nice to have a dog friend this weekend."

"So glad." Another knock sounded at the door, and Sean opened it. "Pizza's here."

I didn't want pizza. I didn't want to hang out anymore where I could feel Ranée's eyes studying my face with the intensity she usually reserved for hunting down her premature gray hairs. I summoned a smile and called softly for Shep who gleefully raced over to greet me at the sofa, his nails clacking on the wood floor.

"Hi, boy," I said, scratching him around his ears.

"Hey, you stole my new boyfriend," Ranée complained.

"Fair trade since you stole my old one."

"I did not!" she yelped as Sean made a Scooby-Doo

sounding, "Ruh-roh."

"Fine, you didn't. But Shep is still my new friend."

"Oh, I almost forgot," Sean said. "Jack sent something for you." He dug a package from his duffel bag and handed it to me. It was flat and rectangular, wrapped in plain brown paper. I opened it and smiled. It was an 8 x 10 framed picture showing a flannel-shirted Jack from behind. He was sitting cross-legged at the edge of a cliff, his man bun on full display. Transcendent Seagull perched next to him, its head tilted thoughtfully as they stared out at a vista.

"Did Jack make you take this?" I asked Sean.

"Yep. What is it with you guys and seagulls?"

"Long story. Hang on. I need you to take a picture of me too." I walked out to our tiny balcony and set the framed photo on the edge. Then I whipped my hair into a messy bun before I sat cross-legged in front of it and stared at the photo the way Jack and the seagull had stared into the distance. "I think you know what to do, Sean. My phone is on the table."

He snorted. "Hang on a second." I heard him rustling behind me, then, "Got it. You guys are so weird."

I rose and took my phone back, smiling again when I saw the picture within a picture my re-enactment of Jack's photo had created. "Perfect." I sent it to Jack.

He responded immediately. `Perfect.`

Sean shook his head and moved the pizza to the counter and pulled down plates. He'd visited often enough to know where to find everything. We sat and ate, and I fought the urge to yell, "Tell me about Jack!" in between each of his sentences. I did such a good job of resisting that I rewarded myself by eating an extra slice before I excused myself at the earliest possible moment to go sulk in my bedroom.

I'd only been burrowing under my comforter for about five minutes when Ranée knocked and walked in.

"Are you okay?" she asked.

"Sure. Why wouldn't I be?"

"Because Jack wasn't with Sean."

"I'm a little bummed, but it's not a big deal."

"That's not what your face said when you saw that dog."

I waved my hand as if brushing away her concerns. "Who can be sad about a cute puppy? It's all good."

She flopped onto my bed. "I don't think so. I think you were more than a little bummed. I'm not here to make you admit it or play I-told-you-so. I just want you to think about something, okay? My grandma told me once that you should make every important decision by playing eenie-meenie-miney-moe."

"Um, no thank you?"

She rolled her eyes. "I wasn't finished. She said the moment you realize what you're getting on 'moe' will tell you how you really feel about it."

"Like that *Friends* episode where Phoebe tricks Rachel into thinking she's not pregnant so Rachel can see what she really wants?"

"Exactly. And when Jack didn't come through that door, I think it told you what you really want." She stood up and straightened her shirt. "I'm going to go hang out with Sean some more. He says Shep is trained, but I'd keep your closet closed and your best shoes up high."

She left, and I stared at the door as she shut it behind her.

A text buzzed my phone, and I opened it.

Jack. Of course. `Did you want it to be me with Sean?`

I set my phone down. I couldn't answer. I wouldn't lie, but I didn't want to tell him the truth.

Saturday morning I got up to make breakfast. "Want an omelet?" I asked Sean as he lay on the couch. Shep had been curled up on his chest, but he hopped down and ran to me, his tail wagging.

"If you're already making one. Thanks."

"No problem." Shep did his best to chase my feet around the kitchen, but I was too used to it from my own dogs growing up to mind. Fifteen minutes later I had omelets plated for both of us, and Shep was crunching on the puppy mix Sean set out for him.

"So you and Jack," he said, causing me to choke on the sip of coffee I'd just taken.

"Excuse me?"

"What's going on with you two?"

"Nothing. We're friends. Did he say something different?"

Sean took a drink of his own coffee and eyed me over the rim of his mug. "Not exactly. But I know him well enough to read between the lines. And here's what I think. Based on what I hear from him, and what I hear from Ranée, you and Jack have spent a lot of time trying to convince yourselves of this friend thing, both of you are failing, and it's totally obvious to the two other people paying attention, so you should probably figure stuff out."

I didn't bother denying it. There was no point. Instead I took a bite of my omelet and refused to meet Sean's eyes.

"He thinks he's serving a penance," Sean said.

He had my full attention. "Who? Jack?"

He nodded. "Yes. We lost a patient that we'd both grown attached to, and everything he's done since for the last two years has been about him trying to atone for that. But he can't. We can't bring her back. And the reality is that it wasn't his fault. He did everything he could—way beyond what anyone else would have tried—and it didn't work. But he doesn't believe it, so he punishes himself."

Shep finished at his bowl and walked over to plop himself on my feet and rest. Sean nudged him with his foot. "Traitor." Shep only panted in response.

"That's so sad." It was true, but also inadequate to describe the way it made me hurt for Jack. I knew him well enough to know that a loss like that had probably killed him inside.

"It was horrible. That's why I've been so relieved to see how Jack is coming to life. It's because of you, if you guys can just figure out what Ranée and I already see."

I traced the rim of my mug for a minute, considering his words. They gave me a different sadness. "There's nothing to figure out. All I can do is be his friend, be a listening ear now that he's started talking a little bit."

"That's the thing. Jack doesn't talk to anybody about anything real *ever*. It's huge that he's talking to you. And what's more, I think you could talk him out of hiding, get him back to the real world."

"You're overestimating our connection. He feels valuable at the clinic. He's not going to leave, and I'm not going to live in the Oregon wilderness. So there you go. Lost cause. Jack and I stay friends. End of story."

"Jack hates working at the clinic."

That startled me. "He didn't sound like he hated it when we talked about it the other night."

"He does. Trust me. I know him extremely well. He's there out of a sense of a duty, but what he's doing, a lot of other doctors could do. What he does in his specialty, it takes guts and genius that exactly one guy has. Jack. He's talked himself into thinking he's doing good where he is, but he could be doing even more good if he went back to oncology. I think part of him wants to. But part of him doesn't think he can tolerate losing another patient. And he would. But he'd save some too. He forgets that because the fight is so lopsided."

I rose and scraped the remaining half of my omelet into the garbage. I'd lost my appetite. "You seem to think I have some kind of power to save Jack. But when it comes right down to it, we're social media friends. We've never even met. I don't have the ability to change his mind about anything. And it's not my job." I wish it were. The strength of that desire startled me, and made me even sadder to know that it wasn't and couldn't be. I wanted to save him, I realized. But it wasn't my place.

"I get that," Sean said. "But I think Jack would change his own mind with the right motivation. He was in a massive low place when he came to Oregon, and I think he's climbed out of it more than he's realized. He's restless, but he's talked himself into believing he's irreplaceable at the clinic because it's the easier path right now. The thing is, he was never an easy-road kind of guy before this. It's just not him. He'll figure that out eventually.

I think, based on the way he tries to ask me casual questions about you, that you've reminded him of the wider world."

"I'm glad I helped, I guess, but what does it say that he didn't jump at the chance to tag along on this trip here? I don't have enough influence on him to drag him back to society when he won't even take a weekend road trip to San Francisco." That was a big part of the heavy feeling in my chest, I admitted. That he could have come, and he didn't.

"I didn't tell him I was coming, Em. You can't blame him for that. Maybe you can't drag him into society, but I think you should come to Oregon and drag him out of the cabin. Or the clinic. I'm trying to convince Ranée she's long overdue for a road trip and when I do, you should come with her. You don't have to save Jack. But I think it'd be good for him to remember that he used to have a different life, that most of it was really, really good, and that there's a whole world of people out there that he can gel with besides me."

I took another sip of coffee while I considered this. "Why do you feel so responsible for him?"

"Because." He sighed. "Because I think I'm leaving soon. I want to go back to nursing full-time, and that means moving back to a city. I'm the one who connected him with the clinic job. I feel responsible for him."

"And you're trying to shift that responsibility to me." I wasn't enough, and it was too humiliating to make that point again.

He finished his last bit of omelet and rose to rinse his dish. "I'm making him sound like a head case. He's not. I think you should come see that for yourself."

"Sean..." His logic sucked but his heart was in the right place, so I tried to think about how to phrase my next thought gently. I couldn't come up with anything, so I said it straight. "You're asking me to be bait, like I'm trying to lure a depressed bear out of his cave or something."

"What exactly do you think we do in Oregon? We don't mess with bears."

"You know what I mean."

He nodded. "I do. And yes, you'd be the medicine he needs, but more like adrenaline than an antidepressant. He's ready. He doesn't see it yet. I'm being selfish and wanting you to go remind him that there's life beyond that little town. It won't be hard to find a doctor ready for semi-retirement who can take over his clinic gig. I'd love to see Jack back in the game. He was one of the best in his field. It's where he belongs."

"It's not my job." I'd never wanted to be anyone's salvation. That felt like a burden far heavier than my shoulders were meant to carry.

"I'll back off," he said. "Sorry."

I shook my head to indicate he didn't need to apologize.

"I'm going to walk Shep. Will you tell Ranée to text me when she gets up?"

"Not until she's had a cup of coffee."

"Good call. Catch you later, Em."

Shep did some kind of Australian Shepherd celebration when he saw the leash. It involved prancing and tail shaking, and a happy bark when Sean opened the door to go outside.

A text came in. Jack again. `Full disclosure: I wanted it to be me with Sean. Maybe you did too.`

`What do we do about that?`

Again, I didn't answer. Because I didn't know.

Chapter 31

Jack's unanswered text nagged at me all day. Luckily, I had a ton of work to do because of the software update, so I worked remotely, answering questions from my team as a handful of them worked overtime and popped into our team chat app with questions. But any time I had a second to breathe, I faced down the same question: what should I say to Jack?

I worked until almost midnight and fell into bed exhausted, only to get up and make myself some instant oatmeal and dive back in again. Sean rolled off the sofa and made coffee, silently filling my mug while I tapped at my keyboard like crazy. I gave him an absent-minded smile and thank you and disappeared into the impossible list of tasks that had to get done before the update went live.

Ranée appeared mid-morning. "We're going to grab brunch. Want to come?"

"Can't. Living on caffeine until we get this update ready."

"I'm bringing something home. And you will eat it."

"As long as I don't have to leave my laptop."

An hour later she was back and deposited a spinach quiche with a side of fresh fruit in front of me.

"Eat," she ordered.

I picked my way through it, not paying attention to anything but my screen until Shep whined. I looked up to see Sean trying to coax him into his carrier. I blinked. "You're leaving?"

"Yeah. Gotta get back for work tomorrow."

"You're making a twenty hour round trip drive to spend a day-and-half with Ranée?"

He looked a little embarrassed. "I wanted her to meet Shep."

"Well, you and Shep are the cutest, then."

He got Shep into the carrier and snapped it closed. "We'll get out of your hair now."

"You were never in it."

He hitched his backpack over one shoulder. "Hey, Emily, I'm sorry. I overstepped on the Jack thing. He wouldn't be thrilled that I said anything. Don't hold it against him, okay? Whatever you two are doing, you both seem to be having fun. I should've stayed out of it."

"Don't worry about it," I said, finally focusing on him. "You're a good friend. I get it."

"I hope so. I think you know if you decided to resign from the real world for a while that Ranée wouldn't let you get away with it. That's all I'm doing here, but you're right: you're not bait. I'll figure out another way to get through to him."

I got up and hugged him. "I'm not mad. Drive safe."

Ranée came out dressed for the barn. "I'll walk you down."

He hefted the carrier and called another goodbye on his way out. I turned back to my laptop, but the screen had timed out and it seemed like a sign to take a short break. Stretch, walk, run in place. Move something besides my fingers.

I did some lunges across the living room to wake my sleepy muscles up and laughed when a seagull fluttered down to scavenge on our micro balcony. Of course a seagull would show up. Of course. "Good luck, buddy."

I picked up my phone and read Jack's last text again. `I wanted it to be me with Sean. Maybe you did too. What do we do about that?`

`Sean seems to think you need rescuing,` I texted him back. `Do you?`

He called almost right away. "Hi. I don't need to be rescued. And if I did, it's not your job."

"That's what I think too."

"So ignore anything he said. I'll kill him when he gets back. In the meantime, how's it going otherwise?"

"I've been working like crazy for the last two days. We've got a huge deadline on Wednesday."

"Are you going to make it?"

"If thirty hours of overtime this week can get it done, then yes."

"Is that how much your team is putting in?"

"No. That's just thirty by myself. The leads are all putting in that much too."

"Wow. Is it always that busy?"

"No. But a couple of times a year, stuff comes up. This is one of those times."

"I used to work a lot of weeks like that. It's tough. How soon do you get a break?"

"I'm sure my boss will give us comp days if the update rolls out without any problems. And then I'll sleep for forty-eight hours straight."

"Come up here."

The words burst out of him so fast I wasn't sure his brain knew what his mouth had said yet. "Excuse me?"

There was a long silence, then I could hear him take a deep breath. "Come up here. On your comp days, I mean. It's quiet. And pretty. And I want to see you."

"Jack..."

"Just think about it."

As if it hadn't suddenly become the only thought in my brain. Go see Jack? I tried to clear my head of the only image it was interested in projecting: me sliding my hands up his shoulders while he leaned down for a—

I cleared my throat. "I don't think that would be a friendly visit. Friendish. Friendlike?" I stopped talking before it turned into nervous chatter.

"No," he said, his voice quiet. "It wouldn't be."

I bounced on the balls of my feet, glad he couldn't see all the nervous energy suddenly spilling out of me. "It's a moot point if I don't meet this deadline."

"Then I'll let you get back to work."

"Coming to Oregon, that's borderline crazy." I bounced faster.

"Think about it anyway."

"Like I'm going to think about anything else now."

"I hope not. I can't."

Chapter 32

And I didn't. I managed to keep my mind running down two tracks, but even at my most focused on work for the next three days, there was an underlying script running in the background. *Come to Oregon. Come to Oregon. That's crazy. Think about it anyway.*

Tuesday night near midnight Ranée wandered out to the kitchen for some water. "Whoa," she said spotting me at the table. "You still working? I thought you guys were set."

"We are. Everything came out fine in QA. I'm just refactoring a few code smells." When she blinked at me, I said, "It's like dotting I's and crossing T's."

"Got it. So it should be fine tomorrow?"

"Should be."

"How are we going to celebrate you surviving your first major project as a manager?"

I shrugged, still distracted by Jack's invitation. "I don't need any more shoes."

"Meet me at Sarno's after work. Drinks are on me."

"I might be too exhausted for that."

"But you have to do something."

Yeah. Like go to Oregon. I shifted in my seat. I hadn't told Ranée about Jack's invitation because I didn't want to hear her input. I wanted to make a clear-headed decision about it. Unfortunately, Ranée had learned to read me too well.

"Something's not right." She sat and peered at me. "What's going on? Work got you down?"

I shook my head. "It's been good. Hard, but this was my first of our biannual hell weeks and I'm getting through it fine."

"So what's up? Why not celebrate?"

"Because..."

She crossed her arms in a way that said she wasn't moving until she got an answer. "Talk to me."

"I'll get a couple of comp days if the rollout goes well tomorrow, which it will." I flicked a glance at my checklist, which I was going through for the fourth time. "I'll get an extra-long weekend. So Jack asked me to come up."

Her jaw dropped, and she gaped for two whole seconds before it shifted into a slow smile. "Well, well, well. When do you leave?"

"I don't think I'm going."

That wiped the smile off her face. "Why not?"

"For all the same reasons as before. Sean says Jack is buried under some sort of avalanche of guilt, and I'm not the rescue crew. It's not my job to save him from himself. I don't have the skills for that."

"The skills? Girl, what do you think it takes to pull someone out of a rut?" She held up one hand, turning it this way and that. "This is all you need. All he needs. A hand up. This doesn't take special training or equipment."

"But this isn't a simple rut. I'm worried if I pull him out that I'm going to have to keep carrying him. I'm not that strong."

"You can't carry the weight or you won't carry the weight?" she asked.

I shrugged. "Doesn't really matter, does it?"

"It does. And what's more, I think you're being overdramatic. Let's imagine you go to Oregon. What's the best-case scenario?"

"Jack and I have perfect chemistry and fall madly in love and he leaves everything behind to live in San Francisco. But you know that's not how my brain works. I'm already thinking ahead to the problems, so I can solve them, but I see no good solutions."

"We'll get to that. Tell me the worst-case scenario."

"I go to Oregon and we don't have any connection."

She lifted an eyebrow. "You think that's a possibility?"

An image of him smiling while he pushed his hair out of his eyes flashed in my mind. "No."

"Tell me your real worst-case scenario."

I knew it too well. "That Jack and I have perfect chemistry and fall madly in love but we both stay exactly where we are, and I get to deal with 'what might have been' for the rest of my life."

"Aren't you there yet?"

My forehead wrinkled. "What do you mean?"

"I mean that if you don't go to Oregon, aren't you going to wonder what might have happened if you had gone?"

There was no arguing with that. She was right.

She leaned forward and rested her hands on my knees,

squeezing them to make her points. “You like him”—squeeze—“and he’s into to you”—squeeze—“and I think you already fell for him”—squeeze—“so any other story you’re telling yourself is a lie”—squeeze—“and so what if he needs a little rescuing? Whatever else you guys may be, you ARE”—squeeze—“friends, and you’d do the same thing for me. But I won’t make out with you, and he will, and you should definitely”—squeeze—“get on that.”

She sat back and crossed her arms again. I rubbed my knees.

She made a good point. If I tried to escape life too long, Ranée would come looking for me. And I would do the same for her. Jack was my friend. He’d become a really good friend. Shouldn’t I do the same for him? Because the thing she was most right about was that I’d always wonder if I didn’t go.

I rubbed my eyes. “I can’t even think about this until we push out the update tomorrow.”

“But you’ll think about it as soon as the update goes live?”

“I’m going to be dead tired when work is done.”

“Emily.” It was a tone of warning.

“I’ll make a decision after work tomorrow.”

“You better, or I’m going to decide for you. Spoiler alert: my decision involves kidnapping you and driving you to Oregon.”

“Go to bed, Ranée. I still have work to do.”

“And decisions to make,” she sang as she obeyed and disappeared down the hallway.

I worked until I napped on my keyboard. Then I put myself to bed for a few hours and headed into the office early.

The update was scheduled to go live at 3:00 AM so that computers could do automatic updates overnight, but I wanted to be there when the East Coast opened for business to track any issues in real time. I was at the office by 6:00 AM, and by mid-morning it was obvious we'd executed the update successfully.

Peter, my boss, tracked me down in the developer's workroom mid-morning. "Just the person I was looking for. Raj," he asked one of the junior developers, "could you bring in two chairs from the conference room, please?"

When Raj returned with the chairs, Peter climbed onto one and held up his hands. "We've been running for seven hours with no error reports, guys. You killed it!"

A cheer went up from my team. Peter turned and extended a hand. "Take a step up, Emily. Let's hear it for your fearless leader," he said, when I climbed on the chair beside him. He high-fived me, and they cheered even louder. "I know you guys have been putting in a lot of overtime to make this happen, so Emily, put together a skeleton crew and take the next two days off. You're not allowed to be on it. The crew will get their comp days next week. If there's anyone on your team that you think deserves longer than two days, consider it approved." That won the loudest cheer of all.

"Really great work. You can take the chairs back, Raj," he said, climbing down.

"Not yet," I said. Peter looked up at me questioningly. "Not until each of them also stands on the Chair of Glory for a high five. Hop up, Raj." Grinning, he did as ordered, and I slapped him five while the other developers scrambled to get in line for theirs.

"This is why you're going to go far, Emily Riker." Peter saluted me before heading back to the executive suite.

I let the developers with the most overtime leave at lunch and hung around with the skeleton crew until the day officially ended at five. We only had two issues come up, and both were user error, easily solved.

A few minutes after five, Hailey stopped by my office. "Someone said you got here at six. You must be wiped. Go home and sleep."

I shook my head. "I know I should be exhausted, but I'm not. And I have a couple of things left to do."

"All right, but I'm out of here. I better not see you back in here before Monday."

"You won't," I promised. I picked up my phone as she shut the door behind her. I had an important call to make, and I couldn't help smiling as I tapped in the Portland area code.

Chapter 33

I slung my suitcase into the trunk of the rental car at the Portland International Airport and settled into the driver's seat, but I hesitated before starting the engine. I took a calming breath. Once I put this car in gear, I would be on the road to Jack.

He didn't know it yet. Sean had offered to pick me up from the airport when I called him to tell him I was surprising Jack and that I needed directions to the clinic. But I wanted my own transportation so that…

Well, so that I could leave the second I wanted to if things didn't go right.

I slid the key into the ignition and took one more deep breath before turning it. Time to do this.

My phone guided me to Highway 26, and I settled in for the drive. *Focus on the journey,* I told myself. I tried to pay attention to the pleasing contrast of modern buildings against the lush Portland greenery, but my attention kept jumping ahead to my destination. What would happen when I got there? How would Jack react?

My lips quirked as I replayed Ranée's prediction when I told her why I needed a ride to the airport. "Yes, girl! You are Princess Charming. He's going to swoon when he sees you."

I tried to focus on the Oregon scenery again, but it was useless. I spent the next hour imagining all the ways this could go wrong or really, really right until I wasn't sure which one had twisted my stomach into an impossible knot by the time I signaled for the exit in Featherton.

Sean told me that Jack took lunch every day around 1:00. That was an hour from now. I drove to the only motel in town, checked in, and freshened up my makeup and hair. And then there was no more stalling. It was time to find Jack.

I found the clinic without any trouble. It was a block off the main street in a low, squat building, but it was covered in new siding and bore a neat little sign reading, "Featherton Health Clinic." I opened the door to a small waiting room. There was no one at the receptionist desk but a sign scrawled in marker read, "Ring bell if you need the doctor," next to a silver call bell.

The only other occupant was an elderly woman sitting in the corner. She had a pile of knitting in her lap, but she wasn't doing anything with it. She smiled at me and massaged her hand absent-mindedly. Maybe that was why she wasn't knitting. "Dr. Hazlett said he's running a little behind, but isn't he always?"

I made a sound that suggested I sympathized.

"Anyway, he's been back there awhile, so he should be out soon. I just need a steroid injection, so I'm sure he'll be with you in no time."

"I'm not in a rush," I assured her. It was the truest thing I'd ever said. Now that I was here, I could see how insane my plan was. I should have told him I was coming, not shown up at his place of work. Or better yet, not come at all. What was I thinking?

I needed to get the heck out of here and at least call to let him know I was in town, so we could decide when and how to meet up. I was halfway out of my chair when the door leading back to the treatment rooms opened.

"—fill this over at the Sandy pharmacy and you'll be—" He caught sight of me and stopped talking.

I offered a tentative smile while I drank in the sight of him. He wore gray jeans that were almost dressy enough to look like business slacks, and a button down blue shirt but with no tie, open at the collar.

He looked delicious.

Um, perfect. I meant he looked perfect.

"Doctor?" The middle-aged woman at his side stared at him expectantly.

He cleared his throat. "Uh, yes, get this filled and you should be good as new in a couple of days."

She coughed into the crook of her arm, thanked him, and left. Jack leaned against the doorframe. "Hi," he said quietly.

"Hi." I gave him a tiny wave. His voice was as warm as it had always sounded over the phone and FaceTime but richer, somehow.

A smile had started working on the corner of his mouth. "Mrs. Castille, I'll take care of you in just a minute. I've had an urgent case come in."

She tilted her head and studied me. "You do look feverish, honey. Your color is high. Go right ahead."

If my cheeks hadn't been hot before, they were flaming

now. Jack didn't even try to hide his grin. "This way, Miss Riker."

He led me to a room that was bare of anything except for a desk and his medical license hanging on the wall. There weren't any photos or personal effects. He pulled a couple of chairs to the same side of the desk and waved me into one before taking the other.

"I can't believe you're here," he said.

"I can't either. Is it…um, are you okay with this?"

"So okay with it. I mean not okay with it. Happy? I'm happy about it."

It sounded almost like a question, and I wondered if I had made a huge mistake in surprising him this way. "Sorry, I should have called."

"Wait, why are you apologizing?"

"You don't seem certain you're happy to see me? Like it was kind of a question?" I hated the insecure way my voice rose at the end of each sentence, but I couldn't seem to stop it from happening.

His eyes widened. "I messed this up. I was trying to think of a way to tell you how happy I am that you're here without completely freaking you out. Um, but the answer is super happy."

"Oh. Good." Relief spread through my chest in a gentle billow, like the soft puff of a newly washed sheet tossed to settle on a bed.

Er. Maybe I needed to focus on different analogies.

"Could I get a do-over?" he asked.

"Sure?" I had no idea what it would entail, but he rose and opened the door, waving me through it.

When I stood on the other side of the open door, he stood

in the office and gave me a sudden look of delight. “Emily? Is that you? Are you really here?”

“Yes, Jack. It’s me. I’m really here.”

“Come right on in,” he said, stepping aside so I could pass him. But this time when I walked into the room, he shut the door behind us and gave me a slow smile.

“Hi, Emily Riker. I’m going to kiss you now. What do you think about that?”

I reached out to catch the edge of his lab coat and tugged lightly. “That’s what I’m here for.”

He backed me against the door and framed my face with his hands. They were warm and steady as he leaned down and brushed his lips against mine, and I slid my hands up to his shoulders to pull him closer. “Hi, Jack Hazlett.”

He kissed me again, a real one this time, and I melted into him as he tangled his fingers through my hair. My lips opened beneath his, an invitation to explore, and he took it, turning the kiss deep and long. I clasped my hands behind his neck for support and disappeared into the wave of heat breaking over me. I didn’t even want to come up for air. For long minutes we didn’t, until he finally broke away to trail kisses along my jaw.

“I’m glad you’re here,” he whispered. I tilted my head to give him better access to my throat, and I managed a soft, “Me too. But wait.”

I pushed against his chest, the lightest pressure, but he immediately gave me space. “I just wanted to inspect this for myself.” I reached out to touch the hair gathered at the nape of his neck.

He wound a strand of mine around his finger. “I like

yours. It's lighter than it looks onscreen."

"I like *this* enough," I said, touching his lips, "to overlook any opinions I have about your crowning girly." And I kissed him before his grin could even spread all the way.

He kissed me breathless, and just as I felt the kiss turning hungry, he pulled away to rest his forehead against mine. "I'm so glad you're here. But I still have to take care of Mrs. Castille."

I blinked at him and then his words registered, and I slipped out of his arms with a gasp. "Oh my gosh, I forgot about her."

"I don't want you to go." He groaned and reached for me, but I stepped out of range.

"No, you're right. Poor thing, sitting there in the waiting room. What time are you done today? Maybe I can meet you after work?"

"It'll take me a few minutes to treat her then I'm free for lunch. I'll call in an order to a place called Annie's and we can eat here."

"Tell me where to pick it up. It'll keep me busy while you take care of your patient." I pointed to the door before he could sweet talk me. "Now you should probably see to Mrs. Castille."

He reached for the handle. "Okay, but you promise you're coming back here?"

I darted over and laid another kiss on him. "Only because you asked nicely." Then I slipped under his arm and headed out to the reception area.

Mrs. Castille glanced up at me. "Now you've got a rash all over," she said, pointing to her mouth. "I hope Dr. Hazlett fixed you up with something good."

"I think I did," he said from behind me, laughter in his voice. I didn't bother turning around and showing him that Mrs. Castille had turned my cheeks red again as I fled to find Annie's.

Chapter 34

When I got back to the clinic, Jack opened the door before I even made it up the stairs. He pulled me in and locked the door behind me.

"Sorry it took so long," I said. "Annie's was busier than I expected for such a small town."

"It's Featherton's best restaurant, that's why. But it worked out great because I called and canceled all my appointments for the rest of the day."

"You didn't need to do that. I don't need to take priority over sick people."

"Don't worry about it. There was nothing urgent. I rescheduled everything. I might still get called in for something, but as of right now, I'm spending the rest of my day with you. Come back to my office."

At his desk, he took the plastic bag of food from my hand and set the boxes on the surface.

"Hungry?" he asked.

I looked from his face to the food and back to him. "Very."

He slid his arms around my waist and kissed me again. "I don't really want lunch." Then his stomach gurgled.

I laughed and pushed his arms away. "Liar. Your French dip is going to get cold."

"I don't really care," he grumbled but sat down and opened his takeout carton, while I did the same to mine. "I got you the chicken salad sandwich which might sound really gross, but it's so good. We can trade if you want."

"This is fine." It did look good, but I didn't touch it. I was more interested in watching Jack. He had an underlying nervousness I wouldn't have expected. I had a feeling he was the kind of guy who had swaggered through the halls of hospitals with the confidence of any *Grey's Anatomy* heartthrob. I'd sensed it in the sure way he'd laughed and kissed me. But there was an endearing eagerness to please in the way he checked on my lunch order and cleared his schedule.

"I can't believe you came up here." He shook his head. "I guess the update went well?"

"No hitches so far. But I definitely needed a break."

"Then we're going to make it a good one. What do you want to do while you're here?"

I raised my eyebrows at him and fought a smile.

He shrugged. "If you insist." Then he reached over and hauled me onto his lap for more kissing.

Several minutes later while I rested my head on his shoulder to recover from a self-diagnosed case of oxygen deprivation, I idly reached up to tug the elastic from his messy knot of hair and let the dark strands fall over my fingers, combing through the soft pieces. I leaned back far enough to see the full effect and shook my head.

"What?" he asked, drawing me back against his chest.

"It's like looking at two different people when your hair is up and when it's down."

"So people tell me."

I toyed with a few more strands until my own stomach grumbled, and I laughed and climbed from his lap to reclaim my chair. "I guess I need to eat too. Tell me what else there is to do around here."

He thought while he took a bite. "Whatever you want. Featherton is your oyster. Tell me what you want to do, and we'll do it."

"Let's do whatever you normally do around here for a first date."

He gave me a look I couldn't interpret. "That could be a little tricky."

"Why? Are we going to bump into all your exes?"

He shook his head. "No. I haven't been out with anyone since I moved here."

"But…" He'd been here for over two years.

"There wasn't anyone I wanted to take out. Now I do." He watched me as I processed that. "Look, I was a head case when I moved here. It's *why* I moved here. I needed to get as far away as possible from all the noise in my life. It worked."

"Except now I'm here…making noise."

"Not that I mind, but while we're on the subject, can I ask why?" he asked, setting his sandwich down. "Why did you decide to come?"

Here we were at the threshold of our first real

conversation in person, the kind you have when you're dating someone, and you want it to go somewhere. "Why did you invite me?"

He studied me for a long moment. "I needed to know," he said. "I've been in a fog for a long time. You've been a steady light. I wanted to know what I'd find if I followed it."

Ranée was wrong. It was Jack who was making me swoon, not the other way around. But even as his words sent a soft, warm glow through me, a flicker of worry trailed it.

"You're frowning." He leaned forward to brush his finger over the furrows on my forehead. "Was that the wrong answer?"

"Not if it's the truth. It's just..." I tried to figure out what the flicker meant. "I don't know. The light in the fog thing. It's rescue imagery, you know? And once you rescue someone or get rescued, there's this moment of intense 'yayness' and then you both move on and that's it."

He looked like he was trying not to smile. "'Yayness?'" he repeated.

"I'm a programmer, not a poet."

"Could've fooled me with talk like 'rescue imagery.' But I get it. It's kind of like how no one wants to be a rebound. You don't want to be a rebound from my hermit life?"

It pulsed like truth where the flicker had been. "Basically."

He took the sandwich from my hands and set it down. "I can't make a single promise. The reality is that we're committed to lives in two different places, and there's nothing we can do about that. But you're here now. I want to be in this moment, for as long as it lasts, before you have to go back to your life. I don't think we can solve anything, and I'm sure if we try we're only going to frustrate ourselves. Let's not do that. Let's just be here, right now, like there is nothing else to worry about, nothing to fix."

I reached up and tucked back a piece of his hair that hadn't made it into the elastic. "I've wanted to do that for weeks."

"Then do it as often as you want this weekend. Deal?"

What else was there to say? He was right. All that mattered was right now because I couldn't do a thing about anything else. "Deal."

And then lunch got cold as we disappeared into countless long, sweet kisses.

Chapter 35

When we finally made it outside, Jack led me to the only vehicle in the parking lot besides my rental car, a black BMW that looked out of place amongst the pickups and SUVs that I'd seen while driving around.

"I've been thinking," he said. "I don't know what a perfect first date is in Featherton, but I know what I want ours to be. I thought we could drive around, I'll show you the sights and the surrounding area, the kind of stuff I like to do, and then we can grab some dinner and I'll show you my place and we can watch that dumb medical show together. In person."

"And I can jab you in the ribs every time you point out what they're doing wrong?"

"Sure. I'll even make sure that you're tucked in next to me so it's easier for you to get me with your elbow."

"Sounds perfect."

Featherton was pretty in early spring, bright with the inevitable Oregon greenery, but this wasn't a town that had dressed itself up to attract any of the resort business from Mt.

Hood. It had a shabby but comfortable feel, with common sense concrete sidewalks instead of cobblestones or bricks. Some of the signs bore faded paint, but they all hung neatly, and every window was clean, and no litter clung to the corners of buildings or street signs, the way it did in San Francisco.

I thought it would take longer to drive as he pointed out different businesses or told me about each place, but apparently, he spent all his time going from Annie's to the tiny grocery store and the laundromat and didn't know much about the rest of the little shops. After two blocks of this, I interrupted him. "Park there, please." I pointed to an empty spot on the street.

He steered into the space without arguing. "Did you need something?"

I grinned and leaned over to kiss him. "That. But also, I can't believe you don't know more about these little places. We're going to explore, and we're starting here."

He glanced at the sign over the door of the business. "At Grove Hardware?"

"Yes. Why not?"

He shook his head but climbed out of the car and met me on my side. "Let's explore the mysteries of the hardware store."

"You laugh but it's pretty mysterious to me. I'm a suburban girl born to parents who kept a handyman on retainer. I honestly don't think I've ever been inside one."

Fifteen minutes later, I left the store as the proud owner of five iron hooks. "There was so much cool stuff in there."

"Remind me why you got the hooks?"

"For coat hooks on our front door."

"You don't already have hooks?"

"Yes, but these are better hooks."

We visited an animal feed store where Jack made me give him the Paul and Ranée update, then we wandered out of the store onto the sidewalk. I stopped short when I saw what the next business was: Mountain Truffles.

Jack glanced back at me to see why I'd stopped. He took one look at my face and burst out laughing. "I guess you want to go in?"

It was the largest business on the street. I could already feel my salivary glands preparing for nirvana. "Please tell me 'mountain truffle' isn't a euphemism like cow patty."

That made him laugh again. "No. It's chocolate, I promise. Their specialty is berry centers made from the ones that grow wild around here."

I grabbed his hand and tugged him toward the store. "I'm so in."

We stepped into a lobby that was half chocolate shop, half receptionist desk. The middle-aged woman seated behind the desk looked up and smiled. "Hi, Dr. Hazlett. What brings you in today?"

I raised my hand. "We're exploring the town. I think I just struck gold."

"Well, there's not much to explore in Featherton, but I can certainly make your trip in here worthwhile. Can I get you some samples?"

I looked around, not sure where to start. Jack watched me with a half-smile. "It looks like your brain is going a mile a minute. What's going on in there?"

"I have to make the strategic choices. You can't abuse the

free sample offer, so I figure four max, and I need to decide which are the best four."

Jack pulled me into his chest for a hug and dropped a kiss on my head. "Marie, can we get Emily here one of everything?"

I loved the feeling of being claimed like that, not in an ownership way but in a declarative way, like, "I'm with her." But I couldn't let him take advantage of the receptionist, so I pushed away to protest.

He tightened his arms as Marie said, "Of course, Doc. I have a grandbaby coming that I'll get to see, thanks to you. Let me make up a box."

This time I extricated myself so I could look at him questioningly. "What did you..."

He shook his head. "Nothing. HIPAA. Can't talk about it. Sorry."

Marie had no qualms about it. "I came in for a wrist sprain and he noticed something wasn't right with my neck. Turned out I had early stage thyroid cancer which is very treatable if you catch it early enough. He called me every day until I went to the specialist in Portland. I was treated and clear within a month and it's been two years without problems. So yes, you get one of everything."

"Thank you," I said, "but honestly, I'm happy to pay you."

"The best currency around here is gossip. Why don't you tell me how you and Dr. Hazlett met? Then I'm going to go tell everyone at Annie's. He hasn't let any of us fix him up since he's been here. And believe me, we've all made our single daughters fake an illness to get an appointment with him."

I grinned at Jack. "Did you know this was going on?"

"I have seen a lot of women in the 25-35 age range with vague symptoms and familiar last names."

"Now you understand why you have to tell me," Marie said.

"It's not that interesting." Jack tried to shepherd me along the length of the display case to distract me with the chocolate. Normally, this would be a smart plan. But I liked Marie, so I stepped closer to the counter where she was tucking truffles into the box.

"Did you know Jack does a little moonlighting?" I asked with a lowered voice.

"With the ski patrol? Sure, everyone knows that."

I threw a look at him over my shoulder. I hadn't. "No, I meant as…" I leaned closer and whispered loudly, "as a male dancer for bachelorette parties. He was the guest of honor for my sorority sister's party a few months ago, and we just had a special connection. He gave me back one of my dollar bills I…you know…" I mimed tucking dollar bills, "at the end of the night with his phone number scrawled on it."

"That's not true, Marie." I would have expected Jack's tone to be the same one my dad used with my mom any time she tried to converse with him after more than two glasses of wine. Instead, Jack sounded like he was choking back laughter. "Excuse me, I think I need to take Emily here back to the clinic and adjust her meds."

"I know it's not true, but I can tell this woman is exactly what you need," Marie said, handing me the box with a grin. "Keep him hopping, girl. It's good for him."

"I will," I said around the truffle I'd already popped into

my mouth. "Oh, dear heavens, I think I'm going to die."

"Yeah, we have that effect on people. Guess it'll be up to Jack to resuscitate you with some mouth—"

"Bye, Marie!" he called over his shoulder as he pushed me out of the door. "You happy with yourself?" he asked once we were on the sidewalk.

"Oh, yeah." I finished off the truffle. "This is the first time I've ever felt like I balanced the scales after those Photoshops. We're finally on even footing."

He pulled me against him and wrapped his arms around me, resting them easily at my waist. "What are you talking about? You've had the upper hand since the start."

"No way." I plucked out another truffle and took a bite. "Caramel," I said, my eyes closing. I savored it for another minute, but more than that, I gave myself over to the happiness of him holding me without any hesitation or worry about who might pass by and see. I opened them to find him staring at me, watching me, like he was assessing and diagnosing. "What?"

"Do you really not see it? That you've always been the one with all the power here?"

I swallowed, my mouth suddenly dry as his eyes bored into mine. "That doesn't sound even a little bit correct. You were the one who set all the rules about what we could talk about, who decided what we did on our dates."

"That's because from the minute you made that joke about my man bun, I knew I was a goner. I was trying to put the brakes on an avalanche."

My smile faded as he handed me the words, plain and true, no hiding. "What are we going to do?" I whispered.

He knew what I meant. I knew he did, but he deliberately misunderstood me and stepped back to take my hand. "We've got a few more businesses for you to embarrass me in."

I let him misdirect. I didn't want to have a conversation about what would happen between us after this weekend. I just wanted to be right here, right now, doing nothing and everything with Jack.

We wandered into a real estate office where the agent also sold handknit goods and used books. I left with a beanie for Ranée and a vintage edition of fairy tales. "I've been collecting these since I was a kid," I said, showing him the watercolor illustrations. "You can tell by the colors that this is one of the ones where they sanitize all the endings and nothing too bad happens to anyone."

"Do they make any other kind?"

"Sure," but I didn't want to talk about those, the ones where the heroes learned tragic lessons and the young beauties died too young. So I pulled him down the street to the next business. We popped into the grocery/bait shop and the post office. I checked to make sure Jack wasn't on the FBI's Most Wanted list posted on the bulletin board among the index cards filled with handwritten requests for people to come work the fields. But as we stepped out of the post office, the novelty was wearing off.

"Next business is the last business," I declared.

He glanced at it. "Linda's Beauty Parlor?"

"Yes," I said, following his gaze. I hadn't known that was next door, but the second I saw the sign, a plan formed in my mind. "It's perfect."

A woman with a shade of red hair someone in the beauty parlor had helped her achieve looked up when we walked in. “Hey, Doc. What can we do you for?”

He held up his hands in an I-don’t-know gesture and pointed at me. “Hey, Linda. I have no idea.”

“Do you guys offer manicures here?”

“Sure. Let me see if Cheryl is free to run over and do that for you. Otherwise we’ll have to make an appointment.”

“Oh, and can we get Jack a blowout?”

“Excuse me?” he said, looking alarmed.

“Wash and a blow dry,” I explained. “It’s about the best thing ever. Every long-haired person should have this done professionally once in a while.”

“That I can do,” Linda said. “Hang on.” She disappeared through an office door in the back for a couple of minutes before she returned and reported with a smile, “I called Cheryl. She’s free for your manicure. Come on back, Dr. Hazlett.”

She had just gotten him settled with a towel around his neck in front of the sole wash basin when the door opened and a woman dressed like a Thanksgiving place setting walked in. She wore her long gray hair in two braids, no makeup, and different layers of linen and cotton in shades of brown and orange. I thought maybe it was a tunic and skirt, but I wasn’t totally sure.

“You’re lucky you caught me when I was over at the bank or I wouldn’t have been in until Monday.”

“Manicure Monday,” Linda said cheerfully. “She’s busy all day long and the women of Featherton are happy again. You’re lucky she came in.”

“Have a seat over here.” Cheryl pointed to a manicure

station tucked into the corner.

I settled into the chair as she pulled out her supplies. “Thank you for taking me last minute.”

“Are you kidding? I wouldn’t miss the chance to get a look at whoever finally snagged the doc.”

Ah. Well, now I knew why Linda hadn’t made the phone call in front of us, and what she’d offered to lure Cheryl: live bait.

“I haven’t snagged anyone,” I said.

“She has,” Jack called.

I glanced over at him, only able to see the underside of his jaw as Linda rinsed his hair. “Just for now,” I said to Cheryl, low enough that he couldn’t hear me. But I didn’t want to think about what happened after the weekend ended, so I smiled and asked her about herself as I studied the small salon. It was a hyphenate, I discovered. Like the grocery-bait shop and the real estate-yarn goods place, this was the salon-beauty supply. Shelves covered the back wall with not just the requisite shampoos and conditioners (she carried only drugstore brands) but a small assortment of nail polishes, cheap cosmetics, lotions, hair elastics, and…shot glasses? I decided not to ask, but I would definitely be picking up one as a souvenir.

I turned back to smile at the manicurist. “I’ll go with a clear coat.”

Linda snorted loudly. “No, you won’t. Cheryl decides what color you’ll get, and you’ll like it or else.”

Cheryl was an artist, I discovered, and didn’t have much use for manicures herself, but it was a nice way to supplement her income from the chainsaw sculptures she made of fallen logs.

“You’re going to answer some questions for me while I

work on your cuticles here, and then I'll pick your color. Now. Let's start with your favorite book of all time."

I answered her questions for the next few minutes, including my preference for milk or dark chocolate, how I liked to spend my days off, and my Myers-Briggs personality profile. Jack shouted the answers to any of the questions he knew, and each time, Cheryl would crook an eyebrow at me, and I would nod that he was right. Because he was.

"I've decided on your color," she said, and plucked a bottle of a coral that verged on orange from her bin.

It was the exact opposite of anything I would have chosen for myself, but I was too scared of her to say anything, so I let her get to work while I watched Jack. "How's it going over there?"

He grunted something I couldn't make out. It sounded like he'd fallen under the spell of Linda's shampooing. I smiled. Having someone else shampoo my hair was one of my favorite luxuries.

I amused myself by studying the rest of the salon. There was no theme to the décor. The floor was a serviceable gray tile, worn but clean. Linda's only cutting station had a plain mirror in an outdated black plastic frame, and a pile of magazines, no gossip rags in the mix. It was all cooking and gardening magazines.

"Done with this hand," Cheryl said. I fixed a polite smile on my face to examine them when she let go of my fingers, but I lost it as my jaw dropped when I looked at my nails. She'd painted them white but stamped them with a pattern of vivid coral rose vines. I'd never had nail art in my life, but I was immediately in love.

"Oh my gosh, I want my nails like this forever." I turned them back and forth to admire them as she went to work on my other hand.

"Now you see why she's always booked up. The ladies all have standing appointments, and she'll only let them come in every two weeks so she can fit everyone in. Even in a place as small as Featherton, they keep her busy."

"You're a genius," I said. "Jack? I want to go to Cheryl's place to see her sculptures tomorrow."

Linda grinned at me. "The poor guy fell asleep."

I looked over to see that Jack's body had indeed relaxed into the chair while Linda massaged his scalp. "If the town is keeping Cheryl busy, they must be running him ragged."

"I don't think so," Cheryl said. "Anybody who needs a specialist goes over to Sandy or even out to Portland if they have to. It's pretty easy to get an appointment with Dr. Hazlett if you need to. Same day, usually. We keep him busy enough for a country doctor, I guess, but just barely."

"Except for flu season," Linda said.

"Except for flu season," Cheryl agreed.

"Flu?" Jack repeated in the groggy voice of someone who dozed off.

"Hush," Linda said. "Relax while I rinse this conditioner out, then we'll get you dried."

By the time she had him settled into the barber chair with a cape around his neck, Cheryl finished my other hand and had started on the top coat. I watched as Linda combed through the long strands of his hair. The water had made it seal-dark and shiny, and it hung past the tops of his shoulders.

"I've been itching to get my hands on this since you got to town," she said, picking up a section of his hair and peering at it more closely.

"You and half the women in Featherton," Cheryl said.

Linda shot her a quelling glance. "I mean in a professional capacity."

"I didn't," Cheryl said, which made Jack squeeze his eyes shut like he thought it would make him invisible, and I laughed.

"Cut it off," I said. "Then maybe the ladies will leave you alone."

"I don't know," Linda mused, combing through it some more. "I kind of worry if we sheared him that none of the single ladies in town will survive a clean-cut Jack."

I rose and came to stand beside her, studying Jack in the mirror as she pulled his hair back. "You're right. Right now, he's barely resistible. I'm in trouble if he goes clean-cut."

He met my eyes in the mirror for a long second, and the jokes drained right out of me. I wasn't kidding anymore. I had almost no defenses against this man or his deep, thoughtful gazes that seemed to see beyond everything I said to all the things I didn't.

"You're safe," he said at last, reaching behind him to undo the Velcro of the cape. "I'm not cutting it."

"Hey, I still need to dry it," Linda protested as he rose from the chair.

"I always just let it air dry," he said. "Don't worry about it. It's getting late, and I need to figure out what to do with this woman for dinner."

"I can draw you a diagram," Cheryl said, and when Linda

hooted with laughter, I wasn't sure whether it was Jack or I who was more embarrassed as he tossed some bills on Linda's counter on our way out of the salon.

"Sorry about that." He smiled down at me when we reached the safety of the sidewalk. "I can't promise it won't happen with someone else. Anyone my mom's age or older around here likes to bust my chops."

"Why won't you cut your hair?" I asked. The question surprised me. I'd wanted to know for almost as long as I'd known Jack, but I hadn't known I was about to ask.

"That's a long story."

"I've got a few days." I held my breath, hoping he wasn't about to retreat again the way he had in so many other conversations.

He tucked a strand of it behind his ear. "Tell you what. Let's grab some stuff at the grocery store and make dinner at my house. I'll tell you the story, and if you're still in the mood we can watch a movie after or something."

"Works for me."

He pulled out his phone. "I'll text you directions because Google Maps doesn't acknowledge its existence. That way you can follow me and leave if you want to."

"Why would I want to?"

But he didn't answer, instead tapping at his phone and nodding when my cell buzzed. "There. Let's hit the grocery store and get this over with."

Chapter 36

Two hours later we sat at the small table in his little cabin in the woods. It was a one-bedroom caretaker's cabin located a hundred yards from a much larger custom log home. The big house belonged to a tech executive who was rich enough to afford it but too busy to use it much, according to Jack. He had the run of the place so long as he kept an eye on things and made sure the cupboards stayed stocked. He'd offered to prep and serve dinner up at the main house, but I wanted to stay in the little cabin, in his space.

I glanced around as I twirled the fettucine on my fork. Jack had made alfredo sauce while I prepped a salad, but I suddenly didn't have much of an appetite. My eyes wandered the cabin for the hundredth time, trying to ferret out more details about Jack, who he was, what went on in his mind. But the small living room and kitchenette told me no more than what he'd shown me weeks ago on FaceTime.

"Something wrong?" he asked, and my attention snapped back to him. His expression was neutral except for his watchful eyes. I had a feeling they didn't miss much—now or ever.

"I'm waiting to hear the story of why you don't cut your hair."

He sighed. "Dinner probably isn't the time for it. It's sad."

"Is there ever going to be a good time for it?"

"I guess not." He pushed his noodles around on his plate. They were good, but he didn't seem to have any interest in the food. "You know I was a pediatric oncologist. I picked that specialty when I was young and dumb because I thought I could make a difference. When I was a kid, I had this best friend named Lucas who lived three houses down, and he died of kidney cancer when we were nine. It sucked. When I did my oncology rotation, something clicked for me. I was young and full of energy and most importantly, wildly arrogant. You have to be to succeed as a specialist."

He took a few bites, lost in his thoughts. I ate quietly and let him wander until he was ready. "I was willing to take risks that older and more seasoned doctors wouldn't. I pushed for experimental treatments that patients could only get at the elite hospitals in the country, but I wanted them here, in Oregon, for kids whose families couldn't uproot everything to go to the Mayo Clinic or Johns-Hopkins. And it worked more than it didn't. The board quit fighting me and started giving me free rein in trying these experimental protocols. It went to my head. I started to believe that I could work miracles."

"Because you were working miracles?" I interjected softly.

He shook his head. "There are no miracles. Only science, and only statistical anomalies that broke my way a few more times than they should have. But I didn't see it at the time. I was unstoppable, and we were sending kids into remission in cases where no one thought we could. Then we got Clara."

He reached up to smooth a hank of hair with the mindless distraction of someone who had made the same gesture a thousand times. "Clara was ten when she came in with an osteosarcoma. Bone cancer," he said, when I shot him a questioning look. "She was a tiny thing and already obsessed with gymnastics. She came to her first appointment in a leotard because the mass was in her hip and she said it would make it easier for us to examine it without having to show everyone her underwear every time." He smiled. "She was a pistol. And gifted. Her mom told me that Clara had already been placed on her gym's athlete development track because her natural talent was so raw that they could already see it."

I knew how this story ended, how it had to have ended for him to go hide on a rural mountainside. But even if I wasn't sitting in the place he'd escaped to, I would have known the outcome because it was carved into every line of his face.

"It was bad," he said. "The conventional protocol was clear. Cut it out, then treat the area with radiation to kill anything that was left behind. But it would have meant taking enough of her hip that she would have to keep getting hip replacement surgeries for the rest of her life."

"And no gymnastics."

"No gymnastics. So I did an insane amount of research, convinced one of the most brilliant surgeons from the hospital where I did my residency to come and operate in a way that left the greatest amount of bone in place, and then put her in a clinical trial for a new immunotherapy treatment. I was convinced it would work. I could have taken a safer route that would have killed the cancer, but this was going to cure her *and* let her keep competing." He pushed the noodles around his plate some more. "Have you ever known anyone with cancer?"

"No one close to me. One of my high school teachers died of breast cancer a couple of years ago, but no one in my family."

"You're lucky. Like wildly lucky, statistically. I'm glad you haven't seen how ugly this disease is up close. It eats people up. That's what it does. It eats away everything healthy and good inside of them, and it is so evil that it will do it even when winning means it kills its own host, and it dies. So it was my job to kill it first. That means my patients are miserable and so sick from the medicines I give them that sometimes they beg to die."

He pushed his plate away and pressed the heels of his hands into his eyes for a minute, the way I sometimes did when I got tension headaches. "Clara, she was terrified. She had this huge mop of curly brown hair, and when it started falling out, I found her crying in her room one day. She told me that the only two things that made her pretty were her gymnastics and her hair, and now she was losing both. So I told her hair was stupid anyway, and I would shave mine off until hers grew back. She said, 'No way. One of us has to stay pretty,' and she made me promise I wouldn't cut mine until hers grew back, and that for every inch hers grew, I'd cut an inch off mine."

"But hers never grew back," I said, guessing the end of the story. I reached over and slipped my hand into his. There was nothing else to say.

"No. Because I was arrogant. Because I didn't follow the protocol that could have saved her. Because I believed I could heal her and keep her competing. And now she'll never do any of it." He pulled his hand from mine and rose, scooping up a light jacket as he reached for the door. "I'm sorry. I need some air. Stay as long as you like, but I understand if you decide to leave."

The door shut behind him, leaving me at the table with two half-eaten meals and a salad neither of us had managed to pick at. I cleared the dishes and put all the food away.

I sat on the sofa to wait for him, studying the sparse cabin again. He'd fled here for refuge, but it had become his prison. He was trapped on this mountain by his pain and his guilt.

I had no idea if and how that would ever change. All I knew for sure was that it needed to. But as long minutes stretched into hours with no sign of Jack and my texts unanswered, the less sure I was that it ever could.

Chapter 37

A little over two hours had ticked past on my watch. I was debating whether or not I should text Sean to ask how worried I should be that Jack still wasn't back when my phone went off.

"Hey," I said, snatching it up as soon as I saw Jack's name on the caller ID. "Are you okay?"

"I'm fine," he said. "I walked the main road so far that I was closer to Sean's place than mine, so I called him, and he picked me up."

It was a gut punch. I'd spent the whole time he was gone trying to figure out how to connect with him, and he'd spent it running away. Again. Like he had from so many of our conversations. "You're with Sean now?"

"Yeah. Look, I'm going to crash with him tonight. I'll be back in the morning, but the roads aren't lighted up there, so go ahead and stay tonight. It's not a great drive into town if you don't know the road. Take my bed or the sofa, whatever you want. I'll see you in the morning, okay?"

"Sure, great." It was all I could get out before I hung up. I turned the phone off completely and dropped it in my purse before I stood and looked around the living room. I could fit on the sofa, but it would be tight. I wandered to Jack's small bedroom. It was as stark as the rest of the house, a double bed with a plain navy comforter on it, bare walls, and a dresser with a small pile of change on top.

I retrieved an afghan from the living room and curled up on top of Jack's comforter. I wanted to make sure he made it home in the morning, and then…

A tear rolled across my nose and dropped to the blanket. More were coming, and I knew it. But it hurt. It hurt that Jack had finally told me about the pain he'd been carrying with him for two years but didn't trust me to share. He'd taken off literally at the first possible second. From his job. From his life.

And now, from me.

While we'd laughed and shared and teased all day, I'd felt a growing sense of need, a desire to know everything about the man whose kisses made me lose all sense of time and place only to find myself in his eyes again. I needed Jack in my life, and my brain had been trying to figure out how to make it work the whole time we were together.

None of that mattered.

Even if I convinced Jack to leave Featherton and bring his talents to San Francisco, I'd never have all of him. He'd bricked himself behind a wall of pain I couldn't break down. Not by jokes and distraction, not by coming to meet him on his turf, and not even by sitting and listening and carrying the weight of his pain with him in the quiet of his home.

At first, I wasn't even sure what I was crying for. Missed

opportunities, maybe. But mostly for the tragic waste of it all, for the brilliant doctor I could see that he'd been and should be again. But he wouldn't be. He was going to stay here, holed up on this mountainside, keeping in all the pain, but also locking away all of his gifts.

I cried it all out, waiting for sleep to overtake me, but it wouldn't come. Instead, I ran through all of our conversations and every single touch, every kiss. Every look. Every word I'd fought to drag from him, then had hoarded and replayed over and over during the last two months.

As evening wore into the deepest part of the night, I admitted the hardest truth: I'd seen this pattern of running from the hard things before. In my mom. I'd watched it play out and wreak havoc on people who hadn't deserved the pain. Like my dad. Like the many who had come after him. I hadn't known how to fix it then, but I'd sworn never to make their mistake.

I had, though.

Now I would pay for it.

***

I'd set my alarm for 6:00 AM so I could be on the road at first light, but it wasn't the alarm that woke me. It was the warm, heavy weight of an arm across my waist. An arm with Jack's watch around its wrist.

Jack had obviously come in at some point and kicked off his shoes before crawling onto the bed next to me. I glanced down to where he'd thrown his leg over mine too. I couldn't believe I'd slept through that, but I'd been up late, staring into the dark and trying to solve an unsolvable problem before I'd fallen into an exhausted sleep. Maybe it wasn't such a surprise that I'd slept through his arrival.

I moved to slide off the bed, but his arm tightened, and he nuzzled his face into my hair, murmuring my name on a soft sigh.

"Jack," I whispered. "I need to go."

He lifted his head to peer down at me. "Where are you going? Stay. I'll make you breakfast." He leaned down and kissed me.

I shouldn't have let him do it. It would only make leaving more difficult, and not just because we were completely tangled up again. "I need…" I tried before immediately losing my train of thought when he murmured an agreement and claimed my mouth.

I ran my hands down his shoulders, still in the shirt he'd been wearing yesterday, lost in the heat and hunger.

"I missed you," he said softly when he pulled away before shifting his attention to my earlobe which he caught with a light nip of his teeth. "I shouldn't have left," he said as I slid my hands through his hair.

It was the feeling of the long strands in my fingers and that last sentence that finally broke through the fog, and I let go of his hair to press my hand against his lips.

"No." I pushed against him and squirmed away, remembering why his hair was so long in the first place. I slid off the bed and found my feet. "No, you don't get to sneak back in here like nothing is wrong."

He dragged himself up until he was sitting with his back against the wall. "I know I shouldn't have left. That's what I'm saying."

"I mean, bonus points for coming back, I guess, but it's not nearly enough to make up the difference," I muttered as I scanned the floor for my shoes. It was light enough to see now. I'd make it back into town without any problem. I'd shower at my hotel, change into fresh clothes, and drive back to Portland. The need to get back home, to where I understood everything happening around me and controlled every bit of it, overwhelmed me, and I hunted for my shoes with greater urgency. I needed to get out of here.

"Can we talk about it at least?" He ran his fingers through his hair which looked like he hadn't brushed it.

"I don't know. Can we? Because it actually seems like we can't. One step forward and two steps back isn't going to get us anywhere, and that's what keeps happening." I finally located the black leather booties I'd paired with my skinny jeans and slid one on.

"You mean two steps forward, one step back."

I straightened and stared at him. "No, I don't. I meant it exactly how I said it. Every time we get a little closer, you push me away again, but it hurts worse every time. I know I'm not a relationship expert, but that's not good. In fact, that's a fatal program bug."

I walked out to the living room and snatched up my purse to rummage for the keys. Jack was right behind me. "So that's it?"

I spun to face him. "If by 'it' you mean how I've spent months trying to coax you to open up, and then I flew up here to surprise you against every ounce of common sense I have, and then it turns out that I never should have come but at least I know that now, so hey, that's a thing that I learned, then yes. I guess that's it."

"You're just giving up?"

"I'm not a quitter! YOU are."

He stepped back like I'd slapped him. I reached out, maybe to snatch back the words, but he flinched, and I let my hand drop. I didn't want to hurt him, but the words were true. "You're hiding, Jack. You're hiding up here when Sean says you can easily find someone in semi-retirement to take over the clinic. You're letting other people fight your battles for you at your old job because it got too hard."

"That's easy to say for someone whose job stakes are whether a program will get a bug or not."

I bent to put on my other boot, and to compose myself. "I will never understand what it's like to lose a patient. But I know quitting when I see it. And so should you, because you're right. I quit this. I can't be a part of this half-life you've made for yourself, and I can already tell you're not going to try to become a part of mine."

"That's not fair," he said.

"Am I wrong? Have you been thinking lately about how you're finally ready to join the wider world again?"

He wouldn't meet my gaze. Instead, he crossed his arms and kept his eyes fixed on the floor. "No. That's not going to happen because I didn't run away from it. I found a different way to help, and it's here. Look." He walked over to the large, sleek monitor I'd seen in the background of so many of our conversations. "This is the only thing I *can* do," he said flipping it on. A minute later, a series of photos filled the screen. "This is why I learned to Photoshop."

I stepped closer to study them. They showed kids in superhero costumes or dressed as powerful knights and warriors. Some looked like ordinary kids. Others bore the clear signs of a fight with cancer; bald heads, steroid-puffed cheeks. I glanced at him, my eyebrows lifted in question.

"I make them heroes in their battles. It lets them visualize a victory. I get dozens of requests a week, and I do them for free."

They were beautiful. Hopeful. And a tremendous gift—from anyone else. If Jack couldn't do the other things he did, this alone would have made me fall a tiny bit in love with him. But he could.

"You have the ability to do so much more for them. These are incredible photos, but you could be changing the outcome in a real way. Treating them. Healing them."

He shut the monitor off. It went black. It was abrupt. Final. "I found a different way to fight. I hate that you can't see it for what it is."

"And I hate that I do." A deep sadness swept over me, smoothing out the angry places and drowning them in regret. "I've never told you much about my parents. They split when I was nine because my mom, she's broken inside. She's always chasing the next romantic high, the shiny new love. It never lasts, because when the new relationship sparkle fades, she can't deal with looking at the real stuff underneath. And for her, it's the feeling that she's never enough." My hands closed around my keys, and I fought the urge to run to the door. "I've watched a string of men try to fix her, put her back together, but it's useless until she patches up some of her own wounds. And still, there's some poor sucker always lining up to try. I swore I'd never do the same thing for someone. But here I am."

A fresh wave of tears threatened, and I closed my eyes against them for a moment.

"Emily—"

I held up my hand. "No, let me say this." I drew a calming breath and refused to let the tears fall. "I should have seen this. But I convinced myself somehow that if I could say the perfect words, behave exactly the right way, find the right sequence of conversations and grand gestures, that this would work out. I swore it wasn't my job to save you, because no one can rescue another person. They have to do it themselves. I know this." I squeezed my eyes shut again. "I used to know this. But I can't control your brokenness. Why did I forget that?" The last part was only a whisper.

"Emily, stay. We've got everything else right between us. There has to be a way to fix this." He shoved his fingers through his hair the way he did when he was stressed. "Please."

"I don't know how." I walked to the door, pausing before I slipped through it. "I have never been so close to something this real. I've done everything I can. And I may have failed, but at least I tried. Goodbye, Jack."

His silence said everything as the door clicked shut behind me, and I started the long drive back to town.

Chapter 38

I pulled into the spot in front of my motel bungalow and parked, resting my head against the back of my seat and closing my eyes, letting the scene I'd just left play on a loop in my mind. I didn't want to go. But there was no point to staying.

When I'd reached that conclusion for the tenth time, I climbed out of my car to change my flight, shower and pack.

A man got out of the car next to me at the same time. I instinctively tightened my hands around my purse strap before a voice I knew called my name softly, and I looked up to find Sean coming around his car.

"Sorry, I didn't mean to scare you. Jack texted me and asked me to check on you, make sure you're okay."

I squeezed my eyes for a second before opening them and staring down at my disheveled self. "Just so you know, this isn't a walk of shame."

"I know. Jack was very clear that he's been an idiot. He said you were pretty upset when you left. He wanted to make sure you got back safely, but he didn't think you'd answer if he called."

"True enough. I'm fine. I'm going to shower and head to the airport."

"I checked the flights while I was waiting for you. If you let me take you to breakfast, you can still make the noon flight."

I hesitated. I just wanted to get home.

He smiled. "I'll even call Ranée and tell her to pick you up and make her promise not to ask any questions."

"Deal."

"Meet me at Annie's in an hour?"

"Stupid Annie's."

He looked startled. "What?"

"Nothing. Yes, I'll be there in an hour."

And I was, feeling cleaner and unwrinkled but somehow no better. I slid into the booth he'd claimed. "Omelet," I said to the waitress, who appeared as soon as I sat. "Whatever the cook likes best. I'll eat anything. And a large cup of coffee. Very strong coffee."

"So it didn't go well?" Sean prompted me.

"No. It really didn't, but honestly, I'm exhausted. I was up late worrying about him, and I don't have the energy to rehash it."

"He told me the whole story, I think."

"Doubt it," I said.

"He told you about Clara, that he failed to save her, the tragic loss forced him to confront his own limits, he looked into a bleak future of losing more kids than he saved, and he couldn't do it anymore, so he ran?"

"Uh, I don't think he put it quite that dramatically. But basically."

"I guess I just added my own personal twist to the story, because that's what it was like for me. I'd been on the floor for two years already when Jack started there. I was in the early stages of burnout, but I didn't know it yet. We worked together for two years, and we lost patients before Clara. But her loss hit us extra hard. Did he tell you why?"

"Because he tried a highly risky treatment so she could still do gymnastics and he lost the gamble when he could have saved her?"

He nodded, slowly. "And because we knew Clara. Before she ever got sick, I mean. Her mom is a surgeon at the hospital. She and Jack had worked on several cases together. Clara had been coming to see her mom at the hospital since she was five, dropping in with her dad so they could eat together in the hospital cafeteria, coming to play with the patients who weren't in isolation. We were all crazy about the kid, which is why Jack wouldn't take the case at first. But Dr. Mendel—Sheila, Clara's mom—begged him to. Wouldn't let him refer her out, said she trusted him."

The waitress returned with my coffee, but I was wide awake now. I took a sip, but I was too riveted by Sean's story to need the caffeine. "And he finally agreed."

"Yeah." Sean scrubbed his hands over his face. "It was a bad idea. She's a formidable woman, and she pushed Jack hard to try the riskier protocol. I think it's because as a surgeon, she knew exactly what Clara was in for if they did the more aggressive excision on the affected bone. And I think she truly believed Jack could pull it off."

"But he didn't."

"It wasn't his fault. No one blamed him when Clara relapsed. She came in for her quarterly screening because she had severe bruising. We all knew that meant the cancer was back, but she'd been clean two months before. None of us expected it to be stage four." He took a sip of his own coffee and stared through the window for a long minute before turning back to me. "That was my worst day as a nurse. The day you find out that there's nothing you can do is even worse than the day you lose them, because you know what's coming."

It was horrible. I couldn't imagine it. I stared into my mug and blinked back tired tears. "That's so hard. No wonder Jack couldn't keep doing that job."

"It wasn't just him. I left first, and when I'd been working for a couple of months here, I started to feel like I could breathe again. I invited him out to spend a week, get re-centered. But instead he got a job. I was the last person who was going to tell him he had to go back to war. So if you're going to judge him for running, I guess you have to judge me too."

His voice had acquired a defensive edge, and I met his eyes, then reached over to lightly touch his sleeve. "I don't judge either of you for leaving. But I'm never going to be enough for him to overcome something like that. I'm not enough to coax him back to life, to leave the safety net he's found here."

"I don't know," Sean said as the server returned to set a plate in front of each of us. "I'm not so sure that's true. You want to know why I was in San Francisco last week?"

"To show Ranée your dog?"

He shook his head. "I didn't tell her because you know how she fixates on stuff, but I had a job interview. I want to get back into nursing, but I want to work for the VA, helping rehabilitate soldiers, maybe apply to physical therapy school."

My jaw dropped. "Sean. That's amazing."

He gave me a shy smile. "Thanks. Eat your omelet. I'll quit bugging you."

The cook had made me a Southwestern omelet, and it was excellent. I'd never met a tragedy that could suppress my appetite yet, and when we'd both cleaned our plates, Sean pulled out some cash and set it on the table. "My treat. I won't keep you anymore. I know you have a flight to catch."

He walked me out to the rental car and paused before opening the driver's door for me. "Hey, Em, none of this has ever been my business, but for what it's worth, I think you should give Jack a little time to come around."

"He's had three years. I don't think I'm the magic bullet that's going to change things."

"I never thought I'd want to get back into nursing full-time, but it looks like I can't shake it. And if I can't, I don't think Jack can either. I think it's just a matter of time."

I slumped against the car. "I don't know. I tried to invite him back to real life, and he made it clear that he'd rather keep half-living than to see if we have a shot."

"You could move here, maybe find a job that you can work remotely."

I glanced the short distance down Main Street and its hodgepodge of hyphenate businesses then met his eyes again.

He sighed. "You're right. You belong in San Francisco. Give me a hug and then get out of here."

I held up my finger. "On one condition. Stop meddling.

No more talking about Jack, even if you move to San Francisco and you're living on our couch indefinitely."

"Agreed." He hauled me in for a hug, and then I got in and drove away, letting Featherton become a green smudge in my rearview mirror.

Chapter 39

Ranée drove me home, and true to his word, Sean had managed to put a muzzle on her. She didn't ask me about anything besides the weather even though I could feel every atom in her straining to squeeze the details out of me. When we got back to the apartment, I headed straight for bed. "I need to sleep."

"Hey!" I turned around in my doorway, waiting for her dam of questions to break. Instead she ran down the hall to grip my shoulders. "You going to be okay?"

"Eventually."

"Then let a nap do its magic."

It was three hours before I woke up and stumbled out again in search of food.

Ranée smiled at me from the sofa. "Hi, sleepyhead. I'll order Mexican."

And somehow, an hour later, we'd settled on the sofa, a shared blanket spread across our laps with a dozen tacos between us. She pulled the whole story out of me before we even got to the flan.

"So he's living his stupid hermit life with his stupid hermit hair in his stupid hermit town," I concluded.

"Team Jack," she said.

"Ranée! You're supposed to be on my side."

She fell quiet, shadows chasing each other across her face. "You okay?" I asked. I'd never seen this expression on her before, like she'd lived a decade in those quiet moments.

She sighed. "I thought I understood how hard Sean's job was because we talked a lot while he was working at that hospital. This was before I even met you. He'd call to decompress, and I'd come up with these motivating pep talks to help him get back in there. So I thought I got it, and that I was being supportive. Now that I work at the barn..."

"I thought you loved volunteering there."

"I do. But it's only been four months and we've already lost some kids. The idea is that they're at-risk and we're trying to connect them to a supportive community, or with these horses because they've been let down by so many people but the animals, they don't judge. Then maybe they can connect to the human part of the community. It works sometimes. But a lot of times it doesn't. These kids, it's not enough for them. The damage runs too deep, and we can't reach them. I mean, how stupid to think we can. We haven't lived a fraction of what they deal with. So they don't die like the kids Sean worked with, but it feels like that a little. One of the caseworkers came in last week and told us this girl I've been teaching every week got picked up by police when they found her half-dead of an overdose under the freeway. They gave her Narcan, so she survived the moment. But for how long? The caseworker says the client won't be back.

And it makes me sick inside. Could I have done something else? Become her mentor?"

She pushed the blanket off and gathered up our empty food containers. "But I can't do anything. And all it showed me is exactly how much I didn't understand what Sean was going through, how much harder it was than I knew."

"But you're sticking it out. You're there and you're feeling and you're trying. Jack isn't. I can't do anything about that."

"Yes. Because I think it works for some of them. But talk to me if I ever get word that one of the kids I've tried to help actually dies. It's hard enough knowing it might only be a matter of time."

She climbed back onto the couch with me. "Look, you know I'll have your back forever. But I don't think it was fair to say Jack isn't trying when you haven't fought the same kind of fights."

"That's not fair. You're acting like I don't understand what it feels like to work hard and fail."

She was unmoved. "I'm not saying you don't work hard. You do. You've faced a lot of challenges, but I don't think you've ever had to face real failure, the kind that cripples you because there's nothing in the world that you can throw at it to fix it." She sighed and smoothed her side of the blanket. "I've only had to deal with that for the first time in the last few weeks, and unless there's some major life story you've never told me, you've never faced the kind of stakes that are so high that it's win or die."

I wanted to tell her she was being dramatic, but something about the quiet way she said it stopped me. Her words about high stakes had echoed Jack's. We sat in silence for a long time, and she didn't try to scrub away the sadness and put on her cheerful face. Finally, I broke the silence. "I had no idea that it was so hard for you sometimes."

"I know. Because I didn't tell you. But Jack tried to."

An ugly, gray feeling crawled up through my stomach and spread through my chest. It was shame. "Ranée…I think I basically told Jack he was weak for running away."

Her gaze sharpened. "Weak? Did you use that word?"

"No, but I basically implied that he was because he was…"

"Being a stupid hermit?"

"Something like that." The shame crawled up the back of my throat like acid reflux.

"But you didn't say that he was weak. And you can come back from that."

"I need to call him and apologize." The urge was overwhelming, almost like panic. "What should I say?"

She pressed me back against the couch as I leaned over to fumble for my phone. "No. Don't call him. You're right that this isn't your problem to fix. That's the first thing you have to see. This is a problem that you can't solve by hammering at it. You can't. He has stuff he needs to work out, and maybe he will. But he might not. Not for a long time, if at all."

I shrank away from her, curling in slightly to protect my core from her gentle words.

"I don't know exactly what you're feeling right now, but I can see on your face that it's hard. And I'm so sorry for that. But you've been overdue for a heartbreak. I would never wish it on you, but I don't think we get to avoid them forever." She leaned over and drew me down to her lap, letting me keep my arms wrapped around myself. It felt like the only thing holding me together when all the pieces inside of me wanted to fall apart, fractured by the unbearable sadness I could finally feel. It wasn't a sadness over things not working out with Jack. It was the tiny glimpse that Sean, then Ranée, had given me of the magnitude of the pain that Jack must be carrying. And if it was enough to curl me into a ball, how was he still standing?

We stayed that way for a long time, an hour or more, just quiet, while I cried. The tears I'd cried the previous night were because I'd been hurt by Jack. These were because I hurt *for* him. They were quieter and infinitely harder.

And when I stopped crying, Ranée sat me up and put her hands on my shoulders, looking me in my swollen eyes. "That's the kind of crying someone does when she's giving up on a relationship. I don't know how you guys can make this work, but just ask yourself if you're ready to quit on something that matters this much to you. And that's all I'm going to say about it."

Then she put on Netflix and watched old episodes of *Murder, She Wrote* in silence until I finally fell asleep again and Ranée made me go back to my bed.

By Saturday afternoon, I felt more human again. I'd made myself a real breakfast, gone to the gym, and run Ranée's insights through my mind so many times that they got enough mileage to qualify for the Boston marathon. For all her bulldozer tendencies, she'd found the kindest possible way to tell me a hard truth: I lacked empathy.

I did. Whether I hadn't had the experiences necessary to develop it was beside the point. It was me who lacked some of the basic emotional skills that a real relationship required, not

Jack.

I sent Jack my first text since walking away from him.

`I'm sorry. I shouldn't have pushed.`

It wasn't meant as an invitation to say we should try again. Nothing had changed except that I realized I'd judged him far too harshly. But that didn't suddenly mean we had a path to move forward. All of the same obstacles blocked it.

But it didn't really matter what I meant, because by the time I was getting ready for bed, he still hadn't answered.

Ranée stopped by my room with a cup of chamomile tea. "I have a feeling you'll need this tonight."

"I'm okay."

"Then why do you look so sad?"

I tapped my cell phone. "I texted Jack a few hours ago, told him that I shouldn't have pushed. He hasn't texted back, and I don't think he's going to."

She sat on the bed. "He's tried in big and little ways to tell you how deep this pain runs for him. He may not believe that you really get it this time."

"That's because I don't. A tiny bit, maybe. More than I did. But nothing like what he must have gone through to walk away from it all." I plucked at the bedspread a couple of times. "About that. I have a plan. But it's hard."

"I'm listening."

"Do you think I should volunteer at Benioff?" That was the children's hospital. "Maybe it would help me understand things better."

She looked thoughtful. "I know Sean mentioned that they were always looking for volunteers at his hospital. The kids need the company or someone to play with them, and the parents need a break. I'm sure every children's hospital is like that. It's going to be hard watching the staff facing down battles that can't be won and fighting them anyway. It's going to wear you out, but...I don't know. My time at the barn has made me softer and stronger at the same time."

I turned the idea over in my head. "It sounds so hard."

"Maybe this is something life is trying to teach you right now. I think you have the right idea." Then she slipped out.

I sat there and thought about nothing else for the rest of the night.

Chapter 40

I snapped a selfie in front of the welcome sign at Benioff Children's Hospital as Sharon Kerns, the volunteer coordinator, walked by. She stopped and smiled. "First shift, right? Are you excited?"

"Nervous," I admitted.

"Don't be. The kids, they'll make it clear if they want company or not. They're used to the volunteers. Sometimes they want you in there but don't want to talk. Just follow their lead. You're doing these parents a huge service. Don't forget that."

"I'll try not to," I said. I was a respite playmate, essentially, on call to keep any of the kids company so their parents could run down to the cafeteria or take a walk without having to worry about leaving their sick kid alone.

"You're going to do great. But don't forget that there are no photos allowed once you're on the floor. Privacy laws."

"I know, I promise. I just need to send a text and then I'll put the phone away."

"Sounds good. Let me know if you need anything," she

said with a short wave as she continued through the double doors leading to the patient rooms.

I stared at my screen, unsure what to say. I hadn't texted Jack since the apology I sent after my disastrous trip up there. That had been a month ago, but I'd put my free time to good use, applying to the hospital's volunteer program and finishing their orientation and training.

`Hi,` I started, then paused, trying to figure out what to say. `I blamed everything on you. I've realized I have some growing to do. Just wanted you to know I'm trying.` Then I attached the picture so he could see my volunteer badge.

It didn't explain everything I wanted to tell him, but I wasn't sure there was anything to say, really. Not when it came down to it. Even if I gained the insight and emotional capacity of Mother Theresa, we might as well be worlds apart as ten hours apart in terms of trying to keep a relationship alive long-distance. But I owed it to him to show him that I'd heard what he said on our last, awful morning together. He'd gotten through.

I turned off the phone, took a deep breath, and pushed through the double doors to do what I could for a dozen kids fighting a battle I could never understand.

All the training in the world couldn't have prepared me for the next three hours. I sat with four different kids while their mom or dad stepped out for a quick dinner. They ranged in age from three to ten, three girls and one boy. Two of the girls, the youngest one and an eight-year-old, didn't want any interaction. I quietly sat and watched TV with them until their parents returned. A four-year-old girl wanted me to work the same twenty-piece unicorn puzzle with her over and over but didn't want to talk. We just put the pieces together then she'd dump them out and say, "Again," and we'd start over.

The ten-year-old was a boy, and he was playing a video game when I stepped into his room. I smiled at his mom. "Hi. Sharon said you requested respite?"

She stood and stretched. "Yeah, thanks. This is Tate. I'm going to go get some dinner." Her eyes flicked down to my name badge. "Emily is here to hang out with you until I get back, Tate. Why don't you tell her about all the stuff you're building?"

He was a skinny blond kid, pale like most of the kids on the ward, with big brown eyes. He flicked me a glance. "Do you like Minecraft?"

"I don't know anything about it," I said, settling into his mother's chair as she slipped out of the room. "Would it be super annoying if I asked you to explain it to me?"

He heaved a tired sigh. "I guess I can do that."

For the next forty minutes he explained all kinds of things like redstone and polished granite. I wasn't much of a gamer, but I didn't have to pretend to be interested. This wasn't as much about shooting or winning stuff as it was about building. He'd made the world's most imaginative superhero lair with cheerful digital cubes of stone, grass, and wood.

When his mom came back, she thanked me again as I left, but I said, "No, thank *you,*" and I meant it.

I turned my phone on as I left the hospital. When I saw a text alert from Jack, my fingers froze. I'd forgotten how it felt to see his name on my screen. It was like the moment when I opened one of my favorite books for a re-read and settled into the sweet comfort of the familiar opening lines.

Hey, Em.

It was as good as, "Mr. and Mrs. Dursley of number four, Privet Drive, were proud to say that they were perfectly normal, thank you very much," as far as happiness endorphins went.

You're amazing. But it is HARD. Don't put yourself through that. You don't have to prove anything to me.

It felt like there should be more, but that was it. I don't know what else I wanted there to be. He didn't sound mad at me. I already knew I'd re-read the part where he called me amazing so many times it would imprint on my eyeballs. But the rest of it...

What was there for him to say, really? I could volunteer every night of the week, but it would change nothing about the fundamentals of our situation.

I tapped out the only reply I could. I think I'm doing this for me.

Tate was the only kid still on the floor when I went back the next week. Volunteers had to commit to a three-hour shift at the same time every week for six months, and I could only do Thursdays, so the coordinator had told us to expect to see a new crop of faces on every visit. Mostly that was a good thing. It usually meant that the kid had been released to go home because they'd stabilized enough or completed a round of treatment.

As much as I wanted to see Tate's new creation, it made me sad that he hadn't been released yet. I poked my head in, and his mom gave me a tired smile. "Perfect. I'll grab some dinner, if that's okay."

“That’s great,” I assured her. “You build any cool new worlds, Tate?”

“I’m making a spaceship out of grass. Want to see?” And I pulled up a chair while he walked me through it.

This time when his mom came back, I turned on my phone long enough to order an ebook about Minecraft basics before I stopped by the next room. I really hoped Tate wouldn’t still be there the next week, but if he was, I wanted to be prepared.

I read it, just to be safe. Tate wasn’t the only kid who liked Minecraft, I’d noticed. It might give me something to talk about with other patients too. But when I saw his name on the card outside his door again the following week, my heart sank. We weren’t supposed to ask about their diagnosis. If the parent or child wanted us to know, they’d tell us. Our job was just to provide a break, and often a big part of the break was not talking about why we were all in a hospital room together.

“Hi, Tate,” I said, stepping into the room.

“Hi, Emily,” he said. He was the first kid to know my name when I walked in, and it made me happy that he remembered but sad that he’d been here long enough to learn it.

“Dinner,” his mom said like she didn’t have the energy to speak a full sentence. I watched her slip out, her shoulders down before I forced a smile on my face and turned back to my patient.

“Hi. So I was thinking about your spaceship. What if you built a secret room with polished andesite?”

He’d been lying back against his pillows, but at this, he raised the back of his bed higher and studied me, a faint glint in his eye. “How do you know about andesite?”

"I'm smart like that. Want to show me how to do it?" And he did. When his mom returned an hour later, I smiled at him. "Thanks, dude. My nieces are going to be so impressed the next time I visit them." I surrendered my seat to his mom and turned back at the doorway. "Hope I don't see you next week, Tate."

He grinned. "Hope I don't see you either."

But I stopped at the store on the way home and bought a Minecraft Lego set just in case. Ranée found me studying the pieces when she came home from a date with Paul.

"What are you doing?" she asked.

"Getting design ideas so I can help one of the kids at the hospital." I picked up some dirt blocks and snapped them to a gray piece to study the effect. "Ironically, although I work for a software company, it turns out that I'm better at building imaginary stuff in analog."

"You like volunteering, huh?"

"It puts things into perspective for sure. Like stuff at work is both less irritating, because I realize that problems I used to think were a big deal are definitely not a big deal, and more irritating, because I constantly want to choke people who are making it a big deal while I chant, 'There are worse things, you idiot.' So that's been interesting."

Ranée laughed. "I get it."

"How was your date with Paul?"

"Fine." She still wasn't comfortable giving me details no matter how often I promised I didn't care. "Speaking of dates..."

"Nothing to speak of," I said. "Haven't checked my app, don't know when I'll feel like it, and Jack hasn't texted, and I don't know if he will."

"Here's a new development. I've been keeping tabs on Jack through Sean, but Sean is moving out of Featherton."

I set down my Legos. "He got the job?"

She grinned. "Yeah. He starts at the VA in two weeks. He wants to know if he can crash on the sofa until he finds an apartment."

"That's so great! Of course he can crash. Tell him congratulations for me."

"I will. But now I won't really have a Jack connection anymore."

"It's okay." She'd passed on Sean's reports about Jack, which amounted to "same old, same old" every time. "I'm sure if something big ever happens to Jack, Sean will let us know." I'd miss getting a more personal account, but I still followed Jack's Twitter feed as he posted his Photoshops, as funny and absurd as ever. Us falling apart hadn't affected his sense of humor. Then again, there hadn't been an "us" for long enough to think it should.

"I still think he'll come around," she said. "Maybe you should text him again?"

But I shook my head. It wasn't pride that stopped me, or that it was his turn. It was something else I couldn't explain. And even if I could understand and work through the feeling that held me back from texting again, I wouldn't know what to say. I'd told him sorry the last time, but now after almost a month at the hospital, I could already sense how paltry that word was for the apology I owed him for not understanding. I wouldn't know how to find the words that captured the realization that was growing in me with each shift I worked.

"I'm starting to get why he doesn't have anything to say to me. It's okay. And now if you'll excuse me, I have to play with my Legos."

The next Thursday, I brought the kit with me. I figured I'd challenge Tate to a build-off, see who could make the coolest thing while his mom got her dinner, him digitally, me with my Legos. But when I got to his door, it wasn't his name there anymore. My heart sank, until I realized it meant he'd been able to go home, and then I smiled. That's exactly what he and his mom had both wanted. What was a bunch of dumb Minecraft Legos compared to that?

I went to deposit them in the playroom for any of the other kids on the floor who wanted to play. Usually the ones in there were the siblings of patients, but they could surely use some novelty too. I passed the nursing station on the way and smiled at the charge nurse, Shelley.

"I see that Tate got to go home. When was he discharged?"

She hesitated and shook her head. "He was released to hospice."

"Oh."

The words didn't register at first.

I checked the respite request list and stopped at the first room, a little five-year-old with an oxygen canula and a woolen beanie over her bald scalp. Her father thanked me and stepped out for some food. The little girl didn't want to talk, so I sat beside her and watched an animated dinosaur movie.

Hospice.

Hospice meant...

I didn't want to think about it.

But when my patient's dad came back, I stopped by Shelley's desk again. "Hospice means they decided to stop treatment?"

"It means there was nothing else to do. And now the family can focus on making him comfortable in the time he has left." Her eyes softened. "This is the first one you've lost?"

I nodded, my throat too tight to push words through.

"I'm sorry," she said. "It doesn't get easier. But we appreciate you being willing to come in here and do this. It's a godsend for these parents."

I could only nod again, afraid that if the knot in my throat loosened it would flood out in tears, and I moved on to the next patient.

When I got home that night, I searched Facebook for Tate's name and found a group his mom had set up to share his journey. I requested to join it, and the next morning before I went to work, I got a notification I'd been approved.

I scrolled through the group whenever I had a free moment at work, going all the way back to the first post where his mom had explained that they'd received a tough diagnosis for Tate, but he was a fighter and they were optimistic that with the love and prayers of the people who loved him and the elite team at Benioff, he was going to beat his illness. I could feel the sincerity and determination in every sentence and in the grinning photos she posted of him from his baseball team and with his little sister.

I checked it every single morning over breakfast before I left for work. Six days later, she posted a picture of Tate asleep in a hospital bed in what looked like a living room, a little girl, maybe three, napping beside him. It said, "Lucy won't leave his side."

I set my phone face down and stared at it.

Sean had arrived two days before, and now he sat down across from me with a toasted bagel in front of him.

"Want to go for a run later?"

His words barely registered as I stared at my phone.

"Whoa," he said, concern creeping into his voice. "You okay?"

I opened the picture and handed it to him. He knew I was volunteering at the hospital because I'd put him down as a reference. "He went on hospice care."

"I'm sorry," he said, handing it back. "Did you work with him much?"

"Not really. Just a couple of times." I made the screen go dark. "I can't believe how bad this feels."

He didn't say anything.

"How did you do this?" I asked.

"That's the thing. I couldn't after a while. It never got easier."

"I committed to a six-month volunteer term," I said. "I don't know how I'm going to do this for six months."

"Ask for a transfer to a different department," he said. "I'm not going to try to tell you to stick this out, and they're used to it. They know oncology isn't for everyone. They'll understand."

"I didn't," I said. "I didn't understand." All I could see was the exhaustion on Tate's mom's face when she would slip out to grab a quick dinner, then the memory of the exhaustion on Jack's during our last conversation. And his words. *I hate that you can't see it for what it is*. I'd blithely told him that I did, proud of myself for coming up with such a good argument-ending comeback before I'd walked away from him.

His words played over and over in my head. He was right. I hadn't seen his retreat for what it was: survival.

It hadn't even been my job to save Tate, and now his name was carved into my heart. How would I feel if it had been my job to cure him? How would it feel if I carried dozens of names the way I would always carry his?

I didn't sleep well, and the next night, when it was my shift at the hospital, I stopped and asked Shelley the question that I should have been asking Jack. "Shelley? How do you do this job when you keep losing kids?" How had Jack been able to do it for as long as he did?

She set down the tablet she'd been working on and gave me a resigned look. "Because sometimes we win. Not enough. But sometimes."

I nodded. "Okay. Thanks." I started down the hall to find the restroom and splash some cold water on my face before I found my next patient.

"Emily?" Shelley called.

I turned to see what she needed.

"You don't have to do this. Most people can't. Talk to the volunteer coordinator and let her know that you want to finish your volunteer term in a different department. It happens a lot. No one will think less of you for it."

"I would," I said quietly.

And I went to find my next patient.

I'd find Sharon later, not to request reassignment, but to

thank her for her work in coordinating. But that wasn't the only thing I needed to take care of.

I owed Jack another apology, a true apology now that I understood what I was apologizing for, even though there weren't any words that could make it right.

Chapter 41

"Sean?" It was Saturday morning, and I had stumbled out of bed to find him at the stove. "When are you getting your own place?"

"Why? You getting sick of me?"

"No." I sniffed the air. French toast. "I don't want you to leave. I get tired of making my own breakfast."

"Thanks, but Shep and I are kind of over living on your couch. I'm trying to work out a roommate situation that's maybe going to be perfect, then I'm out of here." He pulled down a plate and slid two pieces of French toast onto it. "These are yours. I'll make myself more."

"Roommate situation? I know I probably don't need to remind you of this, but don't go with a Craigslist rando. And whoever you move in with, check all their references. If you don't, you might end up living with someone like Ranée. I should have asked more questions."

"Ha," he said dryly. "Thanks, but this is someone I know. Should be fine."

"Oh good." I buttered my French toast and decided to skip

syrup. I'd had Sean's French toast before. It needed no drowning. "Have you talked to Jack lately?"

He paused in dredging another piece of bread in batter and looked at me in surprise. I hadn't asked since he'd gotten here. "Yeah."

"He's okay?"

"Yeah. I think he's doing well, actually."

Because I was a terrible person, that made me sad. I wasn't doing well. I missed him every day, and it hurt that moving on wasn't as hard for him. Then again, maybe it was easier when the person who walked out on you had been thoughtlessly cruel the way I had. But all I said was, "I'm glad to hear it."

I opened Facebook to Tate's page again, hungry for crumbs of information about him but also terrified to see what the newest update might be.

Instead, I found a new picture of Tate in a hospital room I didn't recognize. His dad stood on one side of him and a smiling doctor giving the camera two thumbs up stood on the other. It was timestamped from the night before and captioned, "New doctor, new treatment, new hope."

"Holy..." I muttered, scrolling through the comments for an explanation.

"What's up?" Sean asked.

"Remember that picture I showed you of that kid Tate?"

"Yeah?"

"I think things might be turning around." I found a comment from his mom, explaining the unexpected picture.

"We applied for a clinical trial for Tate that we knew was

a long shot. We didn't tell him or anyone else because we didn't want to get his hopes up, but yesterday morning we got the call. Dr. Bhandari accepted Tate into a clinical trial at Cincinnati Children's Hospital. This is a highly targeted stem cell and chemo protocol that has shown incredible results in pediatric cases. Lucy needs me home, so Derek's amazing boss is allowing him to work remotely from Cincinnati while Tate undergoes treatment. They already checked in, and Derek sent this picture this morning. We'll miss them, but knowing we're finally going to deliver the knockout punch to this illness makes it much easier for Lucy and I cheering at home!"

"I can't believe this," I said, looking up at Sean. "Look at this."

He read through her comment and smiled up at me. "That's a good sign. This doctor wouldn't have taken him on if the little guy didn't have a decent shot."

I accepted my phone from him and read through the two newest posts where Tate's mom described the details of the new treatment plan and a picture of Tate playing Minecraft.

The photo made my eyes sting. I googled the name of the hospital. The whole first page of results showed that it was the top-ranked hospital for pediatric cancer treatment according to several prestigious surveys.

Tate was okay.

For right now, he was okay, and it sounded like he had a chance to get better.

I finished my French toast, cleaned my plate, and laced up my running shoes.

"Want company?" Sean asked as I tightened my laces.

“Maybe tomorrow?” I had something I needed to do today, and I needed to be alone for it.

“Sure.” He went back to his French toast, Shep panting at him for a bite of his own.

I caught the streetcar over to Golden Gate Park but instead of heading for the running trail I liked, I found a quiet spot in the Shakespeare Garden.

I chose an empty bench and pulled my phone from my armband, studying the blank screen like it could tell me what to say instead of vice versa. I’d run over the words a thousand times in my mind, changing the inflection, the order, the verbs. But I couldn’t ever get it exactly right.

That was the thing about perfection. It didn’t exist. No way I could say this in a way that would fix everything. Or even anything. But that didn’t mean I didn’t have to say at least something.

I took a deep breath and opened the messaging app. I pulled up Jack’s name and pressed “Record.”

“Hi. Long time, no talk. I’m in a place called the Shakespeare Garden.” I flipped the camera so he could see it. “It reminded me of our date walking through Hyde Park.” I switched the view again and sighed. “I needed a peaceful place. It shouldn’t surprise me that I chose one connected to you.” I tried to say the next part I planned, but a lump formed in my throat, and I knew I wouldn’t get the words out, so I ended the recording. I sat and took more deep breaths and looked for the courage to try again.

It took several minutes before the pressure of unshed tears eased behind my eyes, and I felt like I could try again. I started the next video message with a smile that was shakier than I wanted it to be, but I was proud I'd managed one, however small.

"I told you I started volunteering at the hospital a month ago. The patients and staff are amazing. Um, but this kid I was working with...I thought he had died." My voice trembled, and I paused a second to pull myself together. "It was hard. I don't even have words for how hard, and I barely knew him. I just found out that I was wrong. I have never, ever been so happy about being wrong. He's gone to Cincinnati for a new clinical trial. But for those couple of days when I thought..."

I stopped the recording, fighting to reorder my thoughts in a way that would make sense to Jack. I pressed record one last time. "I wanted to say I'm sorry again. I'm so sorry. You weren't running away. You weren't hiding. You were so strong to work there for as long as you did. I don't know how you did it. And I'm so sorry for what I said. If this is how it feels when it works out for a kid I barely know, I can't imagine what it was like when it didn't work out for a kid like Clara. I'd love to talk to you. Really talk. I get it if you don't, but if you do, call me?"

I ended the recording and sent it before I could talk myself out of it. I couldn't have said it any worse, but I also didn't know how to say it any better.

It wasn't hard to ignore my phone the rest of the day. I knew he wouldn't call. I wouldn't have.

I went out with Ranée and some girlfriends for dinner, and even though I laughed and joined the conversation, Ranée kept shooting me concerned looks, like she knew exactly how big of a show I was putting on. I tried to keep a cheerful face on. I even agreed to go with them to a nearby pub to listen to some live music, but she kept sending me those worried looks.

Sometime after midnight, she picked up her phone, wrinkled her forehead, and showed it to me.

`This is Jack. Sorry to bug you but I can't get hold of Emily. Could you ask her to check her phone?`

I fumbled my cell from my handbag so fast that it shot out of my hands, and I had to retrieve it from between Ranée's feet on the sticky pub floor. I unlocked, cursing when I realized I had no reception bars but six different notifications from text, voicemail, and FaceTime. All of them were from Jack. I checked the text first.

`Call me.`

"Ranée, it's—" I started to shout over the music.

"Go."

I excused myself from the table and stepped outside to the street to make the call, hesitating before I dialed. The text had come in two hours ago. Maybe it was too late tonight? But the city was full of quiet noise, the soft hum of passing cars and the chatter of people on the sidewalk. Maybe Jack would be awake too. I dialed his number.

It rang twice before he answered it simply, "Em?"

"Hey."

"Hey."

I savored the warm sound of his voice. It was better than the drink Ranée had forced on me when we got to the pub.

"You wanted to talk?" he asked.

"Yeah." I looked around me at the bustle of my city corner,

but I didn't want to wait until I got home where it was quiet. "I've been thinking. I was so wrong about so much when I was up there."

"Em—"

"I need to finish before I lose my nerve."

There was a long pause before a quiet, "Okay."

"I was wrong. And out of line to say the things I said. I'm sorry."

"You don't need to apologize."

"I do. I didn't get it then, but I think I have the tiniest sliver of empathy now. And it's painful. I can't imagine how much harder it was for you, working with those kids and losing them." I paused to pull myself together. Jack let the silence rest, and I was thankful for a minute to think. "So the thing is, I'm hoping you can forgive me."

"There's nothing to—"

"Yes, there is. I'm so sorry I keep interrupting you, but I'm scared I won't say this if I don't blurt it out." I took a deep breath. "I get it now. And I can't believe I was so judgmental. You're strong. You're not a quitter. I'm sorry for everything I said. And I don't know if you still want to make us work. I do. I don't know how, but I was thinking I could spread out my vacation days, so I could take several long weekends through the year to come up and visit you. I've never done long-distance before, but people do it all the time. We can make this work, if…" I realized he hadn't tried to interject for a while. "If you want to?"

A sigh met that. "Emily..."

All that followed was a long silence. I gripped the phone harder. What did I expect? I'd hurt him with words the last time we were together, and once those things were said, it took so much more than simple words to fix the damage.

"Jack?" I knew he was still there, but I didn't know what else to say.

"You have bad timing."

"Oh." His voice was soft, but it felt like a slap. "Okay. I get it. I'll let you go."

"No, it's not—" He broke off with a growl. There was a pause, and he started again. "I don't want to give up on us, but I also don't think long-distance is the right answer. The thing is, it's one in the morning, and conversations tend to go way off the rails when my head isn't clear. Can I call you tomorrow when I've got myself together?"

Considering the way I'd run out on him, it was worse than I'd hoped, but better than I'd feared.

Why did it leave me with such a tight fist of disappointment in my chest? He'd said, *I don't want to give up on us*. But a polite request to talk about it in the morning wasn't exactly a sign that he'd been eaten up with missing me the way I had with him.

I swallowed the disappointment and tried to compose myself. "Of course. Sorry, I shouldn't have called so late."

"You don't have to apologize. I just need…I need to make sure I'm in the right place when we talk about this."

"I get it. Why don't you call me tomorrow when you've had time to think about it?"

"As if I could think about anything else now." He sighed again. "Man, Emily. Whatever I thought you were going to say when you asked me to call you, this wasn't it. Call you tomorrow?"

"Yeah, sure. Good night."

He hung up, and I turned to face the pub behind me and the uncertain future ahead of me.

I tapped a text to Ranée to tell her I was taking an Uber home. I spent the whole ride staring through the window without seeing anything, replaying my video message and our conversation in my head.

The one time when it had really mattered to get the words perfect, I'd failed. But I'd offered him the truth.

And if that wasn't enough, I didn't know what was left to say.

Chapter 42

The next morning, I was cooking breakfast when Sean walked in from taking Shep out.

"I'm taking omelet requests," I said. He didn't answer, and I looked up to find him frowning at his phone. "Sean? Something wrong?"

"Denver," he said. I blinked at him. "My omelet."

I turned to get some ham from the fridge. "You okay?"

"I think my roommate situation just worked out. I'll be out of your hair soon."

"You're not in my hair, but that's great news. When are you moving?"

"Uhh..."

Something about the way he said it made me look up from the eggs I was cracking. "Are you about to tell me it's going to be like a year or something? Because then maybe you'll be getting in my hair." A text sounded on my phone, but I ignored it while I waited for his answer.

"You should probably get that," he said.

"Can't." I wiggled my fingers covered in egg.

He unhooked Shep's leash, walked over to me, and gently steered me to the sink. "You really need to answer your phone," he said and ran water over my fingers.

I washed and dried them while he headed down the hall, calling Ranée's name.

"You're being weird!" I called after him.

"Answer your phone," he called back.

I picked it up as another text came in.

It was from Jack.

Even though I'd dried my hands, my fingers became impossibly slippery as I fumbled the phone trying to unlock it.

It was a selfie, showing only Jack's flannel-clad torso—which I'd know anywhere by now—and his hand holding a cup of coffee and a small bag of Cheetos. But it was the background that dominated everything, because it was the front of my apartment building.

Before I could fully process what that meant, my phone vibrated with another text and a picture of Transcendent Seagull appeared. It said only, "You should buzz Jack up."

I ran to the door and did exactly that, then turned and yelled Sean's name down the hall, with a big, fat question mark behind it.

"Sorry, trying to keep Ranée barricaded in here," he yelled back, muffled by her door. There were some thumps and a few Ranée curses.

A knock sounded at the door, and I flung it open to find Jack standing there. But it was Jack like I'd never seen him. The shirt and jeans were familiar, and so was the smile. Devastatingly so. But…

My hand flew to my mouth. "Your hair."

He reached up to touch it, but there wasn't much left. He'd cut it much shorter, trimmed around his ears and collar. "Linda did it for me. She wanted to leave some length in front, but I figured it would get in the way of the microscope."

"You look..." Incredible. He looked even better than in my constant daydreams by a factor of infinity. "It looks really good. Linda must have loved it when you walked in."

"She did. There was enough to send it to Wigs for Kids." He shifted and cleared his throat. "Can I come in?"

"Of course. Let me just..." I took the Cheetos and coffee and set them on the table. "Um, should we sit?"

"Sure, great."

It was such a stilted conversation, but I couldn't wrap my mind around what it meant that he was here. We settled onto the sofa facing each other.

"So I—"

"Why are you—"

We said at the same time.

"Sorry." He cleared his throat. "You go ahead."

I curled my hands into fists to keep them from fidgeting. "Why are you here, Jack?"

"When you called me last night, I was already in the city. I'd been hoping you'd see me today, but then you called..."

"And you told me I had bad timing." The realization was dawning on me. "But not because you think we're over?"

He smiled. "No. Because you ruined my surprise."

I gave him a smaller smile in return. "Sorry about that.

But I'm glad you're here. There are things I need to say to you in person. More apologies I should have made a while ago."

His expression grew serious, and he shook his head. "When you left Featherton, I was pretty upset. I thought I was mad at you, which is why I didn't text you or call you. I figured you didn't understand anything about me, that I'd read you all wrong, that I was better off without you."

"Jack, I—"

"No, it's okay. Because then you sent that text about how you started volunteering. And it turned everything upside down for me. You've tied me in so many knots since we met that I don't know what's up with anything anymore, even things I thought I knew for absolute truth."

My hands relaxed. "I know how that feels."

"The fact that you were willing to do something that hard, it shook me. Out of complacency. Out of self-righteousness." He reached up to brush back hair that wasn't there anymore, and his hand drifted to his lap as if he was uncertain what to do with it. "Most importantly, it shook me out of self-pity. I realized that I wasn't mad at you when you left. I was mad at myself."

I looked down at my lap. "I still shouldn't have said what I said."

He sighed. "Maybe you should have. You were wrong about me needing to go back to practicing, but you were right about me hiding. I didn't realize how much I'd isolated myself until you came along. You shook me up in ways I needed."

I rested my hand on his knee. "If it's any consolation, you did the same thing to me."

He covered my hand with his, toying with my fingers.

"Yeah?"

I swallowed as little currents ran up my arm from every place he touched me. "I had a perfect life figured out for myself. A plan for my career. For a relationship. Five years, ten years, I saw it all laid out in front of me, clear and simple. You were nowhere in there. And yet..."

"And yet there's no version of the future where I don't see you. How did that happen, Em?"

"I don't know. But it happened to me too."

"That's what I came here to tell you. And then you ruined it with that call last night." Another smile twitched at the corner of his lips.

A warm tendril of hope had unfurled inside me when he'd walked through my door, and now it grew and stretched. "I have faith in you to fix this, doctor."

"Good, because it's my turn to do the fixing," he said. "You took a risk and came up to see me. As happy as that made me, I didn't understand what a huge gamble that was until I packed my life into my car to drive down here to you."

"Your life into your car?" The tendril of hope grew to a flame fueled by wonder. He had done that for me?

He threaded his fingers through mine and met my eyes. "When you told me last night that you were willing to work on this long-distance, and to do whatever it took..." His voice trailed off. He shook his head with an air of disbelief. "I promise you, I planned this grand entrance into your life before you even called. Ask Sean. I've been here since yesterday afternoon."

"A grand entrance into my life," I repeated. "Is that also why you cut your hair?" I touched the close-cropped strands near his temple. Then I remembered something he'd said when he first walked in. "Wait. You said you packed your life into your car. And when you came in you said something about cutting your hair for a microscope?"

"Yeah." He brushed his lips across my knuckles and this time heat shot straight up my arm. "Sean mentioned he needed a roommate, so I figured I'd help him out and move to San Francisco. It kind of worked out since the UC San Francisco School of Medicine offered me a teaching and research position." He watched my face closely, but he didn't need to. He could have seen my jaw drop from the top of Coit Tower, and he smiled at my reaction. "I can't go back to treating patients, but I can work on the problem from a different direction. Have to keep this out of the way of the microscope." He brushed a hand over his hair, clearly still not used to it. "It was time."

Suddenly I was every romance novel cliché at once: pounding heart, sweaty palms, and there was no way my knees would support me if I had to stand. But luckily—so luckily, as Jack reached over to slide his hand around the back of my neck—I didn't have to go anywhere.

"I'm here. I can't go back to the work I did, but I'm not quitting anymore. Not medicine, and not you." He leaned forward, gently touching his forehead to mine. "I love you, Emily."

I slid my arms around his neck, thrilling at the brush of the soft, short bristles of his hair against my fingers. "Jack?" I whispered, a hairsbreadth from his lips.

"Yeah?"

"I love you too. Now shut up and kiss me."

And neither of us paid any attention at all as Ranée and Sean spilled into the hall cheering.

Epilogue

I smoothed down the bodice of my dress as Ranée fastened the last hook in back. "How do I look?"

Ranée peered over my shoulder at our reflections in the full-length mirror. She spread the veil out and let it float back down with a happy sigh. "This dress is amazing. You're amazing."

We grinned at our reflection again. I hadn't dreamed much about my future wedding before Jack, but if I'd thought about it at all, I'd imagined a simple, chic wedding gown. The dress I chose was exactly opposite, a ball gown with a strapless sweetheart bodice, the billowing skirt made of layers of airy chiffon. The dress itself had no embellishment. With the intricate draping of the bodice and the floaty layers of the skirt, it didn't need any, but lace appliques edged the long veil behind me.

Suddenly, Ranée picked up one edge of the veil and peered more closely at the pattern woven into it. "Wait. Are these…is this veil covered in *seagulls*?"

I grinned at her, and she burst out laughing. "That's so perfect."

It felt that way. This dress said everything about how marrying Jack made me feel. It was full and exuberant and gorgeous and unrestrained.

"Are you nervous?" Ranée asked, scooping up her maid-of-honor bouquet.

"Not even a little bit. I've never done anything that felt so right."

She stepped back to study me, tapping a finger against her chin. "You look almost perfect."

"Almost?" I reached up to make sure the veil was fastened correctly, but Ranée caught my hand.

"It's not that. I think the shoes aren't quite right."

I lifted the hem to examine the silk heels my mom had helped me pick out. "I thought you liked these."

"I do, but—" She broke off and rushed to her overnight bag full of hot rollers and makeup. She rustled around in it for a moment before she turned, bearing a familiar shoebox. "*These* would make it perfect," she said, lifting the lid on a pair of gorgeous red high heels. "They deserve a dress like that, and you deserve to wear a pair like these when you marry the man of your dreams."

And as I slipped them on and the full skirt settled down around them, I smiled.

Ranée was right. There was no better pair of shoes to take me down the aisle to Jack.

ACKNOWLEDGMENTS

First and foremost, thank you to my Facebook readers for the encouragement to write and keep this story going every week.

Thank you to Leah Gariott and Tiffany Odekirk for helping me plot out this ridiculous idea on a Starbucks napkin. Thank you to the best critique group in the world for picking through the key scenes and helping me to make the right parts less creepy and the best bits more swoony: Teri Christopherson, Aubrey Hartman, Brittany Larsen, Tiiffany Odekirk, and Jen White. Thank you to Jenilyn Tolley, Leah Garriott, Jeigh Meredith, Tiffany Odekirk, Rosalyn Eves, and Cindy Baldwin for reading through this to make it stronger. Thank you to Camille Maynard, Kathy Spencer, Cindy Ray, and Amy Bennett for proofreading and helping me make it shipshape. Thank you to Jenny Proctor for her patience in formatting this knotty manuscript for me! And thank you to the friends who answered doctor questions for me.

And, as always, thank you to Kenny for his unwavering cheerleading. Maybe I'll lift the household ban on the real thing after all.

KEEP READING FOR
A SNEAK PREVIEW OF
Wedding Belles

WEDDING BELLES

Chapter One

Harper stared at the sample menu in front of her and dug deep into her etiquette training to find a way to say, "Absolutely not," in a way that would make the caterer in front of her feel complimented, not rejected.

"You certainly have fresh ideas, Mr. Choi." There. That was a diplomatic start. She hoped it didn't sound sarcastic since he looked to be her age, in his late twenties at most.

"Call me Zak." He smiled at her. It was a good smile, toothpaste-ad quality, and with the laugh lines crinkling around his dark brown eyes, it could have been irresistible if Harper was looking for a man. But she wasn't.

"But my clientele is very traditional," she continued. And really, her office should have tipped him off. She'd designed it to look like an elegant Charleston sitting room. "I used a caterer last month for a garden party who put Dijon mustard in the potato salad and it created such a ruckus that it upstaged Beth Martin's hundred-year-old hydrangeas. And that was a tragedy I'm not sure Miss Beth will ever recover from. So this…" she waved her hand to encompass the menu, "would push my clients too far. But I wish you good luck finding your client base."

There was no way he was going to find a client base in Charleston with the edgy offerings he'd listed on his menu. At least not with the old money families Harper was targeting on her quest to become Charleston's premiere event planner.

His smile dimmed, and he sat forward and cleared his throat. "I realize that most of this town still considers Julia Child revolutionary for introducing French cooking techniques, but that makes them ripe for the next food revolution. There's a whole world waiting for them if they can evolve past coq au vin."

Harper frowned. She happened to like chicken in wine sauce. The first time she'd had it at a sorority banquet, she'd felt a flush of luxury that was new to her, the little girl from scruffy Goose Creek who got Hamburger Helper on special occasions.

"Sorry." She pushed the menu back across her desk, not sorry at all. "But your information isn't correct. Charleston is full of innovative restaurants who have connected to a customer base that loves what they serve. But I serve a coq au vin crowd and I use caterers who serve coq au vin." Even the name sounded fancy and French, and she liked the way it unfurled on her tongue, unlike . . . what was is it? She flicked her eyes over to his menu again. Ah, yes. *Bulgogi.* Her clients wanted a prime rib, reliably sliced and served with mashed potatoes. If they were feeling adventurous, maybe they'd walk on the wild side and make them garlic mashed.

His smile had disappeared, and his sharp cheekbones suddenly stood out without his smile to soften them. She wondered idly what his ancestry was. Based on the Korean influences in the menu he gave her plus his last name, she'd guess a Korean father, but he didn't look full Korean. Maybe a white mother? They'd each done him a favor and passed on their best bits because even his scowl didn't diminish his good looks. She wondered which one of them was to blame for his short temper.

"Thank you for coming in." She pushed back from her desk to indicate that their meeting was at an end, but when he made no move to leave, she hesitated in an awkward half-crouch above her chair before sitting again. "Was there something else?"

"Do you know what foodways are?" he asked.

She blinked at him. "Is that . . . a grocery chain?"

His lips stretched in a quick smile, a mean cousin to the one he'd offered her only a few minutes before. "Foodways is the history of regional dishes. Port cities—like New York, where I'm from—are prime areas for cultural shifts in cuisines." He made a short sound that was maybe supposed to be a laugh, but it wasn't happy. "Usually. Looks like the oldest port in the country has the oldest taste to go with it."

He ignored the menu she'd pushed back toward him and headed for the exit. "Good news," he said as he reached for the handle. "Your branding is on point. No one is going to accuse you of being hip or fresh."

He was halfway out the door before Harper pulled herself together enough to call in her Bridezilla-wrangling voice, "Pleasure not doing business with you!"

His answer was the jangle of the bell hanging over the entrance. Strange. It usually had a cheerful tinkle.

Whatever. Hip and fresh were code words for trendy. She was all about timeless classics. Who cared what he thought about that? She had enough to handle with her high maintenance clients. The last thing she needed on top of that was a high maintenance caterer.

Speaking of which . . . she glanced down at her watch. Fifteen minutes until the highest maintenance bride of all time appeared.

Harper sighed and pulled out the binder that grew thicker by orders of magnitude after each meeting with the lovely Dahlia Ravenel. It was possible she'd already put in more time planning this wedding than every other event she'd organized since she went solo three years ago. Combined. But Dahlia was a prize, the daughter of one of Charleston's most prominent families, engaged to the son and scion of one of Charleston's other prestigious families. This was the break she'd been working and praying for, the kind of society wedding that the *The Post and Courier* would splash on the cover of the local section with her name attached as the wedding planner.

Of all the types of events she did, weddings were her favorite. They were the biggest paycheck, and she had worked out the perfect network from florists to bakers, mostly other rising new vendors who had the same grit and hustle she did. The Ravenel-Calhoun wedding would be a windfall for all of them, a chance to break into the Charleston upper crust and enjoy the fruits of that very rich pie.

Assuming, of course, that she survived Dahlia Ravenel.

And that was by no means certain.

By the time the blushing bride arrived, the groom and

maid of honor had already been sitting at Harper's desk for twenty minutes making small talk. At least they were easy with each other. From the conversation, it sounded like the three of them had grown up together. The groom was Deacon Calhoun of the Garden District Calhouns, and Lily, the maid of honor, was Dahlia's cousin, born to the same Charleston caste. If there was anything the silver spooners knew, it was how to keep a sparkling conversation going to gloss over any kind of awkward moment, like the tardiness of the bride who'd demanded their attendance in the first place.

Dahlia finally blew in on a gust of exotic perfume and chatter that burst out of her the second her foot was through the door. "Why didn't anyone tell me that show about the vampires was so good?" she said, scolding her way to Harper's desk, who rose to greet her. "I mean, that show makes Charleston almost seem as interesting and gothic as New Orleans. You'd never know we don't have handsome vampires in every mansion. Speaking of," she said swooping down to drop a kiss on Deacon's lips.

"Did you just call me a vampire?" he asked, and Harper couldn't tell if he was amused or confused by the comparison.

"A handsome vampire," Dahlia corrected. "You know, charming with those dark, brooding good looks and a workaholic night owl. You're a perfect candidate, Deacon."

Deacon shook his head. "Are you telling me that you're almost twenty minutes late for an appointment you made because you got distracted by a TV show?"

She fluttered down to the seat next to him and placed a hand on his knee. "Binge-watching, honey. I know it made me late, and I'm sorry about that, but it's exactly the kind of escapism you need right now. You should try it, Deac."

Lily, the maid of honor, had been watching this all with a half-smile on her face and now she patted Deacon's other knee. "You're not dark and brooding," she said, which smoothed out the furrow on his forehead. "And Dahlia, if I have to start picking you up for all these appointments, I will. My shift at the hospital starts at two o'clock sharp. We probably better get down to business."

Harper bet she could binge watch a reality show based on these three. She'd met with Dahlia and Lily once before but having the groom in the mix charged the situation with a new energy. Lily was the peacemaker and problem-solver, she could see right away. That meant she'd need to make Lily her primary ally in wrangling Dahlia, who had demonstrated a fierce commitment to the irrational. There was a shorthand in the way they all spoke and touched one another that would have given away their long friendship even if she hadn't already sensed it before Dahlia arrived.

Harper opened her Ravenel-Calhoun binder. Dahlia had chosen her venue and colors at their previous appointment, when Mrs. Ravenel occupied the seat Deacon took now. That had been a bit of tug-of-war between mother and daughter until Mrs. Ravenel had put her foot down and refused to budge on the William-Aiken House. She'd had it reserved since Deacon and Dahlia had announced their engagement the previous year, and Dahlia had only just decided to balk. Harper knew why she wanted it: it was the most prestigious venue in Charleston, a gorgeous historic mansion on King Street with lush grounds and an airy ballroom. Harper, sensing an unconventional streak in her new client, convinced Dahlia that the bright tangerine-painted walls of the dining room added the touch of whimsy she craved.

That victory had seemed to reassure Mrs. Ravenel that the unknown wedding planner Dahlia had chosen was right for the job, but Harper wondered if Mrs. Ravenel even knew that Dahlia had come in to pick the rest of her vendors. If she were a betting woman, she'd put money on Dahlia blindsiding her mother with her next set of choices.

But Harper was not a betting woman because she had no money to lose. Every penny was tied up in the business and the lease she'd signed three months ago for her storefront on George Street to attract wealthier clients. She'd have to use all her considerable skills to direct Dahlia toward choices that would make Mrs. Ravenel happy enough to still sign the check for Harper's services.

She put on her warmest smile and turned to the second tab. "With the venue decided, we need to choose a photographer. I work with the best in Charleston, and—"

She trailed off as Dahlia waved her words away. "My friend Sutton is doing it."

Harper search her memory but came up blank. "I don't think I've worked with her before."

"You wouldn't have. She gave up shooting weddings a while ago. Very artsy now, but she's my best friend from school, and she agreed to come back to do my wedding."

"That sounds great," Harper said, her smile never slipping. "Artsy" worried her because she didn't think it was a word Mrs. Ravenel would like. But worse, she received a bonus from the vendors she referred, and that meant she could kiss her photographer bonus goodbye. She'd had plans for that money.

Her plans would have to wait, but no hint of her disappointment crept into her voice as she turned to the next tab. "Let's move right on to food."

At this, Deacon straightened and leaned forward for a better look. Lily grinned. "You're speaking his language."

"I particularly love Burnham's Lowcountry Caterers," Harper said. "Their shrimp and grits are to die for and they do such an elegant presentation with their plating. They elevate our humble food into art." The cranky caterer from the morning flashed through her mind. He might think Charleston needed shaking up, but the city was ripe with restaurants sporting James Beard awards and even a couple of Michelin-starred establishments. There were rising stars who innovated *and* chefs who'd made lucrative careers out of the simple goodness of traditional Charleston cuisine.

"I like shrimp and grits," Deacon said, flipping to the next flier. "But who's your steak specialist?"

Harper turned to the flier for Salthouse Catering. "They're amazing with any cut of cow."

Dahlia's nose wrinkled. "Steak, honey? Really? Why don't we just throw a cookout and serve up some burgers?"

Deacon sat back in his chair. "You took the words right out of my mouth. Why don't we?"

Dahlia rolled her eyes. "Because we're not doing the whole hipster redneck revival thing. So help me, if I see anything in a mason jar or bacon-wrapped anything, I will lose it."

Harper privately agreed with her about the overdone "country living" aesthetic, specifically when it was used by wealthy debutantes who disdained real country living. But now Deacon was frowning.

"If there's no bacon, I walk," he said. He was kidding, Harper thought. And about the cookout too. Probably.

"Not only do I not want any bacon, I don't love the idea of meat at the wedding either."

Deacon drew a deep breath. "I think it's great that you're exploring vegetarianism, but you know the Calhoun men are going to drink through every bottle of bourbon at the open bar if they have to sit through a vegetarian wedding dinner."

"Pescatarian," Lily said as Dahlia was drawing breath to argue. "That could work as a compromise. What if you have seafood? Seared scallops, shrimp, that kind of thing, maybe even something wrapped in bacon for the carnivores, but no red meat or poultry. Could you live with that?"

Dahlia didn't look thrilled, but she nodded. Deacon shrugged. "I could live with that."

Harper admired Lily's deft handling and jumped on the solution. "I know a couple of perfect catering options." She popped the right menus out of the binder and handed one to each of them.

"Yum," Lily said.

"Looks good to me," Deacon said.

Dahlia only offered a groan.

"Is something wrong?" Harper asked.

Dahlia's whole face scrunched like Harper had handed her raw sewage instead of a catering brochure. It was the first time Harper had ever seen her look anything less than stunningly gorgeous.

Dahlia pushed the menu back. “I’ve eaten food from all of these caterers at other weddings, and they’re all good and totally boring.”

Lily winced while Deacon shut his eyes for a few seconds. But Dahlia wasn’t finished. “I picked you because you haven’t done the weddings for every single one of my friends, but somehow I’m still having this thing in a boring old mansion, and now I’m going to be serving boring old food. I’m not boring,” she said, slapping her hand on the open binder. “I’m sorry, but I don’t think this is going to work.”

Lily was shooting her an apologetic look, Deacon’s face had gone blank, and Dahlia had hopped up from her seat and taken a step for the door when Harper panicked. She couldn’t let her leave and take her mother’s fat checkbook with her.

The words escaped her before she could think better of it. “If you’re willing to work with a Gordon Ramsay wannabe who has wild ideas about food, I’ve got the guy for you.”

Dahlia sat back down with a relieved smile. “Tell me more. I think I could be persuaded.

Find the rest of *Wedding Belles* exclusively on Amazon.

About the Author

Melanie Bennett Jacobson is an avid reader, amateur cook, and champion shopper. She lives in Southern California with her husband and children and a series of doomed houseplants. She holds a Masters degree in writing for children and young adults and is the author of nine romantic comedies from Covenant Communications as well as several independent projects. You can read more about Melanie at www.melaniejacobson.net.

Made in the USA
Middletown, DE
17 August 2019